VOLUME 1

THE HOME FOR WAYWARD CREATURES

EC GARRETT

TO THE PEOPLE WHO LOOK
TO THE STARS AND SEE
DREAMS AND POSSIBILITIES.

AND FOR LADY AND CALY—
GONE BUT NEVER FORGOTTEN.

BEFORE YOU READ

The Home for Wayward Creatures is a space romantasy with a light spice level. Because of the advanced themes (animal welfare, kidnapping, sexual content) it would be Rated R, but if you have read my books before, I can tell you this is by far my lightest and coziest story. The spice is also built so that the scene can be skipped over, if you desire or if you're reading it with a teen and want to omit. It adds to the story but is not necessary. Below are some possible triggers you will come across in the book. Please review them before reading if you want a preview of the themes and content present in this book.

Hate, Discrimination & Oppression

Classism, Speciesism, Sexism & Misogyny, Alien Slavery & Indentured Servitude, Prison/Prisoner Scenarios

Sexual & Romantic

Age Gap, Slow Burn, One Bed on The Spaceship, He Falls First, Yearning, Making Out, Fingering, Vaginal Penetration, (Mild) Dirty Talk

Mental Health

Anxiety & Anxiety Attacks, ADHD, Panic Attacks, and Grief.

Blood, Injury & Medical

Minor gore depictions.

Death & Loss

Death of a Parent & Guardian, Grief & Loss Depiction.

Violence & Crime

Blackmail, Captivity & confinement, Explosions, Fire & Arson, Imprisonment & Incarceration, Interrogation, Knife & Gun Violence, Attempted murder

War & Genocide

Colonialism, Imperialism, and War themes & military violence

Animal Death and Cruelty

Animal Attack, Animal Cruelty & Abuse, Animal Illness & Injury, Animal Testing & Experimentation, and Animal Auctions.

MUSIC PLAYS AN IMPORTANT
ROLE IN THIS BOOK.

SCAN OR CLICK THE QR CODE BELOW
TO BE TAKEN TO THE OFFICIAL
PLAYLIST OF

THE HOME FOR
WAYWARD CREATURES.

"YOU CANNOT LOOK UP AT THE
NIGHT SKY ON THE PLANET
EARTH AND NOT WONDER
WHAT IT'S LIKE TO BE UP THERE
AMONGST THE STARS."

– TOM HANKS

CHAPTER 1

ALIENS IN A BOOKSTORE

"**T**HERE'S AN ALIEN IN THE BOOKSTORE AGAIN!"

The high-pitched shriek nearly bursts my ear drums, and I wince as I clutch the phone against my ear in one hand and attempt to juggle an iced coffee and three dog leashes in the other—a situation that does not bode well for said iced coffee.

"Okay, okay. Take a breath. Why do you think it's an alien?"

Betty, the manager of my local bookstore, lets out an exasperated exhale at my confusion.

"There is a...strange looking animal in the bookstore. Strange like...the others."

Ah.

In the background, my three dachshunds spot a squirrel and nearly yank my arm off trying to chase after it.

"And what does it look like?" I pant.

Betty's voice raises an entire decibel. "It's goddamn mini pony, Henri! A really weird looking one. It, uh..." Betty pauses, her voice turning shaky, "it has eight legs."

Well. That's fairly conclusive.

"And you don't know how it got there?" I ask, trying to sound calm while wrangling the pack of rabid weenie dogs at my feet, who are still on the eternal hunt for that squirrel.

"I got to the store this morning and everything was fine. We opened and then as we were having our morning coffee while the first few customers of the day began shopping around, there was this *noise* from the office."

It's always a suspicious noise, I nod solemnly to myself.

"Naturally I went to check it out and I don't know HOW but this fucking pony was standing in the office. Then it ran out! The little bastard had the audacity to *shove me out of the way,* Henri! You have to take care of this thing."

Right.

"You said there were customers. Did anyone else besides you and Carolyn see it?" I ask quietly.

"Uh, yeah. A small group of readers." *Shit.* "I told them we're doing a sort of petting zoo thing? But honestly, I don't think they buy it. I'm bribing them into silence with free books."

"Okay, but keep them there."

"What?!" Betty shrieks.

Unfortunately, this isn't the first time this has happened. But it *is* the first time it's been during business hours.

"Yes. Don't let them leave. They cannot know what the pony is. Nobody can know. Do you understand me? Think of the worst possible consequences you can even comprehend, and then times that by a hundred thousand. That's how serious I am."

"No need to be dramatic," Betty mutters, but I can hear the fear in her voice. She understands, even if she doesn't really understand. "I'll keep them here," she tells me. "But you better hurry."

There's another shout.

"OH MY GOD, IT'S EATING THE BOOKS."

That gives me an important clue about the creature's true species.

"I'll be home in 5 minutes and then on the way," I say and quickly hang up the phone.

Today is supposed to be my day off, but there is no such thing when you run the only animal rescue in the entire galaxy.

My geriatric black and tan dachshund Frankie and her co-conspirators, a long-haired brown dachshund named Jinx and a miniature cream dachshund named Barbara, all spot the squirrel at the same time. The squeak that comes out of my mouth is rather undignified as I'm yanked into a shrub.

I groan, trying to brush myself off. Barbara, the little demon, has the *audacity* to look confused as to why I'm on the ground. I glare at her, but she just sticks her tongue out and barks at me.

The others wag their tails and Barbara proceeds to take this moment to lick all of the makeup off my face, while Jinx sticks his tongue up my nose.

"Okay, yep, that's great, thank you so much," I squeal. "I'm very clean now, thank you!"

A glance to the side reveals my iced coffee spilled everywhere and I let out a pained groan.

Not the iced coffee.

Anything but the iced coffee.

My attention span is that of a flea—thanks to my raging ADHD—and the caffeine keeps me focused. But nope, half of it is now on the ground. My hands are coated in sticky, delicious coffee goodness that belongs firmly in my stomach.

I manage to untangle myself from the shrub and stand up, the weenies all happy as could be as if nothing happened. Within minutes, we round the corner and make it back to the house.

From the outside, my house is normal.

Well. It's more like a small mansion, but I hate the m-word.

A large red brick Victorian with a pretty garden and a substantial pasture to the south. Turrets and slanted roofs show its age, but I've maintained it well. Next to it, a huge green area with fruit trees and well-trimmed bushes line the pasture for my two horses.

My neighborhood is quiet and spread-out, but not so much that I'm all by my lonesome. Mable and Bob all munch happily on the grass below their hooves as the sun beats down on their glimmering coats.

Mable spots me and glares. For a single moment, her giant black wings show as they shimmer with an unearthly gleam.

I point a finger at her, and the wings disappear.

Damn aliens. They're all so headstrong!

Yes, my life is perfectly normal.

It's only a *little* bit complicated trying to hide intergalactic species in my basement and spaceships in my backyard. Or the Endorian Pegasus in the pasture...

Oh, and the aquarium in my hallway? It's hiding a pygmy kraken and a pack of Kriblets—shrimp-looking creatures with lobster-like claws—who I'm 99% sure are running an intergalactic crime syndicate, headed by the lead Kriblet, who I have dubbed as 'Kevin'.

Kevin is my arch-nemesis, but we are at a stalemate currently due to the minor fact of my keeping him alive and feeding him bloodworms daily. The worms are Kevin's favorite treat and it's the only reason he listens to me, but he's on the top of my list of suspicious creatures.

My already frizzy blonde and pink hair isn't ready for the

humidity of a Kansas City summer. But it's still springtime, so I'm trying to get outside as much as possible before it becomes hotter than the burning pits of hell.

I keep a simple wardrobe, since I'm always covered in animal fur and other mysterious substances—it comes with the territory. So instead, I occasionally add some fun colors to my hair. Last time it was purple. This time, pink. My hair is a pale golden blonde, making it easy to add pops of color here and there. It washes out after a few showers anyway, so it's low commitment.

Since the rescue is a non-profit, the UGF—better known as the United Galactic Federation—gave me a rather large grant to buy my house. After all, I needed lots of space to hide the aliens and it had to be in a quieter neighborhood outside of the city.

Located north of Kansas City in an affluent neighborhood, most of my neighbors are retirees, which suits me perfectly. All the houses have large porches, many of which are protected with fly netting—something we call a "sunroom"—and each house is surrounded with immaculate, green backyards.

Mr. Johnson and his dog Parker pass us on the other side of the street and Barbara takes this as a direct and personal attack, immediately launching into tiny barks, her small beady eyes wide and angry. Jinx watches with his tongue out, and I contemplate whether or not he has more than one single braincell. Frankie and Jinx follow suit, joining in on the vicious barking.

Watching three 10-pound dachshunds attempt to "intimidate" poor Mr. Johnson and his extremely large Great Dane is, as per usual, horribly embarrassing.

"Barbara! Frankie!" I *shh* them, but they just keep barking. Jinx however has quieted down and now looks at me with wide eyes. "Jinx, control your sisters!"

Jinx's tongue sticks out of his mouth with a happy smile and he sits down, not a care in the world—and not even a little bit controlling his sisters.

I sigh, wincing as I send Mr. Johnson an apology wave and mouth "*Sorry*". He just laughs and continues.

"Do you see that, Barbara? Did you see how Mr. Johnson's dog behaved like a *civilized* being? Frankie, did you see how Mr. Johnson's dog did not bark or lunge? You could learn a thing or two from him, you menaces!" I mutter, continuing my useless lecture as they completely ignore me, and we walk the rest of the way back to the house.

When the front door shuts behind me, I free the weenies from their harnesses and they take off through the house, the sound of their tiny paws like a stampede of elephants.

A spurt of cold water suddenly slaps me in the face.

That's the only warning I get before a red blob is leaping into my arms, tentacles armed and dangerous.

"Hey, buddy," I laugh as Boris the red pygmy kraken wraps his slimy legs around my neck and abdomen in his version of a kraken-hug.

"I gotta go to the bookstore," I tell him. "Which means you're in charge. The weens are on one today; don't let Barbara get into any more trouble, okay?"

Boris' eyes narrow and he lets out a squeak.

I sigh.

"You can't come with me, buddy. Earth is too far behind the rest of the galaxy, remember? It's too hard to explain you away by calling you an octopus."

Boris looks affronted at the thought of someone calling him

an *octopus*, but he reluctantly nods and slides down my body, looking dejected. From the ground, he looks back up at me with his big brown eyes.

I'm such a sucker.

"How about I stop at the candy store on the way back and get your favorite?"

He immediately perks up and makes a happy *squeak*.

"All the tootsie rolls for my best guy, huh?"

Boris, like me, *also* has ongoing beef with Kevin and the Kriblets, so the pygmy kraken prefers a bowl filled with water which we attached some toy cars to.

Boris takes off after the weens and I throw some more official clothes on, which translates to a non-coffee-stained shirt and a light jacket.

"Jace!" I shout.

"What?!" My sister's head pops up from the couch as I walk into the living room. Her chin-length black hair is in disarray.

"Napping on the job again?" I laugh. "Nice bed head."

She rolls her pale blue eyes. "I don't *have* a job, remember? What else am I supposed to do but be depressed and nap a lot?"

Two weeks ago, Jace showed up out of nowhere and announced that the UGF fired her.

Earth is not a part of the UGF—the planet is too young and the people are not ready for the knowledge of just how much is out there. Perhaps in a few centuries they will be ready, but not now.

I've tried to get Jace to tell me more about the job situation, but she just starts mumbling about how the UGF are a bunch of assholes.

"That's it," I announce. "You're coming to the bookstore with me. Get dressed."

"Baby sisters are not supposed to tell their older sisters what to do."

"But bosses are, and as of now, you are the newest employee of the Wayward Creatures Animal Rescue. Time to earn your rent."

Jace glares at me. "*You* don't even pay rent!" she mutters.

"Don't care. Get dressed and get back down here. There's an alien eating the books at Under the Cover."

Jace lets out a horrified gasp. I took her there few weeks prior, and she fell in love.

"NOT THE BOOKS!" Jace shouts, disappearing to change into something more suited for wrangling an unknown alien creature.

In few minutes, we're getting in my beat-up Prius.

Frankie comes with us. Despite the fact that she is old and ornery, she inexplicably loves other creatures—even the scary ones. I've started to bring her on Earth-based retrievals to keep the creature's calm. I strap her into her doggy car seat in the backseat and secure her harness. I give her velvet-soft head a kiss before closing the door and getting in the driver's seat.

"Thank GOD you're here!" Betty runs over, her black and green hair bouncing with every step. Carolyn, the store's owner, is talking with a small crowd of readers in the back.

The store is gorgeous. All shades of purple with rows and rows of colorful books. The floors are covered in vibrant rugs. Neon signs and bookish artwork line the walls.

But my favorite part is the rolling ladders on all of the bookcases.

It's magical, and homey.

And *apparently* a beacon for alien creatures.

"It's in the other room. It went for the mafia romance section. I don't know how much more it's eaten. I was too scared to look."

These books, this store—they're integral not just to the lives of those that work here, but the city as a whole.

"I've got this," I reassure her. "You stay with the readers. We'll get the creature. Keep them here, okay?"

Jace and I parked in the back, so we'll have to herd the creature out.

As I walk through the dim, velvet curtains that line the arch leading to the second room of the bookstore, I halt in my tracks.

Jace runs into my back with an *oomph*. Then she steps around me and halts too.

"Oh my God," I gasp.

"It's so CUTE!" Jace whisper shrieks.

"It's not just cute. Do you know what that is?"

"Not a clue."

I elbow her. "Firstly, your knowledge of creatures in our universe is *abysmal*. Secondly, that's an Armasidian Pony."

Jace stills.

"It's from Armasid? That?" Jace points at the pony.

Armasid is a planet in the Cor Cana system, populated by semi-humanoid centaurs called Armas.

The Centaurs rule with iron hooves—literally, their hooves are made of iron. The UGF has been trying to get them to join the Federation for centuries. But anytime they send emissaries...those emissaries don't return.

Armasidian Ponies are considered a pest to the Armas. Like cockroaches for humans on earth, the ponies get into their farms, destroying crops and eating their food. Their population has dwindled significantly as hunting increases, but the Armas must have started selling the ponies to buyers off planet.

They're *that* desperate.

"They're fairly docile, but they like to eat plants. *Anything* made of plants." I nod to the books.

"Ah, paper from trees," Jace realizes.

"They will resort to eating bark if there aren't enough vegetables and fruits around. It must be starving."

The pony has eight legs and otherwise resembles a small brown Shetland pony from earth, except with giant donkey ears. *Pink* donkey ears. They start off as brown but fade into a bright, shimmery pink at the tips of its ears.

Big brown eyes watch us warily.

Luckily, after Betty told me about the pony eating the books, I took a guess on its species and brought bribes.

All creatures can be bribed with the proper treats.

Pulling out a handful of fresh, bright red strawberries, I pick one up and take a bite. Bending down to the pony's level, I creep closer, slowly, as to not scare it.

"Mmmmm!" I make a happy noise as I munch on the strawberry, showing the pony it's good to eat.

I hold my hand out carefully and the pony's gray velvet lips twitch. Its mane and tail are gray and brown streaked with white. Its coat is thick and velvety with an almost cheetah-like pattern within it, of dark brown and various shades of gray.

The pony is gorgeous—and it's so terribly skinny. No wonder it's eating books. As I suspected upon hearing about the book consumption—the poor thing is starving.

"Have some fruit, friend. I am not here to harm you. I am here to help."

I whisper the quiet words to the pony and its ears twitch.

Most alien creatures are fairly sentient and intelligent—more so than Earth animals. I'd imagine the pony understands me.

"They're called strawberries," I whisper. "They're sweet and delicious. I think you would really like them."

It leans forward, taking a few small steps, until it's hovering just near my hand.

With slow movements, it leans down, eyes still on mine, and slurps the strawberries into its mouth.

I can tell the moment it relaxes. The pony's ears turn forward and its eyes brighten as it steps closer to me. I raise my hand and pet it, thrilled at this progress.

"Now, it's not safe for you here. But I have more strawberries in my car, and at my house I have a big pasture full of fruit trees. You will be safe there. I have two horses too. They would love to be your friend and hangout with you all day every day. But if you stay here, the humans will come for you."

I swear the pony nods.

Jace steps up and I gesture to her. "This is my sister Jace. You can trust her too. She's very safe and nice."

"Hi there! You're a very pretty pony." Jace smiles, "Let's get you out of here, okay?"

The pony snorts and I stand up. It stays right by my side, following me out the back door and leaving a wake of destroyed books behind us. Jace loads the pony into the car and Frankie hops up next to it. The pony is visibly calmed by the presence of the little dog. Most animals have herd tendencies, even alien animals. That's why it helps to have Frankie with me.

"Alright, you stay here with Jace, and I'll be right back. Then we'll go home."

The pony nods as I close the door.

"You got this?" Jace asks with a raised brow as she gets in the passenger seat.

I take a deep breath and nod. "Yup."

"Let me know if you need help," she whispers before closing her door.

I head back into the bookstore and find Betty surveying the pony's damage with tears in her eyes.

"I'm so sorry, Betty. I'll wire transfer you for the cost to replace everything that was damaged."

She sighs. "Thanks. Is the, uh, *creature* okay?"

"Yes. It's starving, which is why it went for the books. It can only eat plant-based foods, and you know...paper comes from trees."

Betty's eyes turn sadder at the knowledge that the pony was likely abused or abandoned.

"I'll take good care of it, and it will be back to perfect health in no time. I promise."

"Good." She nods. Then Carolyn walks in, wringing her hands. Behind her glasses, her eyes are worried.

"What the fuck are we going to tell the customers?!" she whispers.

"I've got that taken care of."

Betty and Carolyn blink. "What does that mean?" Carolyn asks carefully.

"Ah, well...I can do something that will erase their memory of the event."

Another blink.

"So the pony *is* an alien, right?"

I wince."Uhhhh...yes. Yes it is."

"Told you!" Betty whirls to Carolyn and points at her. "I *told* you it was another alien!"

"Shh!" I quiet her. "Remember what we talked about last time? Nobody besides the two of you can know."

Surprisingly, they're both okay with this and nod. They're the only two people I've ever told. It can damage the mind to wipe someone's memory multiple times and after the third alien creature showed up in store...I really couldn't hide it any longer.

"Now, I'm going to wipe the customers' memories and then take the pony back home. Okay?"

They nod and follow behind me.

"Close your eyes when I count to 3," I whisper over my shoulder.

"Dang it, I wanna see." Betty mumbles.

"Not unless you want your mind wiped, too." I mutter back to her.

The group of customers turn to me as I approach them. Putting on my best customer service voice, I begin letting my magic build.

"Thank you so much for your patience. It looks like a nearby petting zoo had a pony get loose and it broke into the store. We've safely rescued it and will be reuniting it with its owner. You're safe to head home."

"Are you sure it was a pony?" someone asks, and the others nod.

"It looked weird!" another said. A chorus of voices chimed in agreement.

I give them a big smile. "I'm very sure! Now, for all rescues we legally have to document the scene, and that includes taking a photo of the witnesses. Would it be okay to take a quick photo for our records? It's completely confidential and will never be shared."

The customers nod, not knowing what else to do.

I hold up my phone as if to take a photo, and let my magic unfurl fully.

Forget the pony. Forget what you saw. Forget everything that happened here except the fact that you came to the bookstore and left.

I repeat the words over and over in my mind, focusing so hard my head begins to pound.

"One," I begin the countdown and hear Carolyn take a sharp breath behind me.

"Two. Three."

I hit the camera shutter and at that same time, my magic explodes from me with a whoosh, coating the customers.

I want to slump over with happiness that the spell actually worked.

Usually, my ADHD is having a time and my focus is too scattered to complete the spell, hence Jace's offer to help.

In some rare moments, when my adrenaline is high, I can focus enough to complete the spell.

The readers freeze and then exit the store quietly, talking amongst themselves like nothing happened.

"WAS THAT MAGIC?" Betty shouts at me the moment the final customer leaves. "Aliens AND magic are real?!"

I turn around and wink at her. "I think the alien reveal is enough secrets for today."

"OH MY GOD YOU HAVE MAGIC DON'T YOU?" Betty shrieks

and hops up and down, giddy with excitement.

"Call me if you see anything else. And send me that bill."

I say goodbye and quickly head out the door, not wanting to make the pony sit in the car too long.

Another creature saved, but damn that was close.

Earth is a Secured planet. The UGF gives a Secured classification to all planets that are at this stage to prevent ecological collapse.

If a civilization were to advance too quickly, or from outside knowledge, it could destroy them from the inside out, leading to wars and worse—mass death.

We've seen it before with other planets.

It can't happen on Earth.

I'm breaking about a thousand rules by telling Betty and Carolyn about the aliens, which is why I'm keeping it to the bare fucking minimum with the details. But it's clear someone keeps dumping alien creatures at the store—or they're just drawn to it for some reason.

Maybe aliens just like smut?

CHAPTER 2

EX-BOYFRIENDS
& FLAMING CATS

The car ride back to the house was uneventful. The pony, which we determined is a girl, quieted down in the back seat after her snack of strawberries.

Jace declared her name to be Petunia.

All was quiet, music playing lightly in the background, until a loud beeping interrupted everything.

Jace and I both glance at the dash, where my phone is connected to the car.

Each of us, at the same time, reads the name and lets out matching angry breaths.

"What the hell does he want?" Jace groans. "Please tell me you're not getting back with him."

"I would rather my naked ass sit on a cactus then get back together with William Fairfax. Sometimes he's the one bringing me animals the UGF finds."

The call keeps ringing and I pout, not wanting to take it but knowing I have to.

I hit the button that connects the call and his voice pipes through the car speakers.

"Henri! How are you, darling?"

I glare at nothing, hoping he can feel my anger through the ether.

"What do you want, William?"

He's always hated when I call him by his first name.

"Aw Henri, don't tell me you're still upset about that one time—"

I nearly swerve off the road in anger.

"Upset?" I ask, aghast. Jace nods next to me, ready to throw down. "Of course I am upset. You left me stranded on a freaking freighter on Centuros Prime! I'm going to be upset about that until I'm dead—and probably in the afterlife too. So don't you 'darling' me, William. What do you want?"

"I see we're in a mood today," William mutters, and I imagine pummeling my fist into his stupidly handsome face. "We have a situation."

"What's the situation?" I grit my teeth. Just hearing the sound of his voice pisses me off.

That's how much I despise William Fairfax. One time boyfriend, now ex and the bane of my entire existence.

"Well, we've got an abandoned litter of Hellcats that just got dropped on the UGF's doorstep. They're far too young to be on their own. Someone found them behind a dumpster on Laxos-9 and they're too little to adopt out. Do you have space for me to bring them by? I can be there by tomorrow."

He just had to pick one of my favorite animals in the entire universe. Hellcats come from Vulcan, an extremely hot and sulfuric planet full of active volcanoes, where warm-blooded species thrive—including those of the furry and fiery variety.

The peace and quiet has been *so* nice, but this is the job I signed up for. And ok, they might be fire hazards, but hellkittens are *so* cute. Wait, speaking of fire hazards...

"As you are surely aware, *William,* hellcats are classified both as one of the UGF's crucially endangered species, and they're also on the list of the most dangerous creatures of the fire variety. So of course, I will take in the hellcats, but as per my contract with the UGF, that handoff will *also* come with $100,000 credits towards protection and insurance. And based on the elemental nature of their power's classification, I will also be getting triple hazard pay."

William Fairfax *thinks* he likes me, but in reality, he's afraid of anyone being smarter—or more capable—than him. Unfortunately for him, I'm a genius. Literally. It's not all that rare, considering my parentage. Novans—the main race of my father's home planet, Proxima Nova—are known for their high intelligence, but I also have a photogenic memory that tends to come in handy. It also makes me good at my job, and it means I can very easily annoy someone if I decide to be a petty bitch.

William Fairfax makes me want to be a petty ass bitch.

He groans. "Gonna make us go bankrupt, Henri!"

"Yeah, that sounds like a *you* problem, not a *me* problem."

Jace smiles next to me and makes a sign like she's counting cash. I fight off a laugh.

Will sighs. "I will transfer your credits for both now; triple hazard pay included."

"Good. I'll get the house ready for the kittens."

"Great, I'll be there around...9:00 A.M. Earth Standard Time tomorrow morning. Can't wait to see you!"

He hangs up and I exhale loudly, reaching over to pet a very soft but smiley Frankie.

"*Can't wait to see you,*" Jace mimics in a rather un-kind voice. "I can't believe you have to deal with that clown. You should have let me shoot his ass."

"Shooting people is not the be-all-end-all solution, Jace. You know this." mMy older sister simply rolls her eyes as we pull into the driveway.

Think of the kittens, I remind myself. *You're getting really cute, flaming kittens.*

Then another thought occurs to me.

"Right, we need to start fireproofing the house. Can you lay down some spells on anything flammable?" I turn to Jace as she unclicks her seatbelt.

Jace nods nonchalantly. "Yup. You get started with the portal for their habitat and I'll make sure the house doesn't burn down because a cute little kitten sneezed."

To my eternal shock, Mable and Bob fell instantly in love with Petunia the moment they saw her. The pony is now happily munching on grass with a large draft horse and the Pegasus, who have deemed themselves the pony's bodyguards.

Meanwhile, I'm downstairs in the basement trying to make a portal to a pocket universe suitable for the kittens.

My powers come with many quirks. I can make a portal to anywhere and anything. But the portal has to be within a stationary doorway.

While most of the portals I create mimic real planets that the creatures in my care come from, or environments that suit their specific needs, all of the portals in my basement connect to a pocket universe. In this instance, even if it *looks* like a certain planet, it is not in fact a portal to that planet.

They are not limitless, the pocket universes. Everything has limits, especially magic. About the size of a baseball field, these pocket universes are able to mimic the environments of known planets, while not actually being on that planet. It means I can make a safe space for animals—with entrances in my basement—where they can essentially live freely. Many of the creatures prefer living in the house, but all of them have a pocket universe portal they can access at any time.

I glare at the offending door.

My basement looks a bit crazy. Dozens of doors line the walls of the big space. Many are open, but the closed ones aren't being used. I'm seated in front of a large brown oak door with a gold doorknob, trying to get the portal to attach to the pocket universe.

Magic is intention. Magic is *will*.

Unfortunately for me, magic is also *focus*.

"Come on, Henri. Focus!" I berate myself. Dropping into a meditation pose, I fixate on the pocket universe and how I want it to look. I focus so hard, my head starts to throb.

Then I let my magic release and form the portal behind the doorway.

Jace's powers are precise and graceful, but mine is more like a giant wave that whooshes out of me.

I open my eyes just as the pink and purple glow seeps into the doorway. There's a flash of light and I feel the magic click into place in my head as the portal activates.

I let out a sigh and unfold my body, pushing up to stand as my bones pop with the movement. I open the door—the knob now warm—and smile when I see the pocket universe that looks exactly like Vulcan.

Volcanos blast in the distance. I can even smell the sulfur. The air is hot and acrid, the sky a dark red with different planets floating above.

It's beautiful, and slightly terrifying; but now the kittens will have a home.

"Henri! Where are you?" my sister shouts from above. "I'm all done up here!"

"I'm in the basement!" I call back.

"I'm coming down!"

A loud noise from a doorway four down from me catches my attention. I smile as a sleepy, fuzzy black head emerges.

"Hi, Harold. Have a good nap?"

Harold the Ursine Bear walks over to me, towering over me. He sits back on his butt and wraps me in his fuzzy bear arms, careful not to catch my skin with his claws.

"Friend," Harold says, his voice low. "Miss friend."

"I missed you too," I whisper into his fur, hugging him tightly.

I am close to all of my creatures, but Boris and Harold are two that I have bonded to the most.

Harold's body shape is similar to a grizzly bear but instead of a hump, he has brown spikes on the top of his back, and his coloring is all black with a light brown face and paws. But it's his warm brown, intelligent eyes that always strike me the most. I've known him so long that the huge scar bisecting the right side of his face that ended in the unfortunate removal of one of his eyes is barely noticeable.

Poor Harold was kidnapped from his home world on Volon-7 and taken to a breeder in Antheri where he was sold, experimented on, and forced to perform in a sort of circus act. He managed to escape when UGF raided the circus, but the injuries he sustained in the fight for freedom went on to scar him physically and emotionally.

His poor nose has a little scar where a large ring once sat. When he first arrived, he would just cower in the corner, not speaking. I spent months just sitting with him, letting him enjoy his space. But once the UGF provided me with the full breakdown of what he went through, I decided to try a new tactic. When I saw him next, I brought a book with me. He perked up and started scooting closer to me. Before long, his head was in my lap. One day he shocked me by repeating the words.

That's when I learned he knew how to read. Since then, I got a library card and regularly go get him a fresh set of books—and a tv. Despite the large forest, he often makes his way upstairs and sleeps in the guestroom next to mine. Waking up to a giant furry bear butt walking past your bedroom door takes some getting used to.

"Hey, nobody told me I was missing on hug time!" my sister calls, her heels clanking down the stairs. Her chin-length black hair is so effortlessly gorgeous. I know I'm the animal lady, but she looks like Snow White. A modern, much cooler Snow White—one that wears ripped jeans, band tees, and converse.

Jace will never admit as much, but she loves the creatures just as much as I do. And she loves Harold the most.

Harold huffs and wraps her in his arms.

"Hey Hare-bear." she says, grinning up at Harold. Her bangs are messed up from his fur, but she couldn't care less. "How was your hibernation?"

Once a month, Ursine Bears go into hibernation. Unlike Earth bears which hibernate for months at a time, Ursine Bears hibernate more regularly, but for shorter periods of time.

When Jace arrived after quitting her job, Harold was deep in hibernation, and neither of us wanted to bother him.

It's nice to see their reunion.

Harold chuffs in a bear laugh, "Sleep good. But Harold miss Jace."

"Aww, I missed you too! But good news; I'm not going anywhere. I get to stay here!" Jace smiles, but I can tell a part of her is sad.

Jace and I both possess *strange* magic. So does our brother Shaye. The UGF had our parents on the watch list, and we're all on it now too. That's part of why Jace and Shaye went to work for the UGF. Not many other galactic companies want to hire people who are listed as 'potentially armed and dangerous'.

Our mom was a Witch, and our dad was a soldier from Proxima Nova, the biggest planet in the Galaxy. Proxima Nova was the capital for all higher activity in the known universe. Well, for the civilizations advanced enough to handle space travel.

Something about both of their magics combined resulted in rather strange abilities in all three of us. Mom and Dad died in a ship crash when I was 15, and Shaye and Jace raised me after that. We fled to Earth to escape potential persecution, and then we all got legal-related jobs with the UGF for protection. When Jace gets overwhelmed, she emotes and turns the minds of all around her to jelly. I always called it mind-melting. If she tried hard enough, she could melt someone's brain. Which is why she was supposed to only use that power in emergencies. In small bursts, it can be reversed, but anyone who survived her mind melting always ended up, uh...rather upset when they discover what happened.

"I can stay...right?" Jace surprises me by whispering. We've talked about this before, but she never asked in those particular words.

"Of course." I wrap my arms around her and join in on the bear hug again. "This is your home too. You're always welcome to stay—and for as long as you want."

Harold nuzzles Jace on her cheek. Jace giggles, smiling as Harold licks her. "Jace friend. This Jace home too. Jace can read to Harold."

Jace laughs, "You know what, buddy, that sounds great. By the way, did you start watching that new show about the dragons and the knights?"

Harold blinks. "Not yet. But Harold would like."

"Yes, you would like! We'll watch it together. I'll make cinnamon apple chips and everything."

Harold's eye goes wide. "Harold love apples."

Jace pumps her fist in the air and pets Harold on the back of the head with her other hand. I laugh, making sure to give Harold a scratch too. But I wrap one arm around Jace, bringing her close. Her hair smells like citrus and sea salt. We don't live near the ocean, but somehow she always reminds me of one.

"Get everything fireproofed?" I ask her and Jace nods. She raises her hands and lets her own magic out. Bright red ropes of magic wind around her hands, glowing like sparklers on an Earth holiday.

"Perfect."

"Now we have...12 hours to figure out how to kill your ex-boyfriend."

I roll my eyes. "We're not killing him."

"I can't shoot him?" Jace asks, pouting her lips. "Ugh, you're so boring!"

"We're not shooting anyone unless they shoot at us first, Jacinda Rochelle Laselle."

Jace cringes at the use of her full name. "Ew, dude. You sound like Mom."

We both laugh, but there's a layer of sadness behind it.

Harold nudges me with his nose. "Henri want Harold to eat William?"

I hold back a laugh so hard I almost explode, "No, buddy, it's okay. We don't need to eat anyone." Harold snuffs, but his one eye is narrowed, and I can tell he's contemplating it.

I wonder if Will knows the mortal danger he's in if my animals see him.

CHAPTER 3

MAN OR [TALKING] BEAR?

The large Victorian that I get to call home has six bedrooms and four bathrooms, not counting the basement. I was able to choose what house would become my place of residence and business. Many papers were signed to ensure I would do my job and that the title would only transfer to me after thirty human years of work.

I picked this house not just because I liked how it looked, with the red bricks and the Victorian architecture, but because it came with 20 acres of land behind it.

I have plenty of room for a barn—and a place well out of the way to hide off-planet guests. With my siblings off world, it's normally just me and the creatures. Sometimes it does get a bit lonely, so it feels nice having Jace under the same roof.

My brother Shaye stops by once or twice a year—he's a scientist for the UGF and my parents' death hit him the hardest. He threw everything into his work, and now he helps the UGF plot courses to new planets and plan where to build new hyperdrives. I think Jace sees him more regularly, but honestly, I haven't asked.

Sometimes it feels like Shaye resents me, but maybe I just remind him too much of Mom. Jace has our father's dark hair, and so does Shaye, but we all have our mother's bright blue eyes. I'm the one who inherited her curly blonde hair too. Shaye is the only one of us who has dark olive skin like Father, making his eyes seem almost luminescent. He's always hidden behind glasses since people have always been a bit hypnotized by his looks.

A giant aquarium bisects my living room and the dining room, which goes into an open kitchen with white marble countertops and a large island. Honestly, the fanciest thing about the house was the kitchen. Something just fine with me. The kitchen used to be white, but I painted it a soft sage green because it needed some color. The pantry door is closed, yet Boris happily chews on a tootsie roll from his bowl on the counter. He can get into the aquarium if he wants. I tried to open a world for him downstairs with an ocean, but he was too scared to use it. Life is hard for a pygmy kraken—his kind can grow as large as a large sailboat, which is why he's been deemed too small to survive in the wild. Instead, I keep bowls around so he can come with me. Although somehow, he always manages to get into the pantry, *closed* or not.

It's the morning after we fireproofed the house and prepped for the kittens, and now we're waiting on Will to arrive. I pad over to the patio door to go out on the back porch, in my usual attire of leggings and a baggy t-shirt. I slide on a pair of barn boots and Jace grabs a spare. Luckily, we have the same shoe size. Before I slide the door shut, I motion to Boris.

"Pond or inside?"

He squeaks and makes his way over, easily sliding across the wood floor with his eight nimble arms. I lean around the corner and make eye contact with what I believe to be the head of the Kriblets. I point towards my eyes with two fingers and then point them at him and mouth, "I'm watching you."

The Kriblet just clicks its claws in a rather rude manner. Boris suddenly slaps a tentacle on their tank and they all squeak, scrambling under their rock. His tentacle goes back to normal as he squeaks across the floor to climb up my leg. Derek, my cat and lifelong companion, watches this with blown out pupils. He lets out a *mrrp* and joins the foray as Frankie, Jinx, and Barbara run around us, all barking and furious.

"You know, I'm still surprised a cat that large can run so fast," Jace says.

"Derek isn't fat—he's just fluffy. Besides, we do not body shame in this household, Jacinda." My sister gags at the use of her full name, looking horrified.

"Ugh stop! You know I hate that shit. I feel like I'm having a PTSD flashback from that time Mom caught me sneaking out with Russel Gordon."

I snicker. "Serves you right. Russel Gordon was a dweeb anyway. I told you those lifted wheels were bad news."

Jace just rolls her eyes with a smile, "If only Russel Gordon knew I only went out with him so I could hang out with his much cooler, much hotter sister." I snort. Poor Russel's head would explode to think he wasn't the center of attention.

Mable sticks her head out of the window and neighs at me, impatient. It's their breakfast time but it's also time for Will to arrive with the hellkittens. The weens trail behind us as we walk towards the barn, having abandoned Derek to a rosebush he enjoys spending his time under. Frankie takes off barking, having convinced himself he sees a squirrel, and Barbara is quick to chase after him, but Jinx stays by my feet.

Boris slithers off my leg and crawls into the small pond I

keep, hiding underneath the lily pads and amongst the croaking frogs.

A weeping willow drapes over the 6-horse, white and blue barn. The second I saw it, I knew this was home. Mable appeared like a normal bay warmblood horse. She's huge, with gorgeous dark brown and black fur and kind eyes. Most people didn't know she's a critically endangered Aseri horse from Endo who can sprout black wings at a moment's notice.

Earth-dwellers would call her kind a "Pegasus" but the proper term is an Endorian Pegasus.

Mable's favorite things are biting me in the butt while I clean her stall, playing with the deflated basketball I gave her as a toy one Christmas, and using her wings to smack her brother in the face.

I enter the barn and Mable and Bob come in. Bob used to be a workhorse for some farmers down south and when they were done with him, they sent him out for slaughter.

A huge draft gelding, with white and gray fur dotted in brown spots, and absolutely no braincells. Bob likes only three things in life: cuddles, food, and Mable.

"Give me one good reason why I shouldn't knock his lights out the moment he steps into this yard, Henri." Jace demands as I feed Mable and Bob. Both are too concerned with eating to notice me as I toss in their hay and pour their grain into their bowls.

I've got a few Kluckies too, and I throw some leftover vegetables in their coop. They run over, wings flapping as they grab the food with one of their four hands, happily cooing. Jace picks one up and it squawks, demanding to be put down.

Kluckies look remarkably like Earth chickens, except for the minor detail of them having t-rex like arms. *Two* sets of them.

"You shouldn't punch him because he works for the UGF and that kind of makes him my boss."

Jace gives me a droll look.

I scoff, "Yes I know, he's not actually my boss. But I can't be too much of a bitch otherwise it could create problems. I don't want to jeopardize the house."

Jace sighs, gently putting the Kluckie on the ground to walk over and put her arm around me. "You're not gonna lose this house over some stupid guy. Then I actually would punch him. But as long as you're taking in animals, your contract is valid. Trust me, I'm the one who validated it."

Jace is a maniac when it comes to laws. It's what made her so good at her job. She, like me, has a photographic memory. We all do actually. Family game nights have always resulted in cataclysmic arguments that involve screaming and someone eventually sweeping all of the cards or game pieces off the table with a dramatic roar.

We're a very competitive family.

Or I guess...we used to be. We didn't do that much anymore with Mom and Dad gone. All of us threw ourselves into work once we graduated college. Luckily our schooling was paid for by a trust our parents had with the UGF, but after that? It was on us to figure that out. Shaye left first as the oldest. Then Jace.

Most of my time is spent alone. Maybe that's why I gravitate toward animals. They're the steadiest company I've ever had. Not that it's a bad thing. Besides, I have Mrs. Johnson .

Wife of the aforementioned Mr. Johnson with the *very* well-behaved great dane, Mrs. Johnson is my elderly neighbor who has taken it upon herself to adopt me as her pseudo-granddaughter. Wife to Mr. Johnson with the poor Great Dane who gets his ears barked off by my three weens. Mrs. Johnson has plenty of grandchildren of her own, with three successful adult children living across the country, but I think she's a bit lonely too. Mrs. Johnson pops by occasionally, prompting me to regularly sound the human alarm to the creatures, which more or less means all the aliens know to either hide or pretend to be very much not an alien species.

It keeps me on my toes, but I'm grateful for her friendship and company.

I've never known for sure, but I've always thought that my magic has to do with animals somehow. I can't talk to them or anything, but they *all* love me. All of them. Even the shy ones. Considering how dangerous most of my animals are and exactly what they've been through? I don't know *what* exactly, but I know without a shadow of a doubt that my magic makes me some sort of creature magnet.

I wipe my hands and brush the dust and hay off as we walk behind the barn.

"I bet he looks horrible," Jace says, eyes narrowed. I laugh as Barbara runs at my feet. I pick her up, cuddling her fluffy body as she kisses my face. Jinx leans against Jace's leg, wagging his fluffy tail so hard it might wag right off.

Suddenly the pressure in the air changes, and my ears pop. A red light shines down in front of us, coating the grass in crimson, and William Fairfax materializes holding a cage of perfect, fuzzy black and gray kittens in his hands.

Of course, he looks handsome. He had to show up all perfectly coiffed and effortless. Frankly, it's unfair to society. William Fairfax could charm the pants off of a rock. *Everyone* is into him. William Fairfax is *everyone's* type, with his perfectly fitted black jeans and the long sleeve gray shirt that clings so tightly to his muscular physique, it might as well be painted on. His shoulder-length black hair only accents his warm brown skin and his dark eyes.

Now I'm the one who wants to punch something.

Barbara licks my cheek again, bringing me back to reality. I sniff and step forward as Will emerges from the light.

"Henri! So good to see you. Wow, you look *amazing.*"

Ugh.

I glare as he turns to my sister, going in for a hug.

Jace just puts her palm up, stopping him. "Nope."

I have to hide my laugh with a cough.

"Jacinda, always a pleasure." Will smirks. "How goes the *forced* leave of absence?"

"I already want to shoot your ass. Don't make me do it twice."

"Enough," I whisper to her.

But Jace only continues. "Bite me, Fairfax."

William Fairfax smiles and runs one hand through his tousled dark brown hair.

I hate him. I hate him so much. I hope a bird poops in his perfect fucking hair.

"Now, if we're done with this very unwanted reunion, give me the hellkittens and you can be on your way."

I grab the cage from his hands quickly as Jace reaches for the other side.

Three tiny black kittens stare back at me. They look like small Maine Coons, but bright red and orange flames light their paws and the tips of their ears. Even the ends of their tails have flames on them.

Their tiny, fuzzy bodies are tucked into a soft, fire-resistant blanket.

They're so young. My heart instantly aches for them.

I gently push my hand in and rub the tip of my pointer finger along one of their heads. The kittens are warmer than usual thanks to the flame, but it doesn't burn my skin when I touch it.

Thank you, Jace, and your fireproofing spell.

Its fur is softer than velvet. The little creature purrs, leaning against my hand. The other two watch quizzically before pushing their heads out and asking for pets too. Hellcats don't breed often, so kittens are rare.

"Henri, can we talk? Please? I want to explain." Will steps forward but I take a step backwards.

"The only time I want to speak with you, William Fairfax, is if it involves a creature that needs a safe place to stay. Otherwise, I have nothing to say to you," I sniff. "Have a safe trip back to the Arc. Let me know if anything comes up."

The Arc, otherwise known as the UGF headquarters, is based on a moon in the Cassiopaean system. Very far away. *Thankfully.*

He sighs. "Yeah, okay. I will. I'm—I'm sorry again, Henri. I wish you'd let me explain, but I'll give you space. Just know I'm sorry."

"You abandoned her in space, Fairfax. Fuck off before I kick your ass." Jace smiles. "Or *worse.*"

"I hate you." Will smirks at her. He turns to face us and tips an imaginary hat. "Ladies, until next time. Call me if you change your mind, Henri. We were good together—we can be good together again."

Then he disappears, the red light fading as he leaves Earth.

"God, he's a prick," Jace hisses. "You should have let me shoot him in the ass!"

I sigh. "He uses a fucking 3-in-1 shampoo too, Jace."

My sister groans and covers her eyes. "Men suck." She grasps her heart in mock pain. "Women are so much better."

I nod. "Yeah, agree."

We've both dated on all sides of the spectrum. Jace is bisexual and I'm...well, I don't really know. I've never met anyone who particularly interested me, if I'm being honest. I've been attracted to people before: men, and some women. But it's been me for so long that I'm not sure I know how to be anything other than single and alone.

It's been years since I went on a date. That was mostly when I was young. Jace is the one that caught me doing the walk of shame after my first time, so she knows I'm no saint.

Dating is harder now. I knew it would be but how can I get to know someone when I have to hide my entire life? I can't risk the biggest secret in the entire universe just for some lousy sex.

I sigh. "It would have to be someone in our business. Then I'd consider it. But I can't hide what I do. It's too much work, and they're too much a part of my life. Besides, you know Boris gets..." I pause and bend down and pick up the squeaking pygmy kraken, his red little body swirling with happy pinks, yellows, and oranges. I cover his small ear holes with my hands. "Separation anxiety," I whisper. "He gets very stressed when left alone too long, but he doesn't like to talk about it. It's a touchy subject."

Boris pulls my hands off him and squirts water at my face, hitting me in the cheek. I squeak and he just laughs, his tentacles swirling happily as he wraps around my upper arm.

Derek is on his back, rolling around in the grass as we walk back to the house. But all it takes is a single tiny *mew* from the kitten cage and he's meowing at my feet, frantic to see the little ones.

"Buddy, they could hurt you. Be careful."

Derek ignores me as we go down into the basement. I wave to Harold as we go through the living room. I'd warned him about the kittens, and he decided that was too much drama for him, so he'd stay upstairs for now.

God, I hope Mrs. Johnson doesn't come by. This would give her a heart attack.

We take the kittens down into the basement and release them into their new habitat. But the kittens just cry, head-butting against the baby gate. I bend over to pet them through my gloves and one of the kittens sneezes.

I wish I could say it was a regular sneeze, but based on the way my eyebrows just burned completely off my face, I'd say the hellkittens are at the fire-breathing stage of their growth.

Just a guess. I look over to my sister as she barely holds in her laughter.

"Not a fucking word, Jacinda. Not. A. Word."

CHAPTER 4

CRAZY ANIMAL LADY

M *mrp.* Derek meows at me for the hundredth time today.

It was a long night watching over the hellkittens. I know they're fine but I always spend the first night with *any* new creature, particularly the younger ones, sleeping at the edge of their enclosure. In this case, right by the door to their habitat.

The kittens must be socialized because they want to climb all over me. My eyebrows never stood a chance. Not even twenty-four hours in and I had to go wake Jace up and ask if she'd reapply another fire-proofing spell.

Of course, she was laughing so hard she couldn't even respond, which led to a slap fight of epic proportions.

"Maybe Shaye can send some potions. He's gotta have some hardcore fireproofing potions in that stupidly expensive lab of his."

Being a scientist, my older brother has dabbled in the alchemical arts, particularly with his unique brand of magic.

Shaye can change the molecular structure of things with merely his will. The UGF forced him to work for them, wanting to keep him forever in sight—and hand.

"Text him yourself," Jace had groaned, face in her pillow.

"He likes you better," I reminded her. "You know we haven't

been close in years." I could hear Jace grumble under her breath as I went downstairs.

That was hours ago, and now I'm in an argument with my oversized cat because he thinks he's the kittens' mother.

"Derek, you can't go in there. The kittens will burn you to a crisp, I'm sorry." The aforementioned feline just looks at me and meows again, absolutely ignoring everything I just said.

Mmrp.

Ugh, he just won't let up. Derek crawls in my lap and gets up on his back legs, putting his soft gray paws on my face as he leans forward to lick my nose.

I can't believe he's using his signature move on me. That little rat! He knows I'll cave if he does this. Derek just purrs louder and rubs his face against mine, getting fur everywhere. But I couldn't care less.

"Listen, you need to be patient. I should have a way to fire-proof you soon."

"The fireproofing tonic just arrived through the Mail," Jace calls as she plops down the stairs, looking much more herself in a pair of loose, old jeans and a band t-shirt.

The Mail is what we call our intergalactic mailbox. I have no idea what kind of magic is powering it, but we're able to receive very small parcels and letters from the Arc through it. It's UGF issued and something I've unfortunately come to love.

I've also spent countless hours with my phone flashlight searching inside of it for some sign of the portal. But for all intents and purposes, it looks like a regular mailbox.

Although Mrs. Johnson has noted on multiple occasions that having a mailbox underneath the apple tree in my backyard doesn't make a lick of sense. I told her it was a bat house but she just made her signature *mhm*, not believing me at all.

"Nice shirt," I laugh, looking at the 90's punk band tee Jace most certainty stole from me.

"You never wear shit like this, so don't even try." She shoves a small glass vial of sparkling purple liquid into my hands.

"Pretty," I mutter, watching the shimmer.

Jace snorts, "Ok, dragon obsessed with sparkly treasure. Drink some and then give the rest to Derek. Since you've been spelled already, you don't need as much."

I nod, grateful for the help.

"And for what it's worth, you're wrong, you know. Shaye loves you, Henri. Just like I do."

I want to believe her. I know Jace loves me. I also know in his own way, Shaye loves me. But I'm...well, I'm not sure he *likes* me.

I pick up Derek and stand. It takes some maneuvering, but I manage to pour most of the potion down his throat before taking a few gulps myself. It tastes like grapefruit and mint but with a weird, metallic aftertaste. Derek meows angrily and claws me. After a stern talking, I open the baby gate and let him interact with the hellkittens. God, I hope the tonic works.

Sure enough, one of the three kittens coughs up a fireball and it hits Derek right in the face, but there's no burnt fur.

I let out a relieved breath. Derek curls up around the kittens and immediately sets to work cleaning them. They all look a bit confused at first, but quickly cuddle up to him, suckling on his ears and burrowing into his thick fur.

Derek's blue eyes cross with happiness. I hear a sniffing noise and look over to see Jace rubbing her eyes. I raise a brow.

"It's just so cute," she admits.

I snort and whisper, "I know, sometimes I just stare at the animals for hours!"

"I don't even want to go upstairs."

I laugh. "It's easier when it's a poison-spitting cobra from Endo or an archidna that likes to eat flesh for breakfast. Not all the creatures are cute and cuddly—or safe. All things considered, fire is a minor hazard compared to what I've had to deal with."

Jace grimaces "God, an archidna? They're nasty pieces of work." I nod. She shakes her head, grossed out.

"Where's Harold?" I ask as we turn and pad back upstairs. I have to shove her along cause we both keep looking back at sweet Derek and his new foster kittens.

"We started watching this new reality show where everyone is naked and left in a jungle, and he's hooked," she replies as we walk into the kitchen and look through to the living room. Harold sits in the middle of the floor, spooning cereal into his mouth. A cinnamon sugar one, by the look of it. But it's the bib tucked around his neck to protect his fur that tops it off.

Jace and I both yank our phones out and sneak pics.

"God, he's so cute," I whisper to her. Jace just nods.

"It's too much to handle!"

"Harold can hear you," Harold's low voice grumbles around his cereal munching.

"Just accept that you're adorable," Jace calls as I start the kettle. We have an espresso machine, but I mostly prefer tea. Jace starts it up and makes herself a mocha. She, like Boris, loves chocolate and sweets. I'm good with my jasmine green tea. The hot water pours over the tea bag, filling up my clear mug as the smell of jasmine wafts up toward me. The scent always calms me down. I squeeze some honey in—might as well since I'm a regular purchaser of the wholesale size 2-pack of raw honey because Harold likes honey on *everything*.

A suction noise followed by wet squeaking is plenty of heads up as Boris peeks his head up from the edge of the counter. Jace laughs as he pulls himself up. I grab a spare bowl—there's one in every room of the house at this point—and fill it with water, setting it behind him so he can be comfortable. Boris jumps in, splashing us both. Jace and I squeal, but mine quickly morphs into laughter at the aghast look on my sister's face.

I hold out a fist and Boris bumps it just like I taught him. "That was a good one, dude."

"Ah ha! Now we know where the bad habits come from, Captain Enabler." Jace points a finger at me, laughter in her eyes.

"I have no idea what you're talking about," I sniff, taking my teabag out of the mug now that it's steeped. That first sip is heavenly. Even the smell of Jace's mocha is great.

"Sit down, I'll cook. I missed having a kitchen," Jace orders and I plop down on the barstool, moving Boris next to me. Frankie and Barbara paw at my leg and I pick them up one at a time and settle them in my lap. Jinx plays with a toy on the floor, content to be on his own.

I pet Frankie's silky ears and spy another gray hair. It's a reminder of how long we've been together and that she won't live forever. None of my creatures will.

Jace is quiet as she pads around the kitchen, pulling out the ingredients for pancakes. My favorite. But—

"Pancakes at three in the afternoon?" I laugh, watching her.

"Yup. Cause we're fucking *adults* and that means if we want pancakes at 3pm, we make the damn pancakes."

The sound of her in the kitchen is so comforting. It reminds me of growing up and watching my parents cook dinner.

As Jace spoons the batter for the first pancake, the air turns warm, smelling deliciously like buttermilk with caramelized bananas.

"Bananas Foster Pancakes?" I gasp. "You're making dad's recipe?"

I can't remember the last time I had these.

Jace gives me a small smile. "I've been craving them since the day I got here, to be honest. I think it's being back on Earth. It...reminds me of them."

I nod. "It does for me too."

We both go quiet while she finishes up the pancakes, each of us lost in our memories. A cold nose rubs against the back of my arm, and I turn to see Harold pushing the other barstool out of the way so he can sit on the floor next to me and lean his head on the counter.

"Don't be sad, friend," he says, patting me on the shoulder. I lean into his giant fuzzy paw, the pups still on my lap. All of the creatures are luckily very friendly with each other.

"Do you remember your parents?" Jace asks gently.

Harold shakes his head. "Harold does not remember much from before. Harold not like to think about it."

I pat his paw, resting my hand over it. "That's understandable."

Jace nods in agreement. "Plus, you've got lots of family now. Right? Harold Laselle has a nice ring to it."

I blink. Harold's brown eyes go wide as he watches Jace.

"Harold...Laselle?" he asks gently. Jace nods. "If you want that and if it's okay with Henri."

"Of course it's okay! I would be honored. But Harold, you don't have to answer now. Either way, this will always be your home and we'll always be your family," I assure him.

"I am...Harold Laselle," he says, a beary smile on his face. I swear his brown eyes even twinkle with happiness. Boris lets out a squeak from his bowl and shoots water into the air in a sort of fireworks display. Barbara groans grumpily but Jinx jumps and bites the water as if it was a toy. I hear a tapping against the glass as the Kriblets even join in, banging their claws against the tank wall in unison.

"Then that's that, you're *officially* family now. The real question is though: do you want your own bedroom or are you going to keep bunking with Jace?" I arch an eyebrow at her even though my question is directed toward Harold. Jace hides a smile.

"I keep Jace safe. It's Harold's job."

Okay then.

As Jace slides two plates stacked high with buttermilk pancakes topped with caramelized bananas and powdered sugar, I can't help but wonder what's going to happen when Jace eventually leaves—and immediately wish that maybe, just maybe, she will actually stay this time. And *never* leave.

CHAPTER 5

CODE KITTEN

"Henrietta, are you back here, honey?" Distantly, I hear the back gate open and close as Mrs. Johnson makes her way along the side of the house. I emerge from the barn, covered in shavings and hay. Mable follows behind.

I don't always let her, but on slow days when I'm working in the garden, I'll leave their gate open since the whole property is fenced in. Do some of my flowers end up as Mable food on those days? Yes. But it's worth it watching her play chase with Barbara and Jinx as Frankie looks on out of her good eye. Bob and Petunia on the other hand just stand behind me creepily, both of them half asleep and half-begging for treats. I pet Bob's soft snout before standing and walking over to Mrs. Johnson.

"Hi, Mrs. Johnson. How was your weekend?"

She tuts. "Busy. I had a bridge tournament down at the Center and that goddamned Roy Sellers kept winning!"

I snort. "Maybe he's cheating."

"Oh, of course he is—and I told him so! In front of everyone! You should have seen how red and angry he got, it was incredible. The old grouch deserves it."

"It sounds like he does. I'm glad you had a good time though. Sounds like a fun day." I smile. "Would you like some tomatoes? I have plenty of extra to share from today's harvest—and some spicy peppers for Mr. Johnson and apples for Parker."

Mrs. Johnson claps her hands together. "Oh! Yes please. Thank you so much dear. There is nothing quite like the taste of fresh vegetables grown with love. Parker loves his apple treats and that husband of mine likes his salsa hotter than the sun, I swear. They'll be so pleased."

I hand Mrs. Johnson a basket I put together of some of today's harvest. Because of the weather in Kansas City, I'm able to grow a lot of my own food all year round. It makes up for the oppressive heat and humidity. I try to give Mrs. Johnson some vegetables and herbs once a week, or at least some flowers. But currently said flowers are in Mable's fat belly, so veggies will have to do.

"I was just thinking about making some salsa. This is perfect, Henrietta. You're such a nice girl." Mrs. Johnson hugs the basket close. She's in her Monday best, a bright teal sweater set that sets off her deep umber complexion beautifully. I hope that as I age, I age like Nancy Johnson.

With smile lines that show a life well lived and full of joy, her rich brown eyes, hidden behind various colorful, chic glasses, are always twinkling with mirth and happiness.

She might annoy me with calling me by my full first name, but it's well worth it when I get her friendship in return. I've long looked up to her positive outlook on life.

Mable comes over and sniffs her shoulder. Mrs. Johnson just raises perfectly manicured brow. "Try to bite me, see what happens."

Mable wisely backs off with a huff. I snicker at this intelligent horse alien being tamed by Mrs. Johnson.

"I don't know how you manage to take care of so many animals alone, Henrietta.”

“She has help this time,” a voice calls from inside. Jace emerges in another band tee and ripped jeans, her short black bob curly from the humidity.

“Jacinda!” Mrs. Johnson calls, wrapping Jace in a big hug. Jace smiles warmly, her blue eyes bright. Her pale cheeks turn slightly red as emotion makes her overwhelmed.

It’s so *adorable* to see.

“When did you get in town. sweetie?”“She arrived this weekend,” I chimed in. “It’s a long drive from Austin, so it was pretty late when she got in.”

We decided previously that if anyone asked, Jace lives in Austin instead of on a freaking moon thousands of light-years away. And that she arrived here in Subaru like a normal person and not via her own spaceship.

There’s nothing normal about us, despite how we might appear.

“How lovely! I’m so glad your back. This house is far too big for poor Henrietta to be all by her lonesome. I’ve been telling her to get a roommate—or a beau. Whatever it is you kids call it.” Mrs. Johnson nods to herself. “Yes, it will be good to have you here. How long are you staying?”

I turn to Jace, unsure of the answer myself.

She bites her lip. “Well, I’m not sure. That depends on how long Henri will have me.”

I walk up to Jace and smack her arm.

“This is your home too, you idiot. You know that.”

“Language!” Mrs. Johnson chastises me.

“Well then,” Jace laughs. “I guess I’m staying for a while then, Mrs. Johnson. Long enough that you can finally teach me how to play Bridge."

"Oh, how *marvelous!*" Mrs. Johnson claps her hands together, looking positively gleeful. "I'm so glad."

Clutching her basket, she gives us both a smile. "These tomatoes are calling my name. I'm going to go make some salsa and I'll bring you girls a jar of it when I'm done."

"How about when you're done, you come back over—bring Mr. Johnson—and we can eat it on the porch. I'll make some mango iced tea," Jace offers. "Henri can get out the cards."

Since Mom and Dad passed, there's been a hole in all of our hearts. Jace and Shaye even more so. Mrs. Johnson has filled that hole for me. It's still there, and I still spend my evenings awake and wishing my parents are still here. But her warmth helps. It's comforting in a way I never could have anticipated. It seems Jace feels the same way.

"That sounds wonderful, honey. I'll go mix this up and be back in an hour." She heads back around the house, sandals slapping against the grass and necklaces jingling with each step. As she opens the gate, she turns. "Don't you go getting into trouble while I'm gone."

"If you only knew," Jace mutters beneath her breath.

"Henri, wake up!"

"It's too early for school, mom," I grumble into my pillow.

I'd fallen asleep early after a few too many spiked mango iced teas—the iced tea courtesy of Jace, and the spiking courtesy of a snickering Mr. Johnson who kept adding liquor when Mrs. Johnson would turn away.

"Five more minutes," I moan, tucking myself harder into the covers. My head is pounding and my mouth dry.

"No school today," I mumble. "Can't do it."

"It's Jace, you ninny. Wake the hell up!"

I roll over and pull the blankets over my head. Barbara is in her usual spot underneath the covers curled at my stomach. She's my own personal heating pad. Jinx is at my feet, Frankie is curled up on the pillow next to me, and Derek is normally tucked beneath my chin, but judging from the lack of fur up my nose and in my eyes, he must be sleeping with the hellkittens.

The blankets are yanked off me and someone bodily shoves me off the bed. I hit the floor with a loud thunk.

"What the fuck?" I groan. "Take back everything I said about you staying here. I'm kicking you out. This is cruel and unusual punishment!"

"This isn't the time, Henrietta." Hearing my full name from her, something that *never* happens, wakes me up quickly.

As do her next words.

"The kittens are gone."

I—wait, what? My mind is sluggish as I blink and take in the dark room. Jace stands in the doorway panting, eyes and hair wild, as if she was electrocuted. She's only in a large t shirt and underwear, her long pale legs making her look even taller than her 5'7" stature. I'm so jealous that she has a whole two inches on me.

"Start over. I'm still waking up. The kittens are gone?"

Jace nods, visibly stressed. She wrings her hands nervously. "They're not in their enclosure."

"Did you check the rest of the house? Kittens are small, they can hide in tiny spaces. I'm sure they're just hiding."

"They're not hiding, Henri. They're gone and whoever took them also took Derek."

"Repeat that," I say as my heart stops beating.

"Derek is gone. Someone took him and the hellkittens."

I stare at her for a good thirty seconds, blinking rapidly as I fight the rage trembling through me. "Henri, someone broke in and stole your fucking cat."

My heart stops beating.

It's like being in the center of a tornado. Everything stops and the world stills as reality hits me with the weight of a thousand semitrucks.

Then everything speeds up and I'm yanked into the present. Words tumble from my lips.

"They...stole my cat? Someone stole Derek?"

Jace winces, "Judging by the neon green smudge near the patio door, they're also um, no longer on this planet."

That does it.

"MY CATS ARE IN SPACE?" I shriek, making the windows wobble. "WHAT THE FUCK?"

"Yeah. *YEAH.* What the hell do we do?" Jace starts pacing. I just throw on the closest clothes I can find and pull my curly hair up in a bun.

"What we do is get them back and then we obliterate the thieves. Nobody touches my cats and lives." I push with my power, making my skin glow.

"Oh shit. Mean Henri is making an appearance."

Siblings are *so* annoying.

"Shut up," I hiss at her. Then another reality hits me. "You know what this means though."

"God, not him. We don't have to call him. One visit was plenty!" Jace whines.

I sigh and grab my sword, lighting it up with a thought. "Believe me, I know."

"Harold will eat intruders. We get fireball cats back. Miss Derek." Harold nods and suddenly more spikes explode from his back, lining all the way down his spine.

Time to call in reinforcements, otherwise known as William Fairfax, galactic fuckboy and unfortunately my ex-boyfriend. *Perfect.*

CHAPTER 6

MEET THE CREATURES

"**A**LRIGHT, here's the deal."

My creatures face me, all of them looking nervous and sleepy. Harold sits with Jace, the weenie dogs at their feet. Even Mable, Bob, and Petunia watch from the yard, their velvet noses flared, their eyes wide.

"Jace and I are going into space; that means you all need to be on your best behavior. I've called Mrs. Johnson, and she will watch you during the day, but under no circumstances will you reveal any alien nature. You are, for all intents and purposes, normal, Earth animals. Got it?"

The creatures nod.

"Now, overnight, you will have some new friends. As you all know, aliens have been showing up at a bookstore in town. I had to read them in, so I've asked that the two women who work there take turns staying here, that way there is someone with you at all times. Now they do know about aliens, but this is all very new and scary for them. Please do not do anything that could startle them, okay? They're probably really nervous."

The doorbell rings and the weenie dogs all set off, barking like we're under siege.

"That will be them. Now, be yourselves, but remember; don't scare them. Kevin," I point at the fishtank where the red Kriblet watches with narrowed eyes. "I'm talking to you. No fucking with the humans. I mean it."

He rolls his eyes and disappears back into his rock hideout. I'm 99% sure there's some sort of portal in his fishtank, but I've never been able to figure it out.

Jace runs down the stairs, a backpack on her shoulder and a duffel bag in one hand. She meets me at the bottom of the stairs and drops the bags to greet the creature-sitters with me.

I eye the duffel bag as it *thunks* to the floor with a suspiciously metallic sound.

"Did you pack an *entire* bag full of guns?" I hiss at her.

Jace stares at me. "Of course. Why wouldn't I? I might have to shoot something...or someone."

I shake my head, unable to deal with my trigger-happy sister.

I open the door and find two, wide-eyed humans.

"We came as soon as we could," Betty squeaks, almost bouncing up and down with excitement.

"Do we get to see a spaceship?" Carolyn whispers. "Or more aliens?"

"Shh!" I grab her arm and yank her inside. Betty follows, dropping her own backpack to the floor.

Both women are dressed in their pajamas—which makes since, considering it's 2:00 in the morning.

"Thank you so much for coming on such short notice," I tell them. "The creatures will be on their best behavior, I promise."

I glare at Kevin's beady eyes peeking out from his rock in the fishtank, just to remind him that I'm watching him.

"Are you kidding?" Betty says. "We get to babysit ALIENS. Of *course* we came."

I smile, grateful for their help—and their enthusiasm.

They're the first full-humans who have been read-in on the whole alien situation…potentially *ever*.

Betty and Carolyn let out twin *gasps* of surprise as we enter the living room.

Harold is joining us on this journey, as backup and emotional support. Which means he's in his assassin best, inspired by my meddling older sister. A velvet blue cape is draped around his shoulders, covering up the spikes that travel down his back. A sword is around his shoulders, the gilded gold hilt peeking out behind his fuzzy ears.

"Hello. Am Harold."

Betty squeals and Carolyn makes a choking sound.

"He—he can talk?" Carolyn sputters.

"Of course he can!" Betty responds. "Because he's a good bear, aren't you, Harold?"

Harold nods solemnly.

Then the weenie dogs make their appearance, stampeding through the living room.

"Okay, time to meet all of the creatures. This is Harold, as you know," I motion to the bear. "The dogs are Frankie, Jinx, and Barbara. In the fishtank, we have Kevin—he's a Kriblet."

I lean closer to the humans and lower my voice, "I'm 99% sure he's the head of some underwater mafia operation so be careful around him, and don't let him see any of your jewelry. He will steal it."

Both humans nod, looking nervous yet excited.

"Outdoors we have the horses. Mable, Bob, and Petunia."

"YOU NAMED THE BOOK EATING PONY PETUNIA?" Betty squeals.

"Actually, I did." Jace says, leaning on Harold in a side hug.

"A good name." Carolyn nods.

"The Kluckies won't bother you; just pretend they're normal chickens."

I give them the full house tour and show them to the guest room before gathering my own bags and saying my goodbyes to the creatures. Betty and Carolyn give us some space, but I know they're listening—and waiting to see the spaceship.

Just as the tour ends and I get ready to tell the creatures goodbye, an airborne missile with tentacles launches at my face. I catch it at the last minute.

"Hi, buddy," I smile, hugging Boris against me. But he squeaks in anger.

"Is that an octopus?!" I hear Betty shriek.

I cover Boris' ear holes. "No, he's a pygmy kraken. He gets very sensitive when you call him an octopus."

Betty's eyes turn serious. "Of course."

I turn my attention back to the creature in my arms. "Boris, you can't come with us. I don't have a travel bowl set up for you." Boris just squeaks again and shoots water at my face. "I'm sorry, buddy. I need you to stay back and keep everyone safe, okay? You're in charge."

Actually, Mrs. Johnson, Betty, and Carolyn are in charge, but he doesn't need to know that.

I swear, Boris actually grumbles angrily before slinking back into the aquarium. I've spent years decorating it with various starfish and other saltwater critters from animal rescues around the country. But Boris enjoys the rock tunnel system the most. He disappears under the gravel, only his two beady eyes left showing as he camouflages and turns blue to match the sand.

I sigh at his dramatic display. "Excuse me for a moment, I have to make a call before we take off."

Betty and Carolyn nod as they sit down on the couch, the weenies instantly jumping into their laps, providing an excellent distraction.

I hit redial on the number in my phone and brace myself.

"Henri! This isn't a great time, can I call you back?" William Fairfax shouts into the phone. What sound like guns echo in the distance. "YEAH, DIE, MOTHERFUCKER!" he screams.

I grind my teeth. "Make it a good time then, because someone stole the hellkittens. Someone not from Earth, William!"

"What did you say?" Will yells, not having heard me. "Someone kidnapped the kittens. Well...that sucks."

My anger rises out of nowhere as I picture his stupidly perfect face. Something like a static shock bursts from me and goes into the phone. I hear a sharp yelp from the other end of the phone.

Well. That's new. But no time to worry about new potential powers.

"That sucks? That SUCKS? It doesn't just suck, you idiot. It's also ILLEGAL. Aliens came to Earth outside of the treaty and stole endangered animals. They stole *Derek*. They're all gone. SO yeah, I guess you could say it sucks. What the fuck are you going to do about it?"

I'm panting by the time I finish, my hands trembling. I haven't let myself lose it or freak out since we found out the cats were gone, but my patience and sanity hang on by a thread.

"Shit. *Shit*. Okay." Will takes a deep breath despite the gunfire in the background. "Get to the Arc as soon as possible. You might be able to get them to help, or at least for them to send a team out to look for them. I can't guarantee they'll help, but it's the best shot you have at finding them."

Of course *he* can't lower himself to help.

"They *might* help?"

"UGF Command *will* help. Get there, find one of the generals, and brief them of the situation. They'll get you outfitted. In the meantime, get on The Menace and get moving before the trail goes cold."

I'm sputtering as he hangs up on me with a click.

How *dare* he! Jace returns as I'm considering hurling my phone against the wall. She carefully takes it from my hands and pats me on the head.

"No destroying anything yet," she says in a cheery voice.

I slap her hand away, protecting my curls from her tangly fingers.

It takes me a few minutes to hug everyone goodbye. I'm openly crying when I finish. Jace wraps her arm around my shoulders, rubbing between my shoulder-blades in a comforting slow circle.

I inhale deeply and wipe the tears off my cheeks. My eyes meet Betty and Carolyn's, and I force a small smile onto my face.

"Okay, *now* you can see the spaceship."

The squeals that follow nearly shatter my eardrums.

I lock up as we make out way outside, through the back yard and into the barn area. Mable watches me with suspicious eyes. Her black mane is covered in shavings. Clearly, I just woke her up. Bob however is snoring louder than the local train. Jace chuckles but I just shush her, not wanting to disturb him.

"I'll be back, Mable. Keep an eye on everything and don't be mean to the humans." She just snorts before turning away. So much for that promise.

"Is she like...a normal horse?" Betty whispers to me.

I laugh softly. "No."

Betty blinks. "Right. Of course."

"Don't get too close to her, or her wings might appear, and she hits harder than a WWE wrestler."

Carolyn trips at that and nearly faceplants on the grass.

"Horses...with wings. Got it."

As we wait for Jace's ship to arrive, my anxiety starts whirling and I'm stuck with one major question. How the hell am I going to find the kittens? And if the UGF can't help...who can?

CHAPTER 7

STOWAWAY

Betty and Carolyn wait with us in the dark. For a few moments, it's terribly awkward.

Harold stands between me and Jace, and the rest of the creatures watch from the barn or from inside the house. The weenies wait at the patio door, their noses pressed against the window.

Boris, however, isn't anywhere to be seen. I try not to be hurt by that but I know he's sad I'm leaving.

I'm most attached to Boris, Derek, and Harold. I love all of my creatures, don't get me wrong, but they're the ones who I have the deepest connection with. None of us like being apart for long, aside from Harold's monthly hibernation.

A noise overhead followed by a bright spotlight announces the ship.

Jace keeps it in orbit around Saturn instead of parking it in the backyard. It's safer that the ship isn't actually ever *on* Earth.

The Menace is a small but powerful spaceship my sister has lovingly restored and upgraded over the past decade. Named after an Earth movie about an order that fights against evil in space, something which she found endlessly amusing. The ship has a primary bedroom with a built-in bathroom, and then two rooms with bunk beds and a shared bathroom. There's a small gym, a mess hall, and a nicely updated kitchen with a hy-droponic greenhouse with regularly growing fruits, vegetables, and herbs. All of my parents' children became green thumbs in some way. I had my back yard, Jace has her greenhouse, and Shaye deals in dried herbs and distillations. Outside of the living quarters was the cockpit, an engineering room, and the cooling system. It wasn't the fanciest ship, but the additions Jace has made have really turned it into something beautiful.

Betty and Carolyn squeal as The Menace lowers, hovering briefly before landing. An automatic walkway lowers.

"Fucking *pinch* me," Betty whispers, followed by a loud, "OUCH!"

"You said to pinch you!" Jace shrugs. "Meet my ship. This is The Menace."

"You named your ship after Star Wars?" Carolyn's jaw drops.

"Duh," Jace nods. "It's a classic for a reason—and we suspect it was highly inspired by my parents, but that's a story for an-other day."

That last part leaves Betty and Carolyn gasping, their eyes wide.

"You have my number, right?"

The humans nod.

I gave them the number for my transponder—a communica-tor and phone that works no matter where we are in the galaxy. I don't ever use it except to talk to Jace when she's off planet, but I want to make sure that they can call us if anything is wrong.

"And you have Mrs. Johnson's information?"

They nod again.

I take a deep breath and wave to the creatures one more time.

"Alright, then we need to get going. Thank you again so much for doing this. I am so grateful and will be forever in your debt."

"Can you like...bring us back some alien-y stuff?"

Now it's my turn to blink.

Jace snorts beside me as she and Harold walk up the ramp.

"I'll try. It's not...touristy the way Earth is, but I'll see what I can do."

"WOO! Space stuff!" Betty high-fives Carolyn, who looks equally excited.

I walk up the ramp before remembering something.

"Oh yes—most of the creatures are aliens."

Carolyn lifts a brow. "You mentioned that."

"No, I mean...they're *intelligent* aliens. So, talk to them the way you would talk to a human. Even if they can't respond in English, almost all of them will understand you."

"SHUT UP!" Betty claps her hands together. "This is the coolest thing TO EVER HAPPEN TO ME!"

I smile.

"Good luck and thank you again."

With that, I wave to them as I enter The Menace and the ramp lifts, closing with a hissing sound and a click.

We drop our stuff in our room—I'll be bunking with Jace while we head to the Arc. After our stuff is situated, Jace instructs the ship to head into orbit while we head to the cockpit as the ship lifts smoothly into the air.

Harold smushes into a seat and buckles himself in. Jace is just starting the full ignition sequence to charge the warp drive when a squeaking noise sounds in the behind us.

My head falls into my hands as I groan, "God, please tell me you didn't."

Boris slides right onto my lap and looks up at me with a loud squeak. I groan again and rub my eyes, hoping this is just some stress-induced mirage.

Boris squeaks again, gently wrapping a tentacle around my fingers. I peak open my eyes and he's still there. Beside him is a plastic container he must have taken from the kitchen. He's drilled holes in the sides and attached some sort of leash thing around it, and there are superglued wheels on the bottom. It's filled with water and a few small keepsakes from his tank.

Boris has snuck onto Jace's ship with a DIY on-the-go fish-tank.

Jace holds back her laughter as I try to look angry.

"Boris, what are you doing here?" I chide. Boris just makes his eyes all wide and puppy-like, crawling up my chest to nuzzle underneath my chin. "You're in so much trouble. So much. I'm talking grounded for life."

Boris just sighs happily and squirts some water in the air.

Jace coughs to cover her laugh. "Are we ready?"

I try to untangle Boris but he holds on tight. I sigh. "Yes, we're all ready."

Jace starts the engine, and we quickly jump out of Earth's atmosphere. We align with the Earth jump-gate, hidden on the dark side of Earth's moon. It takes a few minutes for the gate to warm up, but we all tighten our seatbelts as Jace begins the count down.

"Relax your necks, don't fight it. Take a deep breath," Jace orders.

I try to scoff, but it ends up turning into a choked sound as a countdown appears on the screen.

I've been to space, but not nearly as much as Jace.

It's been *years* since I've experienced warp drive.

FIVE.

FOUR.

Harold takes a deep breath and holds his bear nose.

THREE.

TWO.

Boris curls tighter against me.

ONE.

The countdown ends and we're flung through the cosmos at the speed of light. Everything wavers as reality shifts. I have no idea how long it lasts—seconds, minutes, hours. I know logically it's only a few seconds, but it's so hard to discern. But we pop out just outside of the Cassiopaean jump-gate in one piece. Boris lets out something that sounds like a sigh as Harold gasps for breath.

Jace sets The Menace on autopilot as we make our way to the Arc, which is on a moon called Andromeda that orbits around a huge gas planet called Circe. Life can't survive on Circe, but Andromeda is surprisingly pleasant. It's all sweeping green valleys and thick forests. I've only seen it in person once.

"Okay, boys and girls. It will take a few hours to get to the Arc. I suggest you get some sleep. I'll wake everyone when we're close."

I nod gratefully, situating Boris to take him with me and glancing at Harold.

"Harold stay with Jace," he says. "Harold must watch and protect friends."

"Company would be nice." Jace winks at him. "But if you need a nap, get some sleep! Knights need their energy."

"I will sleep in chair."

I leave them to their conversation and make my way back to

the room as I tug Boris along with his rolling fishtank. I set the tank right next to the bed but Boris climbs out of it, using my body to slither up onto the bed. I lay down, not even bothering to get under the covers. My mind is racing too much. But Boris clearly senses it because he climbs onto my chest and hooks his arms around me so that he's hugging me, with his face pressed against my cheek.

A quiet, gentle squeak leaves him and he vibrates. A kraken's version of purring. It helps, and I nearly fall asleep, but it's restless.

But I won't *truly* be able to rest easy until Derek and the hellkittens are safe.

God, I hope we can get them home safe.

CHAPTER 8

A CAT LADY SCORNED

"Up and at em', folks!" Jace's voice yanks me out of a deep sleep.

"Mom? Where's the syrup?" I mumble, still half-asleep. Cold water hits my face and I squeal, sputtering as Boris chitters and squeaks beside me.

"Ahh! Okay, okay. I'm awake!"

Boris nods his shiny red head and descends into his travel aquarium on the floor.

I'm already dressed in black cargo pants and a long sleeve dark gray top. I reach into my bag and find a wide-tooth comb to do a quick job on my tangled curls, careful not to over brush them. They're frizzy as hell, but that's the least of my worries. I make a quick trip to the restroom to relieve myself. It's small and resembles an airplane bathroom, but with a small shower in one corner and the toilet vestibule at the other.

Wetting my hands, I get my hair just damp enough to scrunch some texture back in. A minute later, and my curls are looking a bit more alive.

That'll have to do.

Boris wiggles a red tentacle at me, scooting his bowl forward with a—

"Is that a remote control?"

Boris nods and holds up a remote control with one tentacle. He hits a button, and the hot wheels roll forward with a light whirring.

A pygmy kraken in space, in an automated hot wheel tupperware aquarium. How is this my life?

"Come on." I motion for the door, and he follows. We make our way to the small kitchen where Harold is chowing down on some waffles. The cinnamon and vanilla in the air makes my mouth instantly water. We're all quiet as we dig in. Jace regularly hands out the fresh waffles until we're full. I'm surprised she has a waffle iron on The Menace, but then again, the Laselles have always taken breakfast rather seriously. Jace finishes making a tall plate of waffles for when we're ready for refills and then sits down at the metal picnic style table to join us. Two jars are shoved my way as I grab two more waffles from the pile. I look at Jace but she's already pouring syrup on her waffles and digging in. I open the jars and smile: *sprinkles.*

Yeah. I like sprinkles on my waffles. Fucking sue me.

Boris watches in awe from my shoulder as I pour purple and blue sprinkles on the waffle. He taps my cheek gently, so I carefully pick him up and place him in the small water bowl. Once he's comfortable, I get a small side bowl that's available on the table and pour sprinkles into it. Boris immediately brings the side bowl so close that it dings off his makeshift tank. They get everywhere and coat his red tentacles, but his happy, delighted squeaks are worth it. We're all giggling in no time.

"He's gonna get a sugar high," Jace says.

I laugh, shrugging. "A pygmy kraken on a sprinkle high, two half-alien sisters, and a talking bear walk into a bar..." I drop off, snorting at my half-ass joke.

Jace just shakes her head. "That was a terrible joke. No—Harold, don't laugh. You're enabling her!"

"Harold like joke."

Jace rolls her eyes.

"See? Boris and Harold think I'm funny. Which means you just have really bad taste in humor."

Jace's jaw drops. "You *dare?*"

I stick my tongue out at her.

"Brat." Jace hisses, and I snicker in response.

Jace finishes her waffle and dusts her hands off before sitting up straight. In the time that I slept—well, *tried* to sleep—Jace has changed into her uniform.

Her wavy black hair is tucked behind her ears, with bangs dotting her forehead. She's wearing a skintight black set that looks like something between athleisure and a superhero suit. Guns and spare ammo are strapped to her thighs, behind her shoulders, and at her waist. A glance down shows guns strapped to both of her black, platform leather combat boots.

Damn, those are cool boots.

"You ready?" she asks, her face hard.

It's always so strange, seeing her like this. *The assassin.*

That's not what her job title with the UGF was. It was something like Personal Liability Officer or some vague-sounding position of that nature.

But I know what her *real* job was.

Taking out highly dangerous targets for the UGF. Most of them, Jace didn't kill. Often her task was simply to capture, but when they realized she was good at the *other* side of that, it changed.

A year ago, something happened and Jace was moved to private security duty for one of the senators of the UGF. The UGF is made up of senators from every planet. However, while they vote and debate subjects of matter, the Victorius rules.

The Victorius is the highest general. The head of the UGF combined forces.

The Victorius rules the UGF, senators included, and everyone knows it.

Which is why it was such an insult to Jace when she was moved to guard a lower-level senator from a non-magical planet.

Somewhere in between then and now, Jace quit her job and ended up on Earth.

...I think.

She hasn't actually told me what happened, just that she's done with the job.

When we get to Andromeda and make it into the Arc, I need to get to UGF Command and read them in so that we can get some help. Hellcats are critically endangered, and the black market trade of any animals from planets under UGF jurisdiction is outlawed. But I've only ever worked with Will. I haven't actually dealt with many other people at UGF outside of my siblings. Speaking of...

"Is Shaye going to meet us? Wait—does he even know we're coming?" We've always called him by a nickname rather than his full name. He hates being called Seamus.

Jace tilts her head. "Yes, and yes."

I don't know why that makes me nervous. It should comfort me. But...what is he going to say? Will he be happy to see me?

We clear our dishes quickly. Jace walks ahead of us to the cockpit and I lean over to whisper in the Ursine Bear's fuzzy black ear.

"Harold, if we have to split up, you stay with Jace and protect her, okay?"

Harold nods, nuzzling me. "Harold keep family safe. Do not worry, Henri friend. We find danger felines…even if they singe Harold's fur." I snort at that. "Harold miss Derek. He funny. He Harold's friend."

I blink rapidly. "Wait, you can talk to Derek?"

Harold nods. "Creature talk to creature."

Oh my God. They can all communicate. For real?

I don't know whether to be jealous, terrified, or in *awe*. A bit of all three, I suppose.

To think that all the animals can talk to each other, when I can only hear Harold makes me a little sad. I wish I could talk to all of them too.

As if he senses my sadness, Harold leans back onto two legs and wraps his giant bear arms around me. I'm buried in thick fur instantly.

I pull back with a smile and look into Harold's eyes, "You're not just my friend, you know. You're my family too, remember? That means you're stuck with me."

Harold leans down and licks my cheek, making me squeak and giggle. Jace pokes her head back into the hallway and laughs before barking at us. "Enough making out, we've entered Circe's orbit and are closing in on Andromeda. We'll enter their atmosphere in 15."

As we reach the cockpit and strap in, the purple, orange, and red skies of Andromeda quickly come into view. Harold gasps. Even Boris makes an awestruck squeak.

"The UGF really lucked out when they won the rights to Andromeda," I mutter, and Jace nods in agreement as she clips her harness together and starts pressing buttons on the command center. "Lucky bastards."

"Looks like the weather is fairly clear, should be an easy descent. Still, make sure you're strapped in tight. You especially, Boris." Jace nods to the pygmy kraken.

Boris crawls up my arms to plop himself in my lap, abandoning his bowl. He reaches a single shaky tentacle down my arm to wrap around my finger, so that we're holding hands—or holding tentacles, I suppose.

"It'll be okay," I whisper, rubbing my free hand along his head. He nuzzles into me with a chirp. "But when we get there, I need you to watch the ship, okay? This is our only way out and our only way to get to the hellkittens and Derek." Boris squeaks angrily, but I keep going, "I wouldn't trust anyone else with this, buddy. No one else can do it but you."

He eventually nods with a little kraken grumble.

"Thank you. Hopefully we aren't gone for long."

"No parties while we're out, okay?" Jace says. Boris waves a tentacle, and we all laugh. "Alright, let's do this." Jace hits a button, and we jump forward as she takes manual control of the steering, using the two side sticks to take us down into the purple skies of Andromeda. As soon as we enter the thick fog of the atmosphere, turbulence rocks the ship. The metal groans as Jace holds the controls with white-knuckled hands.

In a few minutes, it ends, and we all let out grateful breaths. Even Boris deflates a little, relaxing finally.

"That wasn't so bad, right?" Jace smiles.

"I hate you," I tell her and she just laughs.

Harold shakes his head. "Harold like it. Very fun. Harold want to do again."

I snort so hard I actually choke on my own spit, and Boris has to slap his tentacles against my back. I recover but Jace is laughing so hard she has to simply hover the craft because she can't steer. She finally recovers, wiping tears from her eyes in the meantime.

Jace takes us down further and we emerge a few miles from the Arc. The land is lush, with gray and burgundy trees dotting the landscape. Bright red and orange flowers decorate dark green grass along rolling hills. The sky from here is a light pink with swaths of purple. The planet Circe is huge in the sky, with the other moons as dots on the horizon.

It's gorgeous.

We fly over the Arc settlement and the town square. The air here is breathable, thanks to the terraforming done centuries ago. There are parks and lots of outdoor spaces. The entire moon is rather small, and the Arc settlement takes up roughly 40% of the moon. But 25% of that is the multi-level structure known as the Arc. The headquarters of the UGF shoots into the sky like a giant skyscraper-city, but I know for a fact there are at least 20 levels underground as well. A huge landing pad circles the entire base, dotted with various ships and tanks.

Dozens upon dozens of outbuildings surround the landing pad. The lesser army officials stayed in the sky—the higher the rank, the closer you got to the ground, with the generals and department heads in ground-level apartments and houses.

"What floor is Shaye on again?" I ask Jace.

Jace sighs, rubbing her eye. "We would all be on the 2nd floor, technically. But you know how they are. Shaye and his experiments were deemed too...volatile to be performed on the

Arc base, so they built him a big lab on the outskirts of the settlement. He has a fancy-ass place, that bastard. He's driving in to meet us at the dock."

Ah. Yes. The Laselles and the UGF have a rocky history, to say the least. To start with, they've never been our biggest fans due to the unpredictable nature of our magic and our heritage. My parents broke about a dozen rules having us, my father in particular. It exposed a human to the universal truth: aliens exist and Earth is at the bottom of a very tall ladder.

"I'd bet they have the whole place wired with surveillance. But Shaye has almost 15 years with UGF compared to my 10 and your 7. So, unlike us, he's been granted a miniscule amount of trust. Also, it's actually in our contracts that if we have twenty years of good behavior, we get a promotion and the restrictions are lighter."

"It's so annoying when you're right."

Jace smirks. I look over to her as she continues steering us towards the dock.

"Will it be awkward?"

Jace glances at me. "What do you mean?"

I nod towards the base as we close in on it. "I mean this. Will it be weird seeing your ex-bosses and coworkers? Since you quit?"

"Uh, well—" Jace stops, clearing her throat.

"Uh? What do you mean, uh? What does that mean?"

Jace stammers, trying to form words but unable to.

"Did you not quit the UGF? Jacinda Rochelle...were you *fired?*"

"Well, I uh, I wouldn't put it like that exactly."

"Then how *would* you put it?" I demand.

"I also wouldn't...*not* put it like that."

At that same moment we come into view of the landing pad on the dock, where our big brother is currently standing.

Along with an entire fucking regiment of UGF command—a very highly *armed* regiment.

They even have a Denny, an 8 ft tall humanoid robot programmed to neutralize dangerous magical targets.

An alarm sounds in The Menace as we're hailed.

"ATTENTION, THIS IS UGF COMMAND. YOU ARE UNDER ARREST. LAND YOUR CRAFT IMMEDIATELY AND DISEMBARK. THIS IS YOUR ONE AND ONLY WARNING."

I turn my chair to face my big sister, hands in my lap petting Boris.

She turns to face me, guilt written all over her face.

"Alright," I say. "Out with it."

She pushes a few buttons, and the ship begins landing protocols.

"So... you know how we thought that private security demotion was lame and boring?"

I nod.

"Well, it was...at the beginning. Until the Hakkar trials. I was guarding her as we passed by a group of the Hakkan criminals and one of them grabbed Senator Liza's ass!"

I blink.

"I told him to take his hand off the Senator or I would be forced to remove it for him."

Jace bites her lip.

"He did remove his hand...only to lift it to my tits. He squeezed my nipple! He pinched it!"

I wince, knowing exactly what's coming next.

"So, I cooked him. I melted the fuckers brain—and when his companions tried to attack me, I cooked them too."

"Were there any Hakkan left?"

Jace sniffs and looks away.

Damn.

I lean forward and take her hands, "You know what? Fuck them."

Jace's head snaps to mine, her blue eyes wide. "What?" You're not mad?"

"No, I'm not mad. I'm scared for you, because I hate seeing you or Shaye get in trouble. It makes me want to protect you; but no, I'm not mad. You did the right thing. That guy was a fucking douche canoe."

Jace snickers but her eyes are glassy, like she's fighting tears.

"I'm the big sister. I'm supposed to have my shit together."

I shrug. "That's a stupid human norm. We're only half human, so *fuck* the norms. We make our own rules, and those rules are that any of us can be a mess. But we'll always take care of each other regardless. Okay?"

Jace smiles, grateful.

"Now, we're not going to let them arrest you, but I also need to find the cats still. So, I might need you to play nice prisoner for them with Shaye for a few days, okay?"

Jace's smile falls. "Ugh. Fine. But only cause I love you—and Derek."

As the ship lands, I unclick from my seatbelt and lean forward, wrapping my arms around Jace.

"I'm sorry I didn't tell you," she whispers.

"Oh, don't worry," I whisper back. "You're on waffle duty until the end of time for not telling me. But I still love you."

I pull back and sniff, pulling my hair back into a ponytail with a scrunchie I had on my wrist.

Boris is in his bowl and waves at me in some kraken version of a salute. Harold just adjusts his guns and daggers before walking up to me.

"Alright, the two of you are going to do exactly as I say this time, or else I will adopt Stinking Ralos Beetles and unleash them in all of your rooms! Do I make myself clear?"

Harold and Jace look at me with wide eyes. Jace gasps, "God, Henri. That's so mean."

Boris nods in agreement.

Jace clears her throat again. "Crystal clear."

I just shush her as a noise rattles the hull and the main ship door opens a floor below us. "Now here's what we're going to do…"

We're at the open doors, just out of sight, with the soldiers waiting for us. If we take any longer, they'll come in and get us.

"Boris? Ink me." The pygmy kraken's eyes narrow and he nods, taking this seriously.

"Just a tiny bit, right here." I point to my cheek.

He squeaks and slaps his slimy wet tentacle right over my eyes. I jump slightly, even though I knew it would happen. The suckers of his red tentacles feel wildly uncomfortable against my eyes. Luckily unlike his Earthly relatives, kraken ink doesn't have any scent and it's a thicker texture. When Boris ginger-ly removes his tentacle, I know what's left behind resembles something akin to, say, running mascara.

I give my shoulders a little shake and start sniffing. Jace just looks mildly disgusted and terribly amused.

"Showtime," I whisper to myself.

The landing dock opens with a soft *whoosh*. Harold goes first, which is perfect because the second I emerge into the line of sight of the UGF, I burst into hysterical sobs.

"HE'S GONE. MY CAT IS GONE!" I hurl myself across Harold when I make it to the dock, letting my knees give out as I collapse to the floor, sobbing into his thick fur.

The soldiers take a step back, alarmed.

My wail gets even louder.

"MY CATS. SOMEONE KIDNAPPED MY CATS!"

Harold doesn't react at all except to stare deeply at all of the UGF soldiers, making all of them extremely uncomfortable based on their rapid blinking and shuffling.

"DEREK! OH, SWEET DEREK!" I wail in between sobs.

Then come the hiccups. Jace had some lemon candies in the kitchen, that I had Boris nab for me. Indigestion can come in handy in my line of work.

The UGF continues to look uncomfortable until one of them steps forward, rifle still raised. Jace goes still.

"By the order of the UGF, we hereby place one Jacinda Laselle under arrest—"

"You—" I gasp, feigning pure horror. "You would arrest my sister when some ALIEN VIGILANTE is out there with my CAT? CAN'T YOU SEE THIS IS AN EMERGENCY?" My shriek is so high-pitched that many of the soldiers have to lower their weapons to cover their ears.

I knock his rifle aside easily and it slaps another soldier in the face. Jace sniffs hard in a way that tells me she's desperately trying not to laugh—or maybe start crying, it's hard to tell. My finger is already raised, ready to launch into another high-pitched lecture when someone interrupts me.

"My sister is correct," a deep, confident voice says quietly. Everyone stops and turns at once as a tall man with dark black hair and light blue eyes hidden behind trendy glasses walks up to us. The soldiers immediately drop their weapons. "Hellkittens are Class A on the endangered species list, not that I expect any of you *peons* to understand."

Jace and I blink. Damn. Shaye is *pissed*.

"Um, uh, Mr. Laselle—"

"*Doctor* Laselle." Shaye corrects icily, crossing his arms. He's in a white button-down shirt and black pants that are a cross between cargo fatigues and dress pants. Both items are expensive and perfectly tailored. Thick black glasses border bright blue eyes the same shade as Jace's. His dark brown hair is artfully coiffed and *just* falling above his eyes.

Shaye looks like a mad scientist model. Something which Jace and I tease him about relentlessly.

At this moment though, I'm glad for his menacing, I'm-better-than-you aura.

"Right, yes, Doctor Laselle. We have a warrant for the arrest of your sister. She has to c-come with us," the soldier stammers, his cheeks bright red and his eyes wide.

"No," Shaye replies simply. "That will not be happening."

The soldier stares, mouth gaping like a fish out of water. Shaye simply turns to both of us with a nod. "Let's go."

The soldiers lower their weapons and look around at each other awkwardly, so I sniffle loudly and follow my brother,

Harold and Jace at my back.

The second we're out of sight, I hiss at my brother under my breath, "Do you have a plan? If they have a warrant, they won't just let this go, Shaye. I really don't need both of my siblings to get arrested!"

"Nobody is getting arrested, *if* Jace can get a hold on her power. What were you *thinking?*"

I swear a blood vessel almost pops in my eye as my anger rises. Ignoring Shaye for the time being, I look around at the Arc. It's gigantic, almost like being in an airplane hangar, only way cooler.

"Don't you dare yell at her! She was *defending* herself. What, would you prefer she get assaulted?!"

Shaye makes a frustrated noise. "Of course not. But you know the rules! We can't show our true power. Ever. Don't even get me started on what will happen if Prox—" he stops, glancing around. "If our father's family finds us."

Jace lets out a shaky breath next to me. "I know, I'm so sorry, Shaye."

Shaye sighs. "Don't be sorry—I heard what happened. I would have done the same if I was there. But please try not to do it again, *if* you can help it."

Species of all kinds pass us in the halls, some dressed in business formal, many in UGF colors and fatigues. All of them give us weird looks with alarmed, wide eyes.

A cold nose bumps my arm, and I remember that we are traveling with a giant armored bear. Yeah, that does explain some of the weird looks. But still, this place doesn't feel safe. I'm on edge, and not just from the Oscar-winning performance I just put on.

"Henri sad? Harold need to eat someone?" Harold asks and a group passing us in the opposite direction trips, gasping as they realize that yes, the alien bear can indeed talk. Shaye actually stops for a moment and takes a deep breath as if trying desperately not to lose his shit.

I snicker. "Not yet, Harold, not yet. But if Shaye is mean to me, I might change my answer…"

My brother turns and glares at me in that older brother way. I shrug. "What? You never talk to me anymore."

Shaye just sighs again, but his eyes look sad. "I'm a busy man, Hen."

My eyes roll back in my head so hard I'm surprised they don't just pop right out. "Oh, *psh*. We're all busy, Shaye! How about you act like your little sister actually exists for a change? It takes 3 seconds to send me a text. It doesn't need to be a damn epic, just a 'hey sis, hope your day is going well' every month or something."

Shaye *hmms* and Jace smacks him in the back of the head. They're only a year apart so they bicker almost like twins. With their matching black hair, pale eyes, and long legs, they look like twins. Jace is 35 and Shaye is 37, while I'm the baby at 30.

"Be nice to your sister," Jace hisses with venom.

"I did just save your asses from being dropped in the Basement," Shaye says with an icy look. "So cut the crap. We need to get out of sight."

"I need to go to Command."

"Says who?" Shaye asks as we start walking towards the main building that houses Command and Admin.

Jace and I look away, and Harold growls. "Harold eat William Fairfax."

Shaye stops and whirls towards us, his eyes suddenly glow-ing as if he was struck with a bolt of lightning. The hair on my arms stands up, and the air gets heavy. "That little *rat* contacted you? After he abandoned you on Centuros Prime?"

I hold up my hand. "Yes. He brings me creatures from time to time. He happened to be the one to bring me the hellkittens that are now *God knows where* in fucking *space* after being stolen by aliens, along with my precious, angel baby Derek!" I pause, panting. "But I can take care of myself. Besides, Jace already threatened to shoot him."

"Yeah, in the ass," Jace pipes up unhelpfully.

"You saw that fucker too?" Shaye growls, and the static in the air increases. Lightning flickers in the air

"Hey, Father Christmas, dial down the lights," I warn, and he sighs as the air calms down. "This is exactly why the UGF has us all under fucking *watch*. If we keep losing control of our magic, they're going to throw us ALL in the Basement."

Shaye and Jace grumble in annoyance, but they know I'm right. We've always been on the brink of losing our hard-won freedom.

The UGF wanted to work with our parents for decades and tracked them down, trailing them every time they left Earth's atmosphere.

Then came the threats.

The UGF threw everything from imprisonment to floating in a tiny pod in space to die alone from starvation and psychosis.

My parents didn't budge—until the threats started targeting us. Me and my siblings.

Then my parents agreed. They would work with the UGF. And it ended up killing them.

My siblings and I might now work for the UGF, but none of us are fans. Still, they were there for us when our parents died, and a paying job is a lot better than prison.

All citizens from Proxima Nova are already on the red watch list, but when our parents started having kids, and, thus, combined their magics, the UGF grew even more concerned. You could say we're the wildcards of the universe. Despite the many hours of testing, we agreed to as part of our so-called "freedom" deal—otherwise known as being able to live somewhere besides the Arc under constant surveillance—there is just enough about our magic that is unknown and unquantifiable to still put the UGF on edge.

To the UGF, unknown and unquantifiable means unpredictable, and that just won't do.

I glance behind us to note a unit of at least 10 soldiers following us, this time with electro-rifles—guns that can shoot paralyzing beams of electricity not all that different from a really powerful taser.

The escort is unavoidable, but it's still fucking annoying.

"Be nice to your little sister, *Seamus.* Her cat was stolen, for crying out loud." Jace is berating our brother, but he just rolls his eyes and rubs his temples as if we're annoying him to death. "You know how long she's had Derek! Have a fucking soul, for once."

Harold glances over at me.

"Shaye, you keep Jace out of sight while I go to Command." Jace whirls to me, her big eyes wide in pure affront. She opens her mouth to lecture me, her hands on her hips, but I stop her.

"Just shut up for a sec and listen to me. The less you're seen the better. It very well could be Hakkar that stole Derek and the hellkittens, and if that's true, we're going to need weapons and supplies. Something that The Menace doesn't have much of. The easiest and fastest way out of this is to split up. Harold will come with me, and Shaye will keep you alive. Right, Shaye?"

My brother grinds his teeth, but lightning flashes within his blue eyes as he nods.

"Despite what you might think of me," he says, his voice low, "I will always protect you. Both of you." Shaye nods at Jace. "You just tell me what you need, and I'm there."

My heart clenches.

He has no idea how much those words mean, but now isn't the time to tell him.

My sister looks back, conflicted. But she just puts her hand on his arm, nodding back.

Shaye and Jace have always been fairly close.

Then there was me.

Sure, they came back to visit...sometimes. At least Jace did.

Shaye came back to visit a few times but then he stopped about five years ago.

We all used to be so close. But once Mom and Dad died, everything changed.

My brother goes to grab my hand and hesitates. I ignore the pain that hesitation causes, but my heart cracks a little.

I clear my throat. "Good. You two load up on supplies and meet me back here in an hour. We can't waste any more time."

Jace raises a dark brow. "Only an hour? Command is notoriously slow and backlogged. It might be longer than that."

"Fine," I sigh. "Two hours. Maybe...find some food then? And don't get into any trouble. Harold, let's go."

The bear nods solemnly. "Time for Harold to kick ass and take name?"

"*Ungh—*" I trip and almost fall on my face at Harold's comment, causing a very ungraceful grunting noise to wheeze out of me. Jace laughs so hard she starts coughing. Shaye just sighs and looks towards the stars, as if a ship might come and rescue him at any moment.

"Not just yet, but soon." I tell Harold.

Jace shoots daggers at me with her eyes. "Two hours."

"Two hours," I repeat, heading to the Arc Command Center while Shaye and Jace disappear into the distance, likely heading to the armory and supply storage. How the hell Shaye can do stuff like break into the armory without getting caught—or fired—is beyond me.

As we close in on Arc command, it occurs to me that ditching my older siblings might not have been such a great idea. There are way more armed guards surrounding the entire building than I expected. I clear my throat and confidently clip on my official UGF employee badge—something I save only for special occasions because I hate wearing it. My photo on it is terrible. I look like a constipated toad. And okay, yes, I was hungover and having a bad hair day.

"Harold have bad feeling," Harold whispers, pulling me from my thoughts.

I click my tongue as I show the guards my badge. They all murmur and fidget nervously at the sight of Harold, but they let us pass. I notice a few click off their safeties, and I make sure to memorize their nametags and features.

I whisper back to Harold as we enter the building doors, "Yeah, you and me both."

CHAPTER 9

ANDROMEDA & THE BEAST

he Arc houses more than just the UGF Command Center.
It's also the training center for the entire UGF army, the
location of one of their supermax prisons, and the UGF Laboratory.

I pass people and aliens, all of them humanoid, on my way to
the command center. Everything is metal and gray, with horrid
florescent lights.

I push open the double doors to UGF Command, Harold at
my side, and honestly?

I expected a bit of fanfare.

Perhaps some screams of terror—you know, the usual reaction upon seeing a giant bear dressed as a medieval knight.

But no one even notices me. There's not a single moment of
pause at the fact that a giant brown bear with spikes down its
spine is standing in the doorway.

What the hell?

"Uh, excuse me?" I ask, but no one responds. "Excuse me?
Can someone help me?"

I repeat my words again, but still, no one hears me. The
room is teeming with frantic energy as people run around in
matching UGF branded fatigues. Large holographs light up the
command room, drawing the attention of many. Males huddle

around diagrams of galaxies and planets as they scream into their coms about moving around their fighters.

I knew the situation with the rebel planets was dire, but I didn't realize it was this bad.

This...this is *war* planning. And with war, comes death. A deep sense of dread washes over me.

Ecosystems destroyed by the blasting heat of nuclear bombs. Entire populations decimated. Animals displaced, if not rendered completely extinct.

That's what war means.

Loss. It means great, irreplaceable losses.

Harold noses my arm, sensing the upset warring within me. I wrap my arm around his head, digging my fingers into his thick neck fur beneath his velvet cape. The feeling of his soft fur, of his deep heartbeat thudding beneath my fingers, of knowing I'm not alone; it grounds me.

Derek needs me.

The kittens need me.

Time to put my adult panties on.

"I need to talk to whoever is in charge here," I say louder. "RIGHT NOW!"

Okay, maybe that last part came out as a scream.

Still, no one pays attention.

The *audacity!* Now I'm getting offended.

Which is when Harold takes a deep breath, rocks back on his hind legs and stands up—which makes his giant body look *even* bigger—opens his mouth, and roars so loud it shakes the windows.

When the roar stops, everything is silent.

That lasts for about five seconds and then the room is filled by the sound of everyone simultaneously reaching for their guns.

"Thanks," I whisper to Harold before clearing my throat. "My name is Henrietta Laselle. I am a UGF level 3 employee and member of the Earth Pact. I'm here to report a violation to both the Creature Protection Act and the Earth Pact. Approximately 10 hours ago, an unknown alien entity entered Earth's atmosphere, broke into The Home for Wayward Creatures estate and stole UGF property. I'm invoking the recovery protocol as per subsection 17.a of the CPA."

Ha! Take that! I finish my speech and put my hands on my hips.

"Ms. Laselle." A tall blonde man approaches me. Older, with white flecks in his reddish beard, the man exudes power. His fatigues are different. Nicer, more polished.

He's not from Earth, but another humanoid planet. I don't sense any magic on him, so he's not from Proxima Nova.

"I am General Sirius."

"Nice to meet you." I reach my hand out and he stares at it as if my hand offends him.

"Laselle as in Dr. Seamus Laselle?"

Uh-oh. I nod at his question.

"You must be the youngest sibling, then."

I lift my chin, unwilling to be embarrassed or ashamed of my parentage.

"The youngest, but not the weakest," I say with a tart voice and a smile.

"I'm sure." General Sirius smiles back, but there is nothing friendly about it.

"As you can see," he motions behind him as the room picks back up into more frenzy, "we're a bit busy at the moment. This is not a place you can just *waltz* into and demand help. We are at war, Ms. Laselle."

"But you're obligated to help me. That's what the APA is. An endangered animal has been stolen. You have a duty to help!" My voice is laden with desperation. *"Please."*

General Sirius sighs. "I'm sorry. But we don't have anyone to spare. War has started, Ms. Laselle, and we're going to win it."

"But that's—"

He stops me with a raised hand. "I said no. In wartime, all other pacts can be superseded by military need. There is nothing we can do."

Then he walks away.

Anger roars within me.

"WAIT!" I scream, and the room goes quiet again. "You have to help. How else will we find them?"

General Sirius turns around and crosses his arms, staring at me. "Scream at me again, and I'll throw you in supermax prison for verbally assaulting a commanding officer *and* refusing to comply to orders."

My jaw drops.

"Now get the fuck out of my command center, or else I will *remove* you myself."

That *asshole!*

Harold's lips pull back as he bears his teeth in a fierce growl.

My throat clogs and I fight the urge to cry as I tug lightly on Harold's fur. "Come on, let's find Jace and Shaye and get the hell out of here. We'll find the kittens on our own...somehow."

How the hell am I going to find Derek and the kittens without any help? Especially when we've just declared war against the rebel planets. What if it's one of them who took Derek and the kittens?

All of this is going to make getting them back that much harder.

We walk out of the room, the doors shutting behind us and closing off the shouts of the command center. I stroke Harold's fur.

"Fuck the UGF," I whisper to him. "We don't need those stupid assholes. Let's go find Derek and the kittens ourselves."

With my head held high and my back straight, I turn to go back the way we came.

I've only been to Arc a few times before, but not enough to be familiar with the layout.

"I think this is the right way," I mutter, turning left when the hallway forks.

Harold ambles beside me, his lips smacking happily.

"Do you know the way out?" I ask, and Harold looks up at me.

"No. Harold not good with directions."

"Same," I mutter.

This hallway doesn't lead outside; it leads to a mess hall.

I let out an angry sigh as we pass the mess hall and turn right.

I don't know how long we're in the Arc but eventually we find out way outside.

"Thank God," I groan as Harold nudges the doors open.

It's not like I'm terribly claustrophobic, it's more than being stuck in a building with condescending, egotistical males who talk down to me that makes me want to rip my hair out.

The planet Circe is huge on the horizon, painting the sky in a wash of pink, purple, and orange. Andromeda's rings break up the view of the planet, creating a glowing white line across the night sky.

We walk onto the tarmac surrounding the Arc. This side seems to be a storage area. Big containers full of supplies line the edges, but the rest is fairly open. Not seeing any cars or ships, I sigh and walk across the tarmac.

I need space. Which feels grossly ironic to think since I'm *in* space. But knowing I won't get any help from UGF Command…

It sucks.

"I don't know what to do," I whisper to Harold who ambles at my side.

"Harold sorry. Harold does not like when Henri is upset."

I snort sadly. "Thanks, buddy. I'm just scared. I'm going to try to find them myself, but I don't even know where to start."

I turn and face the watercolor sky. The sun is setting and it's making the colorful sight above me even more vibrant. Closing my eyes, I try to calm my mind and find some sort of center, because freaking out and melting down won't find Derek.

I take a step back, adjusting my balance, and run into a wall.

Must be a cargo container.

Leaning into it, I allow my mind to go quiet and focus on my five senses.

I'm on Andromeda.

Harold is next to me, with his soft fur.

The sky is pink and purple.

The air smells like…musk?

I open my eyes, unsure, but I see nothing. Harold sits at my feet, looking up at the sky just like me, so I close my eyes again.

Huh. Okay. Sure. The air smells like musk. Sexy, citrusy musk.

The cargo container behind me feels warm from the sun.

"What's a girl like you doing on a moon like this?" a deep voice behind me asks.

What kind of pickup line is that? I keep my eyes closed, ignoring it.

"Are you alright?" the voice asks again, but this time there's genuine concern in it.

I sigh, eyes still closed. "Not really."

Everything goes quiet and I assume the person has walked away.

"What's wrong?"

Oh, they're still here. They seem genuinely interested and concerned. It makes me feel...safe. I open my eyes and gaze up at the sky, trying to not let my thoughts race.

"My hellkittens got kidnapped. So did my cat Derek. I asked Command for help but they said no. Now I have to figure out how to hunt them down and rescue them by myself."

The voice waits a beat. "That sounds quite stressful."

I glance to the side, expecting to see the person speaking to me but I don't see anything.

That's *weird.*

I look down at Harold who is now playing with his paws.

"It is stressful," I say hesitantly, trying to find who is talking to me. I take a step forward which is when I realize the cargo container I was leaning on wasn't just warm; it was *hot.*

The loss of it is an icy warning.

I turn around, ready to meet this stranger and nearly fall on my ass.

Oh.

My.

God.

"You—" I choke, taking in the sight before me.

"Yes?"

The giant black dragon smiles, showing a mouthful of giant white teeth longer than my forearms.

CHAPTER 10

WORLDKILLER

The dragon rests its head back on its front claws, never taking its eyes off me.

I, however, am stunned into frozen stupidity.

"Are you alright?" the dragon asks, sounding rather concerned.

Words continue to fail me. It's huge, with resplendent black scales that shimmer like stars. Dark purple veins bisect the scales, and eyes of glimmering amethyst watch me carefully. Horns curl up from its head like an onyx crown.

The dragon sighs and deep purple smoke wafts from its nostrils, hitting me lightly in the face. I expect to cough but the smell of citrus and musk gets stronger.

"Your heart is racing," the dragon notes casually. "You're afraid."

The dragon can talk. The dragon can talk and it's *talking to me. Ohmygod.*

There's this...*thing* that happens to me when I see a cute animal. Even if they're scary, if I see an animal and it's even just the tiniest bit 'cute', my brain sort of shuts down and I turn into a 3-year-old child.

An undetermined squeal comes out of my mouth and before I can even think of why it might not be the best idea, I'm leaping at the dragon's snout and wrapping my arms around it.

The dragon's eyes go wide, and it jerks back.

"What is happening?" the dragon says in an aghast voice.

"I've always wanted to meet a dragon, but I never thought it was possible!" I lean back and smile, looking it in the eyes.

"You're *not* scared?" The dragon tilts its head, careful not to jostle me. I caress its soft scales, marveling at the smooth, warm feel.

"Oh, I'm terrified, but I'm more in awe. You're incredible," I whisper, and wrap my arms around its snout. "I'm so sorry if this is inappropriate but you have to understand, this is literally a dream come true."

The dragon laughs lightly. "You surprise me. Most think that coming face to face with me is a nightmare, not a dream. Most of them would be right."

"Well, they're wrong then."

The dragon snorts. "You are a very strange human."

"*Half*-human," I mumble, my face pressed against the dragon's soft snout. "May I see your wings?" I ask politely.

The dragon looks down at me for a moment before nodding. Still seated, two black wings lift from its back. It unleashes them and I gasp as the sky is blocked, turning everything dark and shadowy. Its wings are huge, with thin membranes that glow with shades of pink, purple, and deep blue like an aurora.

"Wow."

"Do you feel suitably impressed?"

"Yes." I nod happily. "You may put your wings back."

"How kind of you to give me permission."

I laugh.

I should be terrified. I know I should be. But *damnit,* this is the coolest moment of my entire LIFE.

"HENRI! STEP AWAY FROM THAT DRAGON!"

I turn and watch as my siblings, followed by some very terrified looking UGF soldiers, sprint across the tarmac to get me.

"Go away," I shout back. "I'm busy bonding with it!"

"HENRIETTA, NO!"

Why is my brother so angry?

"Why do you look like you might throw up?" I shout back. "Oh, Did you have dairy again? How many times do we have to remind you that you're lactose intolerant, Shaye! You can't just go around drinking milk. And it's kind of gross, drinking the milk of another creature. Do you know we're the only species in the entire galaxy to do that? It's a bit *suspicious,* if you ask me."

Jace looks like she can't decide whether to laugh so hard she might fall over or smack me in the face for having this entire conversation at shouting-decibels.

"Henri, shut the fuck up." Shaye points at the dragon behind me. "Just shut up and walk towards me."

I roll my eyes. "Why? Clearly the dragon is harmless."

"Shh!" Shaye shushes me, then turns and points at the dragon. "Harmless? My sister thinks you're HARMLESS? You slimy motherfucker! You stay away from my baby sister, you hear me? Disgusting *perv.*"

The dragon huffs. "I wondered why she smelled like you."

That's...weird. I glance between them.

"Do you know each other?"

"No," Shaye answers at the same time that the dragon says, "Yes."

"Uh huh." Jace nods. "How about we all calm down. Henri, come over here where you can't get eaten alive."

"Nobody is getting eaten," I tell them.

"Harold hungry. Harold would like to eat something. Harold eat soldier?" Harold sweetly asks, staring at the soldiers.

"No, not right now buddy." I cringe as Jace replies to him with a bloodthirsty tone. "But maybe later."

"Uh how about *nobody* gets eaten?" Shaye mutters.

"There goes my plan." The dragon sighs.

"Shut up!" Shaye hisses at the Dragon. "And you stay away from my sister." My brother is glaring at the dragon so intensely I'm surprised laser beams aren't shooting out of his eyeballs.

"God, Shaye. You're being so dramatic. The dragon won't hurt me, will you, gorgeous?" I smile at him.

Shaye makes a choking sound.

Crossing my arms, I stare down my brother. Harold has joined Shaye and stands in between him and my older sister.

"She's right, I will not hurt her."

I smile proudly at the dragon's proclamation.

"Orion, leave her alone," Shaye growls, no longer sounding scared, but furious.

I glance up at the dragon. "Orion. Is that your name?"

The dragon smiles at me and I hear my sister make a squeak of fear at the sight of its fangs.

"It is."

"YOU MOTHERFUCKER." Jace has to hold Shaye back from charging the dragon.

What the fuck is my brother's problem?!

There's a shout from behind all of us and we turn, watching as General Sirius and a battalion of soldiers jog over to us. The General does not look too pleased.

Uh-oh. What now?

"I'll handle this," I tell them all, fury rising in me at the reminder that the UGF rejected my plea for help. How *dare* they get mad at me now, when I came to *them* begging for assistance?

However, I get too ahead of myself and as I step forward, I trip over something and nearly fall on my face.

There's a bright flash of light and arms catch me just before my face hits the cement tarmac.

"Careful."

The voice is the same, but lower and mortal.

Arms pull me up to stand and suddenly I'm standing chest to chest with a man.

The man has black hair that gleams in the light, and vibrant amethyst eyes that stare at me with such unveiled curiosity, it gives me goosebumps.

Amethyst eyes.

"D-dragon?" I force the word off my tongue. "You're th-the dragon?"

Orion smiles and I catch a flash of white fangs.

"Hello there."

Even in this smaller, more mortal looking shell, the man radiates power and danger like I've never experienced before.

"It's nice to meet you, Henri."

"Step away from my sister, dragon."

A hand grabs my arm and yanks me away from Orion. I'm suddenly behind my older brother.

General Sirius approaches and we're surrounded by soldiers with guns, all pointing at Orion.

Orion, however, doesn't look the least bit worried.

I can't stop looking at him.

He winks at me, and I nearly choke on my own spit.

A dragon. A dragon that can shift into a *man!*

"Worldkiller, you're not on duty. How many times do I have to tell you to disperse immediately? Laselles, you're staying here."

At the last part, the General stares at my sister and I realize she's in far more trouble than I previously imagined.

"I heard you rejected Henri's plea for help, *Leonard.*" Orion stares at the General.

Oh shit. He first named him!

The General grinds his teeth. "Why are you here, Worldkiller? Go back to your lodgings and stop bothering me."

"But that's no fun," Orion smiles. "I do so *enjoy* our little chats."

General Sirius's face turns red. "I said, disperse. Now!"

Orion picks off invisible lint from the fine black shirt he wears. "I wanted to sun my wings. Now, however, I am intrigued. What have you been hiding, *Leonard?*"

The General takes a step forward and I notice the soldiers getting their guns ready for use.

This is a bomb ready to go off and I need to diffuse it, *STAT.*

"The aliens that took them left a glowing green goo behind," I suddenly add, realizing I never said that. "I don't know where they went but that's all I have to go off of."

"I know where they went."

My head nearly falls off as I whirl to look at Orion.

"You do?"

He nods. "There is only one species that secretes green goo; Antheriens."

My heart drops.

"Th-they're on Antheri?"

Orion nods.

Right. Well...that makes things infinitely more difficult. Panic descends, but I notice nobody *else* is panicking. Why is no one PANICKING?!

"There are other concerns at the present moment," the General snaps. "Disperse, now."

Orion lifts an inky brow. "Are you saying you're going to do *nothing* about Antheri entering a neutral, pre-stage planet? Why, General, that doesn't sound very legal."

"I have bigger problems to deal with, Worldkiller. Now shut your lizard mouth and DISPERSE!"

Orion smiles. "No."

"Give me a good reason to kill you," General Sirius snarls.

"You know you can't." Orion smiles back. "But you *can* let me help Henri Laselle find her cats."

I nearly swallow my own tongue out of shock.

"What?" I breathe.

"Absolutely *not.*" Shaye growls.

Jace says nothing. She just clicks the safeties off of her guns.

"You're clearly deranged," the General snarls at Orion, who is still smiling and looking rather un-worried.

"I accept!" I shout.

My siblings immediately protest but I hold a hand up, shushing them. Clearing my throat, I step closer to the dragon, ignoring the guns pointed at my head. "I accept your help, dragon."

Orion towers over me by almost a foot and a half, and I'm a pretty average height at 5'5". Broad shoulders and arms corded so thickly with muscle, hands tucked into the pockets of his pants. To say he's in a pair of dress pants and a dress top would be an utter *shame* to fashion. Both are made with expensive silky fabrics and tailored to perfection.

Plenty of his chest is on display, and it's equally as muscular as his arms, based on the definition I see. However, black tattoos in the shape of scales crawl up his neck, framing his face.

As he moves and his muscles flex, the scales *shimmer* and move, as if a reflection of his true form.

His shirt sleeves are rolled up, showing more scales covering his arms, which is when I realize I've been staring at him. I jump and glance back up—to see him watching me with a wicked glint in his amethyst eyes.

Oh God. He knows I was checking him out.

Orion flashes pearly white fangs. "I've been to Antheri many times. I will get us in and out without being seen."

"Under no circumstance are you going with him, Henrietta."

Shaye's order has me seeing *red*.

Whirling on my brother I stalk towards him and poke my pointer finger into his chest. "I am thirty years old. You don't get to order me around like a damn *child*. Plus, it's not like you or Jace can help me. Jace is basically under arrest, and I'm guessing you're not allowed to go galivanting across the universe into enemy territory, which means the options are I go to Antheri alone, or you pull the stick out of your ass and accept that someone actually wants to help me. What's it going to be?"

Jace flashes me a thumbs up and a wide smile.

Shaye deflates slightly, looking quite guilty. "Fine. But this is a bad idea. You shouldn't trust him, Henri. He's not what you think."

"He's the only one willing to help and for now, that's enough," I tell him, and my brother reluctantly nods.

I face General Sirius and lift my chin. "The dragon Orion is coming with me, and we're getting my cats back."

"If you're caught, we will not save you," is all he says before turning to my sister. "You, though? You're staying right here."

The air turns electric, and I realize we're on the brink of disaster.

Jace sighs and waves our brother down. "Stop that. It's fine, I'll go with them—*for now.* But only because I have nothing else to do currently. However, when you get back, I am leaving with you. Got that, General Fuckface?"

Shaye lets out a loud laugh at that.

Jace starts to go with them, much to my displeasure, when a voice causes the soldiers to halt.

"Henri! You're here!" A voice calls and I freeze, every muscle in my body going still as dread pools in my belly.

William Fairfax. My archnemesis.

"Tell me right now why I shouldn't kill him," Shaye growls, back to being furious, but this time for a reason I very much approve of.

"Because it would draw attention and I'm guessing you don't want that," Orion's voice travels over to us and Shaye sighs.

"I hate you."

Orion winks at him.

Oh yeah, they definitely know each other.

But Orion is right. We can't kill William Fairfax...*unfortunately.*

My eyes close as I sigh audibly, grinding my teeth together so hard I'm surprised they don't crack. When I open them, the dragon continues to simply watch me. He looks at me the way I suspect humans look at polar bears in a zoo exhibit—with extreme curiosity.

I turn around to face the person behind that stupid, sexy voice.

William Fairfax, in a skin-tight space suit that leaves literally nothing to the imagination, is walking towards me.

I glance up towards the sky, hopeful that the laws of physics might just somehow stop for a few seconds so that I can be taken out by a lightning bolt or something. I don't see Will for four years, and now, twice within the span of a week.

I mentally make note to ask Shaye about a potion to erase whatever horrible curse has been wrought on me.

"Harold eat bad man?" The bear steps up to my left side, and the dragon steps to my other.

I sigh, looking at all of the guards around. Not to mention the freaking dragon is right next to me. My right eye twitches, the eyelashes fluttering out of my control. I slap a hand over my eye, grumbling in frustration at the stress response.

"No eating him. Yet." I mumble the last part.

"I came as soon as I could," Will says, not even out of breath after his power walk down the landing field.

I glare, suspicious. "I thought you were busy."

"As did I." The dragon surprises me so much that I almost jump. "If I remember correctly, you aren't due to check in for another week, Fairfax. Did you abandon your post?"

The soldiers around us all go still and turn to face Will in unison.

"We finished our mission early." Will smiles, but it's full of tension. "I got to the jump-gate the first moment I could. Are you okay?" He turns his warm brown eyes on me, concern evident on his face. "Stay away from the dragon. He's dangerous."

"Hmm, let's see..." My voice is venomous as I respond, "My best friend—no, my *family* member was stolen by a cruel and aggressive alien race along with three innocent newborn kittens who are just nearly the last of their kind. And now my ex-boyfriend who *abandoned me in space* is trying to warn me away from the only person willing to help. No, I am not okay!"

Will blinks, staring at me with wide eyes.

"Um, I—" My heart races as I take a deep breath and try to get myself together. Which is when Will focuses in on Orion.

"Why are you standing next to her? Fuck off, lizard."

"Don't talk to him that way," I snarl, furious at how rude Will is being.

"And here I thought you'd be happy to see me," Orion purrs. He steps forward, stopping when he reaches my side. "I would say it's good to see you, William, but that would be a lie."

I fight off a laugh at the furious look on William's face.

"He's dangerous, Henri. Don't trust him," Will says in an icy tone. "You should have been executed, Worldkiller."

Then Will grabs my arm and pulls me towards him.

Or he tries to.

Just before William's hand reaches my arm, Harold takes that moment to sneeze. But the sneeze is particularly aggressive, which leaves a wad of spit and snot flying right into William's face.

"I do not need your help, William." I reply, my voice dark.

"That's bullshit. You called *me*, remember? Who else is going to help you but me?"

I realize now I might have played myself into William's corner.

"An unfortunate moment of weakness on my part," I admit.

"I also was unaware the UGF was actively at *war,* William. That changes things. Besides, I don't trust you."

"Henri is correct," the dragon drawls.

William's eyes turn stony. "Piss off, Orion."

The dragon glares at the man before his violet eyes flick down to me, his gaze softening.

"We should leave soon before the trail gets cold, Henri."

"HE'S HELPING YOU?" William shouts and approaches me again. Harold quickly moves between us and growls at William.

"You don't get a say in anything I do," I remind him. "I would rather work with a giant dragon than you *any* day, you fucking asshole."

I turn and look at Orion, whispering, "You really want to help?"

The dragon nods. That aura of power and wisdom turns into something much more dangerous. The dragon's eyes turn to reptilian diamonds and the fire within them spreads, growing brighter and more furious as he turns to look at William with a sinister smile. But William just stares at me.

"Your sister has a warrant out for her arrest, and I'll guarantee Arc Command is making her stay here. You think you can get to a rebel planet alone? You'll be shot down before you even enter their atmosphere. This ancient lizard won't help. Work with him and you'll doom your sister to a life in prison."

I narrow my eyes at William, well aware of the threats in his tone.

I lift my chin. "Jace will stay here with Shaye. I'm going to Antheri with Orion. And yes, I trust this stranger more than I trust you. He at least hasn't *abandoned* me in space. And William? If you touch a single hair on my siblings while I'm gone, there will be hell to pay."

William ignores me.

"You're insane. This is going to get you killed, Henri."

"Great. Now leave me alone," I tell him.

Shaye appears and grabs William's arm, dragging him away. "You're so lucky I can't kill you," my brother snarls.

"I'll make sure no one is murdered," Orion says, sounding tired. He follows my brother and Will before glancing back at me. "We'll take my ship. I'll meet you in the Hanger at 8:00 Universal time." Orion doesn't even raise his voice, and yet I can hear his voice right in my ear and feel his breath upon my neck. The scent of his cologne is still in my nostrils and it's addling my ability to think logically.

"Dragon man scare Harold," my beary companion whispers to me.

"Don't worry buddy, you don't need to be scared," I say, yet internally all I hear is *Liar, liar, pants on fire*. "If you think that's scary, you clearly haven't seen Jace when someone tells her no."

CHAPTER 11

LAST RESORT

After a long—and very tense—walk to the hanger where The Menace is parked, Orion disappeared to pack, leaving us to wait.

Jace and Shaye sit on two small cargo tubs. Jace is very animatedly telling some story and Shaye has his head in his hands, with his glasses pushed up on his head.

It doesn't pass by my notice that Jace is strapped to the nines. Guns on both legs, with spare ammo on her belt and—

"When did you get a machete?"

Jace glances at me and smirks.

"Jace, you said you would go with them!"

She shrugs. "I did. I never said I'd go quietly though."

Shaye takes the glasses off his head and pinches the bridge of his nose.

I look at my brother. Stress lines, subtle but present on his otherwise perfect face. Shaye is what I'm sure others consider very attractive.

Dark circles under his eyes tell me he's still battling insomnia. Shaye has always had trouble sleeping.

Shaye shakes his head, but I see the subtle glint of humor in his pale blue eyes.

"Henny, I—" he hesitates, putting his glasses back on. "I'm

sorry."

It's been a long time since he called me that. When I was a child, I idolized my brother. He called me 'Henny'. And hearing it again after so long melts my heart.

Without hesitation I walk over to him, crouch slightly, and wrap my arms around him.

He smells like a summer storm, fresh and wild. It instantly comforts me. Yet again my tears threaten to make an appearance, but through sheer will I force them back.

"I needed to hear that. I love you. Always. But maybe you could visit more, and text me sometimes, okay? I don't want to constantly be missing my brother and wondering if he's okay."

Shaye holds me tighter, burying his face in my curly blonde hair with a shuddered breath.

"It gets lonely," I admit to him in a voice so quiet, I know Jace can't even hear. "It would be nice to have you *both* there more often. To be together again. Just sometimes, at least."

Shaye shudders and presses a kiss against my temple, pulling me into his lap the way we used to do when I was a kid. Maybe it seems silly do to so as grown adults, but I don't care.

"It's lonely here too, Henny bug. I promise, I'll come visit more. I miss Earth."

I pat his shoulder before gently pulling away.

"Good. The creatures will be so happy to see you. You know you're Barbara and Frankie's favorite."

Shaye smiles softly but I see sadness in his eyes. "I do miss my fur nieces and nephew."

I focus on his dark circles again. "Are you okay, Shaye? I know I'm your baby sister, but I'm here for you too."

He pulls back and looks away, pushing his glasses up the

bridge of his nose and righting his hair. "I'm fine, Henny. Don't worry about me."

I put my hand on his arm again and squeeze gently before letting it fall back at my side, "That's a silly request. You're my brother, Shaye. I'll always worry about you."

"Yeah, but I'm your big brother, I should be taking care of you—"

"Stop. Don't do that, Shaye. You *did* take care of me. Both of you did." I turn to Jace, who has approached us. "But I'm not a kid anymore, so now I get to take care of you both, too."

"As cute as this little reunion is, we do need to be going. The less time those creatures spend on Antheri, the better." Orion's voice suddenly projects across the hanger, and lighting erupts in Shaye's eyes. Jace turns to steel and not-so-subtly grabs both guns, flipping off the safeties.

"I still don't like this." Shaye says, his voice neither loud, nor booming, but I can hear the explosion of thunder and the smell of burnt ozone within his voice.

Lightning sparks in his irises; a storm about to land.

"Your dislike is noted." Orion appears next to me. I didn't even hear him approach. "When I return your sister to you safe and sound, remember this moment as I'm saying, 'I told you so'."

"I swear to fuck, I will knock you out—"

I shove my hand in Shaye's face, ending his tirade. "Okay then! That's enough of that. Let's get going."

Orion addresses both of my siblings who stand, their arms crossed in matching poses of barely suppressed suspicion and rage.

"I will keep your sister safe—I promise."

"Why should we trust you?" Jace's hand twitches near her weapons. "Other than your promise, which means *nothing* until you return."

Orion smiles darkly and I blanch at the sight of his pearly white fangs. "Why? Because you have no other choice. You three," he waves his hand at us, "are at the top of the UGF watch list. I am not asking, Ms. Laselle." I cringe as he continues, "I'm going with your sister to ensure that she doesn't cause a galactic meltdown that causes further war, and I will bring her back in one piece. Is that understood?"

Shaye has to wrap his arms around Jace, whose blue eyes are quickly turning red.

"It's fine, Jace," I say quickly, shoving away from Orion and hugging my sister. "I'm bringing a tracker," I whisper in her ear, "If anything happens, I'll send the SOS signal, okay?"

"The trip should take a few weeks, depending on how things go after we make it through the jump gate." Orion informs us.

"If you have one scratch on your blonde head, I'm going to melt his lizard brain," Jace snarls in my ear before letting me go.

"You can try." Orion winks, and I don't need to look at him to know there's a dangerous glint in his starry eyes.

"Yes she can, although I happen to have some solutions for melting dragon scales that might come in handy as well," Shaye says, and I fight the urge to smack him on the back of his head again.

Despite all of this, there *is* another problem with this plan, though. One I'm a bit more concerned about at the moment.

A problem with red tentacles and a penchant for candy.

CHAPTER 12

RELEASE THE KRAKEN

For the past five minutes, I've been frantically thinking of how to explain all of this to my tentacled friend.

How the fuck do I tell Boris that I met a dragon and now I'm going off into space with him? *Without* Boris?

No, that won't go well. Nobody has noticed the way I keep looking around nervously.

My thoughts are racing, and my palms are hot and sweaty.

Oh my God—do dragons like seafood?

WILL HE TRY TO EAT BORIS LIKE AN ALL-YOU-CAN-EAT SUSHI BUFFET?

I feel a sudden warmth in my stomach, and I shove my feelings into a box, forcing my heart to stop racing.

Nothing good happens when a Laselle panics. I cannot afford to panic and lose control of my magic.

I clear my throat. "Right, do we have everything we need, then?"

Orion watches me, he's *always* watching—and it's a bit unsettling since he doesn't seem to blink much. Must be a dragon thing.

"We will take my ship as The Menace isn't equipped with the proper cloaking technology to get past the Pollux gate unnoticed. Rest assured, it's stocked with everything we could need."

There's an indignant squawk from behind me. Jace doesn't like when her ship is insulted.

"Not all of us can afford to upgrade our tech twice a year," she sneers at him.

Just then, there's a cold nose against my back. I turn and Harold is inches away from my face.

"Hey, buddy. Everything okay?" I ask, concerned.

Harold just leans into me, rubbing his bear face against mine. "Henri worried. I feel it. Harold think Mr. Lizard-man is okay now. He protect you from bad guy."

I blink. He thinks Orion is okay? Oh. The bad guy is William!

"That's true," I nod. "I guess you're right."

"I thought you wanted to eat him, Harold?" Jace says loudly and I wince. "What happened to that part? Can we get back to that?!"

"Harold needed snack. Harold hungry. But lizard-man is nice..." he pauses and I throw my arms around him, burying my hands in his thick black fur. "Harold heard of him. Before."

Jace and I lock eyes.

Harold heard of Orion?

"Of course you did, but not for good reasons, Harold." My brother is the one to respond. He glares at Orion. "The dragon is a criminal."

Orion crosses his arms. "I got off on good behavior centuries ago, which you well know. We don't have time for my entire history."

Jace narrows her eyes at the dragon but nods, reluctantly.

"It's fine, Shaye. It'll be fine. Harold says we can trust him, right Harold?"

The bear nods, looking up at me with his dark blue eyes.

"Thanks, buddy," I say, kissing him on his cold nose.

"Harold friend. Harold family."

"Damn straight," I reply. With a deep breath, I step back. Jace hugs me tight one more time and Shaye gives me a pat on the head, ruffling my hair.

"Stop that," I snarl, as his fingers get caught in my curls.

He just smiles, "Be safe—and don't trust him. He's danger-ous, bug. I mean it."

"I'll be safe."

That's the only promise I make, though.

I take another deep breath and turn to Orion, willing confi-dence into my eyes.

"Alright, I'm ready. I just need to grab my things from The Menace."

Orion nods and waves me forward.

Here we go.

We walk over to where The Menace is parked and I walk up the ramp to the loading door, Orion following right behind.

"So, there's something you need to know. I did not exactly come alone, uh, to Andromeda."

He simply watches me. "Okay. Who else came with you?"

"That...would be Boris." I take a deep breath and hit the but-ton to open the loading door.

At first, there's nothing. Just the mechanical whirring of the door lifting.

Then I take a step inside, and Orion does the same.

One moment, it's quiet, and the next, I'm plastered against something that feels vaguely like jelly but smells like bad seafood. Then there's a roar like something from the depths of hell and I distantly hear people scream on the landing tarmac. That's when the jelly holding me hostage lets me go and I drop to the floor with a thump.

Why did the jelly let me go?

Because it—*Boris*—is now outside the ship...and he's super-sized.

"WHAT THE HELL, HENRI!" Shaye shouts as something explodes in the distance. I cough and run down the ramp only to stop and watch in horror as a giant red kraken takes Orion and swings him around like a cat with a mouse toy.

"BORIS! HE'S NOT A BAD GUY! PUT HIM DOWN THIS IN-STANT!" I scream.

Jace just watches, looking highly amused. "I wondered if he would supersize."

Although the smallest of their species, pygmy kraken have a very distinct power. When scared, they can grow up to 50 sizes larger than their true form *instantly.*

Boris bubbles happily while continuing to toss around Orion.

Then, something *else* happens.

Orion somehow escapes, or perhaps Boris dropped him, and there's a giant explosion of lights and shimmering colors. We all cover our eyes against the burning bright rays.

Seeing Orion transform back into his huge dragon form, stand, and spread his wings renders me speechless yet again.

"Holy fuck," Jace breathes.

Shaye slaps her on the back with a grunt. "Miserable prick."

"You're just jealous of that wingspan," Jace teases him and there's a sharp *oof* as he elbows her.

Orion flaps his wings, showing off his gloriously huge wingspan, and roars to the sky with a mouthful of razor-sharp fangs.

Then Boris slaps the dragon across the face with a tentacle.

I gasp.

Orion growls and headbutts Boris.

I step forward, ready to fight. "DON'T YOU HURT MY KRAK-EN!"

With a loud squeak, Boris leaps, wrapping himself around Orion But the dragon doesn't take off or try to escape. Instead, he rolls over and...

Wait. Are they...wrestling?

They roll around on the landing tarmac, squeaking and grunting and growling. But not once does Orion bite or scratch Boris. And not once does Boris open his mouth, where giant pincers that could take a chunk out of Orion wait.

I think...they're *playing*.

"Pinch me," I mutter under my breath. Then there's a sharp pain in my ass and I squeak.

"You said to pinch you," Jace says as I smack her on the arm.

"Rude!"

We stand and watch for at least ten minutes as Boris and the dragon *wrestle*. There's lots of growling and posturing, but no actual wounds.

I must be drugged. Because this can't be real.

"Uh, sorry to break this up but, we do have kittens to rescue!" I shout at them. Boris stops at once and slithers over to me, shrinking down to his normal, everyday size. By the time he makes it over to me, he's back to the size of small dog. He crawls up my leg and cradles himself around my neck, squeaking and bubbling happily. There is another explosion of light as Orion transforms back into his two-legged form.

There's not a hair out of place on his perfect head.

I stare at him in shock. A light pink rises on his cheeks.

Is he embarrassed? That's horribly cute.

Orion clears his throat and looks towards my siblings. "Discuss what you just witnessed with anyone, and I'll eat you."

Shaye flips him off. "You can try!"

Jace has to press her lips together to hide the laugh that is bubbling out. "That was very enlightening."

Orion exhales in annoyance. "Let's go."

With a snaps his fingers, my stuff appears right in front of me.

"Wait, why didn't you just do that in the first place?" I ask, confused.

"I was being polite," he says, before picking up my bags and walking away. I scramble to follow him, ignoring the fact that the bags he's carrying are so heavy Jace and I could barely carry them together. Yet his arm muscles aren't even bulging. He's barely trying.

Not that I'm looking at his arm muscles that closely or anything. We walk to the other end of the landing pad and approach a private ship station. Orion places his hand on an ID reader that scans his palm, and the door whooshes open and—*oh my God.*

Well. I can see why we're taking his ship.

Orion looks back at me with a smile full of manly pride. "Meet Starfire."

CHAPTER 13

DANGER, HENRI LASELLE

Starfire, a class E battleship, is so brand-new I'm actually scared to touch anything.

"Love you," Jace whispers in my ear. "I know it's a neurotic big sister thing to say, but please be careful. Trust your instincts, and if it's all going to hell, you get out of there right away."

I make a muffled sound of agreement, suddenly too emotional for words.

Jace takes a deep breath and caresses my head before pulling back and giving me a gentle shove forward into Harold's arms. I inhale the woodsy, sweet smell of his fur, imprinting it into my memory.

"See you soon, buddy."

"Harold miss Henri already." His deep voice is tinged with sadness.

"I miss you already too."

Pulling away before the tears start flowing, I turn and face Shaye. He darts in to gives me a quick hug and I let out a surprised *oof*.

"Be careful with the dragon," Shaye grumbles. For a moment, I resist. Then I melt into my brother's arms as my mind and body relaxes.

"I will, I promise."

Shaye nods and lets me go.

Then it's time to go. Orion is inside the ship already.

I walk up the ramp, Boris at my side. Orion leans against the wall just inside, waiting for me.

"I put your things in your room."

"That was fast."

He smirks.

"Right...dragon," I remember aloud, and Orion flashes a hint of fang.

Class E ships haven't even been released yet. The newest ones on market are Class D. The Menace is a Class B, but in immaculate condition for its age.

Starfire, though, is a masterpiece of metal and technology. All perfectly trimmed metals. It's beautiful. A *click* behind us tells me the ramp is closed.

There's no going back now.

"Starfire?" Orion asks and I look around, confused.

A female AI voice suddenly sounds from an invisible speaker, "Yes, Orion?"

"Take us into orbit and set a course for the Pollux jump gate."

It's so smooth as the ship powers on and lifts off the ground that I don't even lose my balance. If it weren't for Orion's order, I'm not sure I'd even realize the ship was moving.

Orion motions for me to follow as he begins a tour of the ship.

I pay attention, but mostly I'm in awe of just how much this all cost.

Orion is clearly rich.

Like, *really* rich. Potentially richer than the UGF, which is almost incomprehensible.

Orion stops and turns, taking in the bewildered look on my face. "This floor is just the holding area and maintenance. The nuclear engine is to the right. Living quarters and the kitchen are one floor up, and the top floor is the cockpit, navigation, and weapons storage."

It's then that I realize we're standing in front of an open door with a small cylindrical room. Almost like a—

"You have an *elevator* in your spaceship?"

Orion blinks. "Of course."

He enters the small space, and I follow, Boris slithering along at my feet. In order to get in the elevator, I have to stand so close to Orion our arms brush. I'm hyperaware of his presence, of each centimeter of his body touching mine.

Boris takes this moment to climb up my leg.

The metal of the elevator walls is so shiny I can see our reflection.

Orion watches me with his amethyst eyes.

I keep reminding myself that the man before me is a dragon.

A *dragon!*

Boris suddenly squeaks and Orion looks down at him, "Yes, I agree."

I choke as the elevator doors opens. "You can talk to him?"

"Yes."

I'm left sputtering as I hurry to catch up. My mind races with possibility.

"Can you talk to all animals?" I ask. "Is this a dragon thing?"

Orion doesn't respond as he continues down the very clean but industrial corridor. Metal walls and shades of gray and white are everywhere. It's pristinely clean, and brand new but there's no art. No decoration. No sense of who he is as a person—erm, *dragon.*

It's just a ship. It might be fancy, but at least The Menace feels like a home.

It makes me strangely sad for Orion, who stops and presses a button on a door. The door slides open to show a giant king-sized bed with a panoramic glass view of space.

Oh wow.

Boris slides off my leg and races into the bathroom. I hear the sound of a water faucet. He must be filling up the sink.

I put his travel aquarium in my bag for now, but as soon as I get settled, I'll fill it up so that he can use it to get around. It's very important that pygmy krakens keep their skin damp at all times.

I pad over to the window.

There's the sound of soft footsteps and I realize Orion must have taken off his shoes. I look down at my dirty boots, instantly embarrassed.

"Don't be embarrassed." My head snaps up as I look at him. His face is gentle but there's a firm order in his eyes. "Don't ever be embarrassed about who you are, Henri. Not around me."

I scoff. "You say that as if I know you, but I don't, and you don't know me."

"I know more than you think," Orion says carefully. "And you trust me." His head tilts as he takes me in, trying to make sense of me.

I blink at his words. "To be honest, I don't really know if I trust you. I just met you what, 30 minutes ago?"

"And now you're on my ship. That requires some trust."

"All that means is that you were my best hope of finding my creatures alive. I trust that you will try to help me, but that is all."

Orion nods thoughtfully.

"You are unlike any human I've ever met, Henrietta Laselle."

"Henri," I correct him. "It's Henri, *please.*"

How does he even know my full name?

Shaye must have mentioned it before. Still, suspicion has me on edge.

I watch as the ship leaves the atmosphere of Andromeda, and the stars appear fully. All the while, I'm hyperaware of the being standing a foot away from me.

I can *feel* him watching me. Feel the trace of his eyes along my skin, almost like a brand.

The view is beautiful but...I'm only half paying attention to it. How can I, when a dragon looms behind me?

I turn and realize Orion is still staring at me, as if the sight of the stars is of little interest.

"Why do you not like your name?"

His question surprises me.

I bite my lip, unsure how honest I want to be. "I do. It's just..." I pause for a moment. I look back out at the night sky and reach my hand up to the thick glass window. "My parents used to call me that. Hearing that name reminds me of them. I hear my name and I can hear them calling me downstairs for breakfast or asking if I finished my homework."

I exhale and trace my finger across the stars in the distance.

"I've always felt more like Henri, anyways."

My heart is always a bit heavy, at least since Mom and Dad died. But in some moments, that heaviness is more prominent than others. Now is one of those moments.

"Grief is strange, isn't it?" Orion says softly. I turn and meet his starry gaze, realizing it's brighter than the view outside the bedroom window. The light from the stars and the fading planet reflect off his face, showing the planes of his high cheekbones and carving out his sharp jawline.

"You are familiar with grief?" I ask quietly, and the dragon gives a small, closed lip smile.

"I am. Far too well, I suspect."

I nod. "I'm sorry."

Orion looks at me, "Don't be. I am old. Very old, Henri. Grief is simply a part of life. It means we've lived, and we've loved. But for one as young as you to know grief so intimately...it is a tragedy. I am sorry you know it as well as I."

I don't even realize I'm crying until a single tear escapes my eyes at his words. He takes his large, tattooed hand and gently wipes away the tears that are now free flowing.

Then he takes his hand, damp with my tears, and *licks* it with a—*ohmygod*—a forked *tongue*. His eyes never leave mine, but he nods, making a *hmm* sound as if tasting the answers he was looking for within my tears.

Orion looks to the bedroom behind us. "This room is mine, but I stripped the other cabins since no one ever travels with me. You can stay here, and I will take the daybed in the living room. We will be at the Pollux gate in the next two hours."

He walks out, showing me a button on the wall, "If you need anything, press this and ask Starfire. She can help."

"I—" I start, and Orion looks back at me. He's so beautiful it scrambles my brain.

"Yes?" Orion smiles and it shocks my brain into activity.

"Nothing. Never mind."

What is wrong with me? Oh my God, Henri, get it together!

He nods. "As you wish."

I'm always the confident one. I know how to act in any situation and can easily take control. But suddenly I feel like a damn fish out of water. I'm out of my depth, in space, with a giant dragon who can turn into a man.

A man who is messing with my head.

Orion smiles and it takes my breath away. "Starfire will tell you where I am. But you don't need to look if you want to find me. All you need to do is say my name."

"Okay?"

"Dragons are known for their exceptional eyesight and hearing. If you say my name loud enough, I will hear you, regardless of where I am on the ship."

Oh. His hearing is that good?

I guess that makes sense. The desire to brush up on dragon lore courses through me.

The door closes and I'm left alone, in silence. I take a few steps and flop onto the bed, groaning at the way the sheets smell of Orion's delicious musk.

"Of course he has to smell good too," I sigh. "This is bad. This is so, so bad."

One thing's for sure: my siblings are *not* going to like this.

But the problem is, well...I'm not sure I care.

CHAPTER 14

A DRAGON IN SHEEP'S CLOTHING

*S*queak!

Boris happily splashes in the sink while I get changed. I took half an hour to vent my frustrations into the ether, otherwise known as grumbling to myself while my face is smushed into the sheets of Orion's insanely comfortable and delicious smelling bed.

"I wish Derek was here," I say to Boris as I bring my small bag of toiletries into the bathroom. Enclosed glass shelves of expensive product surprise me.

Orion is rich in a way I've truly never experienced. Not even a little bit.

One small tentacle wraps around my finger.

Squeak, squeak.

"I know you miss him too. We're going to find him and bring him home. I just—" my voice cracks, "What if it's too late?"

Boris makes an angry *SQUEAK* and a jet of water hits me in the face.

"I'm trying to stay positive! But Derek and Frankie have been with me since Mom and Dad died. I can't lose them—I can't lose *any* of you. I promised you I would always keep you safe, Boris. I made the same promise to Derek. I will tear apart this entire goddamned universe to keep that promise."

Boris squeezes my finger before letting go and continuing to play in the water. I stand up and pad over to my bag.

I might have suspected that Boris might follow me...so I *did* pack a few toys. I toss them into the sink, along with some wrapped tootsie rolls. He squeaks happily and gobbles down the tootsie rolls, wrapper and all.

"Dude, that's so gross," I say. He just flips a tentacle at me which I assume is the kraken version of giving a middle finger.

I laugh but it's cut off by an extremely loud bubbling noise in my stomach.

Boris stops and looks at me with wide eyes.

Squeak.

"I know, you're right. I do need to eat something. Thank you for reminding me."

Boris knows my ADHD well.

One of the hardest things for me is remembering to eat. I *tell* myself I need to eat, and logically I know that I need to and want to eat, but suddenly the day is gone and I haven't had anything other than a large coffee and a few pieces of stale sour candy!

A few years ago, the creatures started helping to remind me. While we can't speak, I know him well enough to interpret his squeaks and body language.

"Do you want me to grab you anything?"

Squeak. He splashes happily.

I smile at him. "More candy and some shrimp. Got it. We'll see if he has that. Speaking of, do you want to talk about that little WWE display you put on? What happened to protecting me from the big bad monster?"

Boris looks away.

"You like him, don't you?" I accuse. "Boris, no! How can you like him if you don't even know him? I know he's a glorious, gorgeous dragon with the most incredible eyes I've ever see—"

Boris lifts an invisible brow at me and I cough. "I'm just saying, we don't know him."

Boris makes an indignant squeak that makes me pause.

"Do you know him?"

Boris makes a lower, softer squeak that I imagine is his version of a sigh. He shakes his head no but then *also* shakes his head yes.

"Okay, no you don't know him…but there is something about him you *do* know?"

Boris nods in affirmation.

"What you know about him, is it good or bad?"

I've taught him to nod once for the first answer and twice for the second answer if we're playing a game of questions.

Boris nods once.

Interesting.

My stomach grumbles so loud it makes both of us jump.

"Okay. I want to know more about this, but clearly I do need to eat some real food." *Real* food is subjective here because space food is *never* all that good. "I'm going to go get something to eat before the jump and then I'll be right back, okay? I'll bring your shrimp."

Boris squeaks and goes back to playing, happy to ignore me and play with his toys.

"Starfire?" I ask the room.

A voice responds, "Yes, Henri?"

My jaw drops. She knows who I am?

Huh.

"Tell me about Orion the Worldkiller" I order.

"Certainly. Orion. Male. Age not on record, estimated to be over 10,000 by some experts. Species: dragon. Threat Level: Black. Nickname: The Worldkiller—" Starfire continues but I start at the threat level. Only three other beings in the known universe have ever been given the status of Threat Level Black. Hakkars aren't even Threat Level Black. They're just Red.

What can he do that's so dangerous? I tune back into what Starfire is saying as she prattles out more facts on Orion.

"—Powers: Not on record."

Hmm.

"Does he have any family?" I ask, tired of the endless list of facts.

"No," Starfire responds. "All remaining dragons are deceased. Orion is the last of his line and the only remaining dragon alive, as per UGF records."

That's so sad.

"Starfire, why is he considered so dangerous?"

"Dangerous. Searching..." she's quiet for a moment, "1 record, found. In the Galactic Year 57,800—" I grimace, I hate the galactic calendar. But that would be about...five thousand years ago?

"—the dragon Orion destroyed the planet Argos in the Hesperides system."

My heart stops. "Argos?"

"Yes," Starfire replies.

He destroyed a *whole* planet. And why have I never heard of Argos?

"What's on Argos?"

"Answer not found. Please try again."

Damnit. I sigh and ask a different question. "It doesn't say how he destroyed it?"

"No, Henri."

"What happened after that?"

"After Orion destroyed Argos, he was hunted for 2,000 years. The UGF finally caught Orion on a freighter going to Allune. Orion was sentenced to life in prison and taken to the Supermax prison on Praxis-6."

Woah.

"How did he get out of prison? Nobody leaves Praxis. Never."

Starfire thinks for a few seconds before replying. "Information found: Orion Worldkiller left Praxis after 400 years due to good behavior. His release was contingent upon entering into required employment with the UGF, where he works to this day."

"What does Orion do for the UGF?"

"Information: classified."

Hmm.

Maybe I need to try another angle.

"Who is Orion's direct superior?"

"The direct superior of the dragon Orion is General Sirius, Vice President of the UGF," Starfire says.

Holy shit.

"Who are you, Orion?" My suspicions can't be ignored.

But...Harold knows Orion. Knew *of* him. And Boris can apparently read someone's soul. I have to trust their intuition. It's not led me astray so far.

I just don't know if I can trust my own feelings.

"Starfire, monitor Boris, the pygmy kraken, and let me know if he needs anything, please. Can you show me where the kitchen is, too?"

"Certainly. Leave your room and turn right. The kitchen is 50 steps away."

I nod and take a deep breath, steeling myself against whatever is to come. I press the button to open the door and am assaulted with the most mouth-watering smell.

Blindly, I follow my nose to the right and walk into the kitchen where Orion is cooking.

"Hungry?" he asks without turning.

"Very." I slide into one of the barstools across from the stove where he stands with his back turned, giving me ample time to check him out.

And my *Lord*, there's a lot to check out, particularly in those tight pants of his.

I rub my eyes with my hands, trying to get the image of his perfect ass out of my head, but it doesn't work.

"Spaghetti and meatballs," he announces, and I open my eyes to see a giant plate of steaming hot spaghetti with red sauce and meatballs in front of me.

My jaw nearly detaches from my face. Orion walks around the kitchen humming something beneath his breath as he makes his own plate and takes a seat next to me.

But unfortunately, I can't eat that. Which is exactly what I say.

Orion simply blinks. "I read in your file that you do not consume meat, so I stocked some substitutes. I, however, am a strict carnivore, so you will have to tell me if it is unsuitable and I can make you something else."

The dragon likes to cook?

"The one time I went to Earth, I had this dish, so I thought it might be something you would enjoy."

I—the dragon is cooking for *me.*

What. The. Fuck?

"It's perfect. Thank you."

Orion looks supremely smug as I dig in, moaning at the burst of flavors on my tongue. The pasta is perfectly cooked, not too mushy with just enough texture. And the sauce! My god, the sauce. The rich tomato flavor mixed with garlic and cheese bursts in my mouth.

"*Thisissogoodholyshit,*" I moan around another mouthful.

There's a clattering and I pause around another bite, realizing I've been shoveling the food down my mouth as fast as possible which must have been hideous to witness.

But Orion just watches me with wide eyes that sparkle brighter than usual. "I'm very glad you like it, Henri." He reaches a hand up to wipe next to my mouth.

Embarrassment courses through me again. My God, I was eating like a starved wildebeest!

"I, uh, I haven't had a meal in...well since before we left Earth. I didn't realize I was so hungry."

Orion smiles at me. "I am glad you like it."

I take a deep breath and continue eating. Using a small knife, I cut into the vegan meatball, shocked to see the crispy exterior and how real it looks.

We eat in silence for a moment, both too busy chewing to talk. But as much as I hate to admit it, the dragon is a damn good cook. Something beeps and Orion's head pops up. "Ah, that's the garlic bread and my steak."

"Y-you made garlic bread?" I ask, instantly salivating.

"Of course. Your file said it was one of your favorites."

Ah.

"You read my file? That's such an invasion of privacy!" I hiss at him.

"Normally, yes. But I read all your files when they moved Shaye into my home. I had to ensure that my roommate could be trusted."

I nearly choke on the pasta. "You and my brother are ROOM-MATES?"

Orion turns around, a perfectly seared steak on a plate in one hand, and slices of buttery garlic bread in a bowl in the other.

"Yes. You did not know?"

"No—I mean, obviously not. For how long?" I breathe. "I—I didn't even know Shaye *lived* with anyone. We don't talk often."

Orion makes a *hmm*-ing sound as he takes this in. "Around a decade and a half, give or take a few months."

"YOU'VE LIVED WITH MY BROTHER FOR 15 YEARS?"

Orion's eyes twinkle with mirth at my shock and outburst. "Yes."

"I'm going to punch him in his *stupid* face," I snarl. "Why would he keep something like that a secret? Especially while letting me get on a spaceship with, you!"

Orion tilts his head. "He does not wish for me to know you."

This stops me.

That...seems true. Shaye was definitely not happy about Orion's presence around me.

"Why would he do that?"

Orion's face and body do not outwardly change, but one moment I'm looking at the man, and the next, I am looking at a dragon in mortal skin.

"I covet rare treasures, Henri."

I blink rapidly at his words.

His eyes burn with an inner flame as he stares at me.

Overwhelmed, I busy myself with a piece of garlic bread. Another moan leaves me as the hot, buttery bread coats my tongue.

There's a low growl and a loud, metallic groan like something just hit the ship. My eyes crack open but all I see is Orion clutching the kitchen counter for dear life as he watches my lips with reverence.

Does he want to eat me?

Oh my God, are my happy food noises teasing the predator in him?!

"Do you eat humans?" I burst after swallowing my garlic bread.

Orion's eyes widen in shock and he lets out a loud laugh, smiling widely.

"No, Henri, I do not eat humans," he chuckles. "Well. Not anymore."

I freeze mid-reach for another slice of garlic bread when his words hit me.

"So you've...you've eaten a human before?"

Orion shrugs. "It was a long time ago. You do not need to worry, Henri. Humans do not taste good. Though...I get the feeling everything about you tastes good."

I choke on air and he smirks, taking a bite of his steak and chewing slowly, licking his lips afterwords. The entire time, he keeps those burning amethyst eyes on me.

Orion wants me. I'm not one to assume without verbal confirmation, but the meaning in his words was clear.

The dragon—the dragon *wants* me.

With a sharp breath at the realization, I look down at my

pasta and try to finish eating, but hunger isn't burning through me anymore.

Something *else* is.

Something hotter and more volatile.

Something suspiciously like need.

I haven't been with anyone in a few years. I don't…I don't know that I remember how to flirt, even. I know that's stupid and silly, but in this moment, I haven't got a clue what to do.

"Would you like a piece?" I ask and I'm embarrassed to note how breathy my voice is. Orion finishes his stake in record time and sighs happily. He stretches his arms a bit and walks around the counter to where I hold the bowl of garlic bread.

I'm holding it almost like a shield, as if that alone will protect me from him.

"No, Henri, thank you though."

I gasp as he leans forward and lifts his thumb to my lips, brushing a stray crumb from the corner of my mouth.

Lick him.

My intrusive thoughts fight for dominance, and it leaves me trembling.

What is happening?

"You're a dangerous creature, aren't you?" he murmurs before pulling away. "Finish eating and meet me in the Nav center. We'll be at the gate in 15 minutes."

"Yep, cool, that's totally cool, sounds great," I ramble with a slightly hysterical voice.

I try to force my thoughts into some semblance of order, but my skin still *burns* where Orion touched me.

And this is *not* the time for burning. It's the time for finding Derek and the kittens. That's it.

Yes.

I *pretend* logic prevails and simply ignore the burning need coursing through me.

CHAPTER 15

THE BLACK HOLE INCIDENT™

"**N**ow approaching the Pollux Gate. Please make your way to the cockpit and secure for jump."

The UGF has hundreds of jump gates throughout the known universe. They're always adding more to make space travel more efficient.

I make my way up to the cockpit which is above the kitchen.

I press the button to the elevator. There's a light *ding* as the doors slide open.

It only takes a few seconds for the elevator to lift me up to the cockpit. When the doors open, I'm surprised to see Orion already in in the navigation seat.

A holographic map of Antheri glows in the air in front of him. Antheri is located in the Hesperides System. It's one of the largest individual solar systems within the galaxy. 30 planets, a mix of gas giants and desert planets, Antheri is one of only two terrestrial planets in the entire system. Orbiting around a massive, ancient star 10x the size of Earth's, Antheri's location is also guarded by a massive asteroid field.

It's why they've been able to resist the UGF so intensely for so long.

"You said you've been there before?" I murmur, walking closer.

It's a dangerous path.

It's exactly why I agreed to his help.

"Yes. Though it was long ago, Hesperides is still the same. I studied it while you changed."

Okay. The dragon is a bit of a nerd.

Orion glances over his shoulder, his violet eyes aglow. "Take a seat. We're almost ready to jump. Starfire?"

"Yes, Orion?" The ship responds, and Orion nods.

"Initiate warp drive sequence."

I walk over to the empty seat next to Orion and sit down, sighing at the plush feel.

Of *course*, the seats are comfortable too.

The seatbelt is different than the ones I'm used to, and I fumble around trying to figure out how to put it on.

"Here," Orion says softly. He unclicks his own seatbelt and stands, hovering over me. Orion grabs the silky fabric from my hands and lifts my left arm, sliding it through the hole. He repeats the action on the other side.

The hot feeling of his touch makes my heart race.

I look up and meet his gaze just as he reaches between my legs.

His fingers only *graze* my thighs as he grabs the seat belt, but it's enough to set me on fire.

My lips open and I inhale sharply as Orion lifts the belt and clicks it into the center, matching the other two, creating a large metal triangle on my chest.

He reaches down again, never taking his eyes off me, and tightens the belt.

Danger, Danger, Danger. I see the warning signs flashing in my head but I can't look away. My heart *thuds* in my chest so hard that I can feel it vibrating against my bones.

"Safety first," he purrs, sounding more feline than dragon. "I did promise to return you to your siblings safely, and Shaye is horrible to be around when he doesn't get his way."

I let out a ghost of a laugh.

I still can't believe my brother has a roommate and never told me. I wonder if Jace knew?

My thoughts begin to wander but I'm yanked back into the present as Orion suddenly tightens the seatbelt even more. He moves the fabric until it's hitting right *there* and my mouth opens with a sharp inhale.

The blood in my body starts to rush and—Orion leans back without a word, going back to prepping the ship.

I'm left staring at him moon-eyed, my mouth ajar.

GET. IT. TOGETHER. HENRI! He was just buckling you in and helping. You're reading into things!

Inhaling again, I try to calm down. But my heart continues to race.

"Something wrong, Henri?" Orion asks

I open my mouth before I second-guess myself. "You are the dangerous one."

I meant my voice to sound strong and confident, but my words come out slightly shaky. I pretend that it's just because he's a dragon and not because of the way he's *staring* at me.

"A little danger never hurt anyone." Orion shrugs. His inky black hair falls into his eyes and I want to lean forward and brush it off his forehead—*what the? No! Bad brain!*

"Am I in danger with you, Orion?" I blurt.

I've always been bad at keeping my thoughts to myself. It's why I like to be alone.

Orion's eyes begin to glow slightly, and he leans forward until I can feel his breath on my face.

"Oh yes. Terrible danger," he whispers. "But I will never hurt you, Henri. I promise."

Orion leans back and I let out a long, shaky breath.

The dragon's face turns emotionless as he glances at the cockpit dash, hitting a few buttons.

Orion spins the holograph and sets our destination.

Starfire comes over the speaker. "Pollux Gate locked. Warp drive ready. Awaiting your orders, Orion."

"Thank you, Starfire. Initiate warp and enter the jump."

The spaceship powers up.

I watch as the gate—a set of 3 rings made out of an ancient ore mined from the deepest reaches of space—powers up around us, beginning to spin faster and faster. Then they begin to hum as the air around us turns electric. I can taste iron on my tongue.

"Are you afraid?" Orion asks, his voice not judgmental, but curious.

"Yes," I admit.

Before Orion can respond, warp drive starts and we hurtle through space, leaving the jump gate behind.

Starfire shakes and groans.

I'm suddenly glad for the tight seatbelt because otherwise, I would be thrown around.

Wait.

"Boris!" I shriek, turning to Orion. "Is he safe?"

"Starfire," Orion shouts. "Kraken update."

"The pygmy kraken safe in bathtub in the primary suite. The being appears to be unmoved by the turbulence of warp drive."

Thank God.

"Please let me know if he seems scared at all, or anything happens," I add.

"Yes, Henri," Starfire responds.

The cockpit descends into silence, and I watch as the stars fly past us, creating streaks of bright colors, like shooting stars.

If it weren't for the turbulence, I'd be lulled to sleep.

At that thought, the shaking increases.

"Approaching debris field," Starfire announces.

Orion makes a surprised noise. "That's new. Put a zero gravity lock on the bathroom Boris is in."

"Yes, Orion."

"Zero grav?" I ask. "What's happening?"

"I'm not entirely sure," Orion says in a completely unworried voice. "Something seems to be impeding the jump."

"I thought that wasn't possible?"

Orion shrugs. "It isn't usually possible. But this is space, Henri. The possibilities are endless."

Starfire suddenly veers, groans, and thuds like it's running up against something.

"Starfire!" Orion shouts. "Status update!"

"The debris field is too dense. We have to leave warp."

"Shit." Orion looks at me. "I'm sorry, we have no choice." He glances up and asks, "How many days from here to Antheri, Starfire?"

"Two weeks," Starfire replies, and now it's my turn to curse.

The ship veers again and my stomach turns.

The metal exterior shakes so hard, it sounds like the entire ship might come apart at any moment.

"Do it," I bite out, and Orion grabs hold of the steering.

"Switch to manual!" he roars, yanking the wheel to the side.

We're all thrown around as the ship drops out of warp, throwing us on the edge of a giant black hole.

"That's not good," I whisper, looking at the black hole in horror as its gravitational field grabs hold of us. Starfire shudders, its metal hull groaning as we begin to float towards the black hole. The lights on the ship go in and out.

"I will take care of this," Orion unbuckles himself and stands. "You will need to take over the cockpit, but Starfire has automatic capabilities. Tell her what you want and she will do it."

Then he leans over, reaches between my legs, undoes my seatbelt, grabs me around the waist—to which I let out a rather undignified shriek—and plops me down in the pilot's chair.

"Y-you—" I tremble with rage. He thinks he can *man* handle me? The audacity!

"You got this, Stardust?"

I nod, frozen by the situation, too scared to be mad about the silly nickname.

One blink and Orion is gone.

Then there's a strange sound. Something like a hatch opening.

"Starfire! What is Orion doing?"

"Going outside," she responds calmly.

My jaw drops but the ship shakes harder as the black hole pulls us in closer towards its center.

Fuck this.

I look at the dashboard, unsure what anything means, but the steering console seems simple enough. I grab hold of the wheel and turn it the opposite way of the black hole.

"Starfire, start the ignition."

"The ignition is already on, Henri."

Well, shit.

"Then increase it!"

"Increasing ignition speed now."

I keep turning the wheel, trying to wrench us away from the black hole but the pull is too strong.

"No change," Starfire reports. "We are still falling closer to the black hole."

"I can see that!" I grunt, putting my entire body weight into my attempt at steering, but nothing is happening.

Something flashes in my peripheral view, and I watch, shocked, as a giant black dragon hovers in front of the ship.

Large talons carefully grab hold of Starfire. Orion flares his wings, pulling us away from the black hole in the direction I was steering.

It's slow. The black hole is so strong, and there is no wind for Orion to use. Still, he flaps his wings, trying to pull us away.

Orion lets out a loud roar, his arms and wings trembling, but after a few minutes, we finally make it out of the black hole's gravity field.

Panting, I watch as Orion lets out a deep breath, relieved.

I smile at him, and he gives me a toothy dragon smile back.

That was close. Too close.

I lean back in the seat and take a deep inhale, relaxing.

It's so fast I can't even see it. One second, I'm looking at Orion, the next, a space rock shoots smack into his scaled head.

Orion's blinks in shock and then and I watch in horror as he falls unconscious, his eyes closing and his body going limp.

Then the dragon begins to float towards the black hole.

CHAPTER 16

KRAKENS IN SPACE

"**O**h no." My heart stops beating and I watch as the black hole slowly pulls Orion's huge dragon body closer. He's bigger than the entire ship but the farther away he gets, the smaller the dragon becomes.

If we linger much longer, the ship will get caught in the black hole's gravitational field again.

I watch helplessly as Orion floats closer to the black hole.

Frantically, I look around, hoping to find something that can help.

"Starfire! Can you send out a rope and pull him in?"

"I do not have a rope."

Shit.

There is only one way out of this.

I have to use my magic.

I unbuckle from the captain's seat and stand.

Cracking my neck, I prepare to unleash potential destruction in order to save the dragon. Rubbing my fingers together, I open my palms and face them up.

Sparks flare in the center of my palms.

I try to empty my mind but my thoughts are *racing*.

Come on, you can do this.

Just as I'm about to release my spell and try to pull the dragon closer, something flashes in the corner of my eye, pulling me out of my thoughts. The sparks in my palms die as my hands fall to my sides.

Oh. My. *GOD.*

Boris floats by the spaceship. He waves a large red tentacle at me and I sputter, unable to form words.

Then he does the thing.

The thing that makes pygmy krakens so rare, and so special.

He *grows.* Not just a little bit, but in an instant he goes from small enough to sit on my lap to as large as Starfire.

Boris rarely grows, preferring his smaller size, but *wow.* It's a sight to behold.

"He-he—" My brain is quite literally exploding a la' the Jacinda Laselle special as I watch my kraken float towards a giant black hole to save a space dragon the size of Earth's *moon.*

Except now my worry has tripled. I scramble closer to the window and watch as Boris approaches Orion and uses his tentacles to grab hold of the dragon's legs. For a moment, they don't move. The force from the black hole is so great that Boris has to attach more tentacles to Orion, pulling as hard as he can.

Finally, they begin to pull away from the black hole.

I breathe a sigh of relief and slump back in my seat. Sweat drips down my forehead, turning my vision blurry.

Or that could be the tears that just decided to escape.

"You're in so much trouble!" I shout at Boris through the glass as they pass by the ship. "You get back into this ship right now, Boris Laselle!"

I swear Boris rolls his eyes at me before he floats out of sight, the unconscious dragon in tow behind him.

A loud clanking sound a few seconds later announces their

arrival.

"Orion and the kraken are entering the hatch," Starfire announces.

"Great," I sigh. "No need to invoke the wrath of the UGF today!"

I stand up on trembling, jelly legs and hurry down to the hatch. By the time I get there, Boris is waiting for me, a prone Orion, now in mortal form, on the floor next to him.

"How did you get him to shift?" I ask, flinging myself at my kraken friend.

Boris squeaks in my ear, nuzzling me before pulling back. He wiggles his tentacles at me in answer.

A kraken secret, it seems.

Orion is face down, allowing me a clear view of the *crater* of a wound in the back of his head.

"Shit. Shit! That's not good."

I swear and Boris frowns, making a low gurgling noise.

"I'm the adult here, I can swear," I tell him. "Speaking of"—I crouch down—"you're in so much trouble. You could have gotten really hurt, Boris. I was so scared."

The pygmy kraken looks down and waddles his two front tentacles, looking rather ashamed. Guilt instantly floods me.

"I'm not actually mad, buddy, I'm just glad you're okay. You scared me so much!" I whisper. "All that matters is that you're safe."

The kraken looks back up at me and wiggles his tentacles. *Squeak!* Boris crawls over to me and climbs up my leg. He plasters himself against my face, nearly strangling me.

"It's okay," I whisper, petting his soft, slimy flesh. "You're alright, sweetheart. We're all okay, thanks to you."

Squeak! Boris shakes a tentacle at the dragon on the ground.

"Yes, and him," I admit. "Now, can you help me carry him into the med bay?"

Squeak squeak! Boris hugs me tighter and I caress his tentacles.

I press a kiss against his slimy head. "My *hero.*"

Boris bubbles happily. I have a feeling that if krakens could blush, his cheeks would be bright pink. After a few seconds, he crawls back down my body and together we pull the dragon's unconscious mortal body into the med bay.

"Good *Lord,*" I curse. "What is he made out of, bricks? An entire fucking *meteor?*"

Boris squeaks and I swear it sounds like an agreement.

"He might as well of stayed in dragon form!" I groan, muscles straining.

Boris nods, pulling harder and letting out very cute little squeaks.

I'm glad Jace isn't around, because trying to get Orion onto the med bay table ends up with Orion likely getting *more* injured than he was before. I wince as his head hits the bed pad again with a heavy *thunk.*

"God, what if we killed him?" I ask, starting to panic.

Boris slaps me with his tentacle, and I sputter for a moment before nodding, "Right. Thanks. No freaking out."

Boris nods and then looks at the ship. I know he's trying to tell me something as we roll Orion's body over, putting him on his back. I pant heavily and want to slide to the ground as we get him situated.

"Starfire, Orion was injured. Can you please do a full health workup and CT scan?" I ask, unsure of the ship's capabilities.

The med bay flares to life. A glass shield descends over the bed and holographs appear along the surface.

"Analyzing. Time until completion: 30 minutes."

I sigh and look around the room. There's one bed and a large chair in the corner.

"Starfire, how long do you think Orion will be unconscious?"

The ship responds instantly. "At least 10 hours. He is reading positive for a concussion and has some brain damage. It will heal, but dragons go into stasis when healing wounds of this caliber."

"How long can stasis last?"

"Up to 72 hours," Starfire answers.

Son of a bitch! I have to sit around for 72 hours?

Worry at how behind we will be, at the thought of losing Derek and the kittens for good, takes over. But there's nothing I can do.

I know many things, but I do not know how to truly power a spaceship. Starfire might be automated, but I don't even know where we are.

"I guess...I'll just wait then."

The ship suddenly feels so quiet.

"If you are looking for something to do," Starfire says, surprising me, "might I recommend the library?"

I blink, shocked. "Uh-what? You have a library?"

"Yes."

I glance over at the prone dragon. I've got time to kill, and nobody is around to tell me "no".

"Okay," I nod. "Show me the library."

CHAPTER 17
CURIOSITY KILLED THE WITCH

O rion slept for exactly 10 hours.

"Henri, Orion is waking up."

At Starfire's voice, I close my book, tucking it below my arm, and set off to the med bay.

I turned the corner, ready to unleash on the tirade I've spent the past 9 hours and 15 minutes working on, but I stumble to a halt. My tongue goes numb and heavy in my mouth as I watch Orion changing. He must store fresh clothes down here.

He faces away from me, showing off his muscular back. Tattooed wings that resemble his dragon wings decorate his shoulders in shades of black and purple. Scales decorate his skin like patches, shimmering in the light.

Orion Worldkiller is *gorgeous.*

Focus, Henri.

I try to keep my cool, but my eyes can't stray from his figure. He's muscular but not in a bulky way. Everything about him seems *purposeful...*and dangerous.

"I can hear your heartbeat," Orion says without looking. His voice is lower and scratchier than usual from the long sleep. As he slides on a shirt, he turns to me, showing me just a hint of his defined abdomen.

How *dare* he be so sexy when I'm angry at him!

I stomp over to him and poke him in the chest.

Orion doesn't move, unsurprisingly. It's like poking a mammoth. I'm not sure Orion even noticed.

"Why are you poking me?" he asks in a wry voice.

"Shut up and sit down," I hiss, holding my book tight against my chest and glaring at him. Orion looks down and sees the book in my arms and a certain *knowing* enters his violet, starry gaze.

"I see that you have questions," he says carefully, taking a seat in the chair near the bed.

"You're damn right I do," I lift my chin and slap the book down on his lap, pointing at the cover. "Starting with *this.*"

A History of Argos, Kingdom of the Dragons faces up at us, the brown leather tome thick with ancient paper.

Orion looks up at me, unaffected. "Ask your questions, Henri."

"You're a KING?" I'm surprised my shriek doesn't shake the walls of the ship. But Orion, in all of his dragon-induced audacity, simply shrugs.

"It's of no consequence," he says. "My people are gone. A king is not a king if they have no one to rule over."

I glare at him. "Yes, I read all about how your family has ruled over dragonkind since the universe first began."

"What can I say? I'm an old soul." He winks at me, and I want to slap him.

Or kiss him.

I'm not really sure, but I hope it's the former.

"So, you're King of the dragons and you have the power to destroy entire worlds. Yet there is *nothing* about that day in *any* of your history books. The day you earned the name 'Worldkiller';

there is no mention of it. Yet it clearly happened."

"And?" Orion asks with a smile.

"And, that means someone *tampered* with the histories. That's very, very illegal."

"Yes, it is," Orion nods and stands, approaching me. "It would take someone very powerful to do so. Or something."

I back up, hitting a counter but Orion doesn't stop his stalking until we're nearly chest to chest. I pant, overwhelmed at the closeness of his presence.

"Thank you for saving me, Henri," Orion reaches forward and draws his finger along my cheek. "I owe you my life."

"It wasn't me," I mutter. "It was Boris."

"You could have taken the ship and left," Orion says.

I purse my lips. That hadn't occurred to me, and it should have. I *could* have stolen his ship.

"Don't go getting any ideas," he chuckles.

It's so fast I barely catch it when Orion leans down and brushes his lips against my cheek. He's warm and *so, so close*. The feel of his breath against my cheek is enough to send my brain spiraling out of my skull.

"Thank you," he whispers before pulling back.

"You're welcome," I breathe unable to look away from his piercing eyes. "But it was a practical decision. You know your way around Antheri, I don't."

"Mhmm..." Orion nods, not looking the least bit convinced. "Is that all?"

"Yes, it is!" I lift my chin.

"You're cute when you're mad."

My jaw drops open and I make a surprised noise.

Orion winks at me and steps back more fully. "I have moon-rock dust everywhere, so I'm going to go shower, then let's get back on route."

I nod, shaken up from the shift in his moods. With a soft smile, Orion turns and walks out of the room. I reach up and trace my cheek remembering his touch, when Orion stops and glances back, catching me in the act. His eyes narrow in on my lips and the entire room heats.

"I'm glad to know you think of me as much as I think of you, Henri."

My jaw drops. "What?"

The bastard smirks. "Reading about me while I'm unconscious, hmm? Seems a bit *obsessed,* Candy."

I gasp in outrage. "How *dare* you! That isn't—I *wasn't*—"

Orion winks and the noise that leaves my throat is somewhere between a choke, a shriek, and a gasp.

I'm left coughing and choking as Orion's laughter drifts down the hallway as he walks towards the main living floor.

Great.

9 hours and 15 minutes of curiosity and preparation and I WILT under the dragon's gaze like a submissive flower.

I was going to interrogate him and get some real answers. Instead, all he did was confirm that yes, he's the fucking King of the dragons, and yes, he's aware that the day of his namesake was removed from the histories.

But *why?* What the hell is he hiding?

Why do you care so much? The stupid voice of logic bursts into my thoughts and I grind my teeth.

The memory of Orion's heated words gives me goosebumps that decorate my arms and shoulders.

I *want* to be responsible, but it's a *little* bit difficult to do so when my brain is screaming, "STRANGER DANGER!" while my body is begging for Orion to touch me.

"Starfire?" I say aloud.

"Yes, Henri?" Starfire responds happily.

"I'm so fucked."

CHAPTER 18

BEWARE THE DRAGON

I head to the cockpit to wait for Orion. It's only a few minutes before he joins me. He smells clean and delicious. There's something about his scent that almost smells...electric.

Taking a shaky breath, I force myself to focus on something else. *Anything* else.

Kittens. Fuzzy kittens. Purring and laying on me. Playing with my hair.

That calms me, but I'm still hyperaware of Orion, and a part of me hates it.

"I had Starfire run diagnostics while I was in the shower. The nuclear reactor got damaged. We can make it to Antheri...but we currently can't enter warp."

I hear what he's not saying.

We can't get home.

Silence descends, and in that silence, I begin to panic. I glance over at Orion. "We have to stop at Hades, don't we?"

Orion nods.

The Hades Outpost. The furthest waystation in the Galaxy. Set in enemy territory, near multiple systems with planets who refuse to bow to UGF law, the Hades Outpost is a neutral, giant floating city, surrounded by freighters.

Theft, fighting, orgies; it all happened in Hades. It's a

free-for-all and an escape. Perfect for criminals and anyone hiding from the law.

Speaking of laws, in Hades, there's only one.

Never upset the Warden.

"It's likely someone there has heard of the hellkittens' whereabouts," Orion says as he charts a course to Hades. "We should get some sleep. It's 18 hours to Hades and we'll need to be quick."

Orion watches me closely, swiveling his chair so that I'm standing between his legs. "Sleep well, Henri. I hope you have sweet dreams."

Instantly, my mind is flooded with images of us. Of his lips on mine...

"Stop that." I point at him and poke him in his—God—his unbelievably hard chest.

"I'm afraid I don't know what you mean." He smirks, stepping away with an innocent look on his face.

"You know exactly what I mean," I glare at him and straighten my shirt before lifting my chin. "Goodnight, dragon."

Even when I turn and walk away, I feel his eyes on my back the entire time as he follows my every step. A quick glance over my shoulder confirms Orion is still watching me, with a hungry look in his eyes.

I hurry around the corner and practically sprint into the elevator. It takes a few moments to go one level down, but I can't get to the room fast enough.

I close the door behind me, panting, and let my legs fold as I slide down to the floor. The room has thick, luscious carpet and I sink into it, leaning my head against the door.

Boris peeks his head out of the bathroom and wiggles over to me, crawling into my lap. He looks at me with those big brown eyes and gently touches one tentacle to my cheek.

"I'm fine." I whisper, but I don't mean it.

I'm not fine.

I'm *confused.* I'm scared about so many things. Derek, not getting home, revealing myself to the wrong person and—

Orion.

Boris wiggles his tentacle, pulling me out of my spiral.

"You're the best, you know that? I don't know what I'd do without you. I know I got mad that you came but...I'm glad you're here, you naughty thing."

Boris squeaks happily, rubbing his tentacle against me again before crawling off me and heading back into the bathroom. A splash follows, which tells me he's playing in the tub.

I force myself to stand and head over to the large bed. It feels so strange to get into someone else's bed. Someone else's sacred *space.*

I rummage through my bag and grab a clean shirt. Sliding my clothes off, I sigh happily at the feeling of the cold, cotton fabric against my warm skin. Forgoing pants, I pull on a clean pair of underwear and my favorite thick socks and jump into bed.

Quickly getting under the covers, as if someone might catch me in the act of something naughty, I'm assaulted with the scent of Orion. It's like he's all around me. My heart *thuds* in response.

"I don't like him," I whisper to myself. "I don't. I *can't.*"

Yes.

Yes. I repeat the words in my head over and over until I feel they're true. The habit hypnotizes and relaxes my mind. Sleep comes quickly, but my dreams are full of terrors. I wake hours later, covered in sweat and no more rested than I was when I got in bed.

"Boris?" I croak.

I hear a wet thunk and a *splash* as he quickly crawls out of the bathtub and wiggles onto the bed. His red head appears as he wraps himself around me, eyes wide and concerned.

Squeak!

"I had a nightmare," I breathe. Boris makes a soft bubbling sound as he settles in, tentacles around my body and his head on my chest.

I manage to fall back asleep thanks to the weight of my small kraken, but it's light and fitful.

Eventually, I give up on sleep and I pull myself from the comfort of Orion's bed, forcing myself to dress.

"Starfire, is there a gym here?" I ask the ship as I survey my limited clothing options.

"Yes, Henri. One floor down you will find a fully equipped gym and training area."

Perfect.

I need to do *something* to keep my mind off Derek and the animals. Maybe moving my body will quiet my mind.

Pulling on some leggings, a sports bra, and some sneakers, I head out of the room. A squeaking sound follows, and I glance back to see Boris following me in his traveling aquarium.

"Are you joining me?" I ask, and the small red kraken nods. "Let's go then. Hopefully we can avoid Orion."

Water hits me in the face, and I sputter.

Boris chitters, clacking his beak together in a sort of kraken-laugh.

"Bad kraken!"

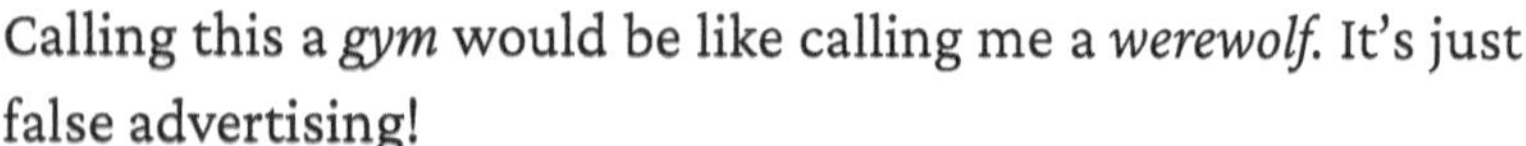

Calling this a *gym* would be like calling me a *werewolf*. It's just false advertising!

The room is gigantic, full of state-of-the-art exercise equipment. Weapons cover the walls, lit up from below to emphasize their beauty. A full-size pool is in the back, next to an enclosed room with titanium-plated walls and a locking door.

But none of that, *none of that*, compares to the sight of Orion Worldkiller, shirtless and covered in sweat as he punches and kicks the air in a martial arts display like something straight out of a movie.

He's wearing shorts that show off thickly muscled thighs decorated with scale tattoos all the way down to his bare feet.

Even his feet are sexy.

Henri, you're clearly losing it!

Orion stops, barely winded and not even panting. He walks over to a small kitchenette and grabs a towel, wiping it over his face.

"Enjoying the show?" he asks, not even looking at me.

I let out a shocked squeak and clear my throat. "It was...adequate."

"I see." He glances over his shoulder at me. "I shall have to try harder to impress you, then."

My heart skips a beat at his words, and I walk past him on trembling legs as I head for the treadmill.

"You're a runner?" he asks.

"Absolutely not," I respond tartly. "But I do strut."

He blinks, looking rather befuddled.

I sigh, "I walk. I mean that I like to walk, Orion."

Orion's answering laughter isn't mocking, but pleasantly surprised. "Ah, I see."

"There is nothing wrong with a good walk!" I shout back at him playfully.

"Nothing wrong, indeed." His voice is low. "When I am planet-side, I enjoy long walks. It's a treat I don't often get to indulge in."

The words are sad, and it almost makes me pause, but I force my arms to keep going as I press some buttons on the treadmill, and it springs to life.

The mat beneath me begins to move and I start a pre-set 3-mile walk.

"Do you have music?" I glance over my shoulder and ask.

Orion nods as he begins taping his hands. "Ask Starfire to play whatever you like."

"Cool," I nod and look up. "Starfire? Can you play something upbeat and good for running?"

"Of course, Henri. Playing upbeat music that's good for running."

Seconds later, a thumpy pop-song with a heavy beat and catchy lyrics blasts through the gym speakers.

I bounce along, strutting to the tune. The music eases my mind and within minutes I'm in the zone, enjoying the moment. Soon, my neck is covered in sweat, causing my hair to stick to it, which is a feeling I cannot stand. Grabbing the ponytail I slid around my wrist, I toss my curly hair up in a messy bun on top of my head.

Behind the sound of the music, the sound of something

heavy hitting the ground catches my attention.

I pause the treadmill and glance back to see Orion glaring at a weight that hit his foot.

Turning forward, I ignore him and let my mind go still again, only focusing on the music and the move of my muscles. It puts me in a trance and soon, the treadmill is slowing as I enter the cooldown.

"Does this contraption not bore you?" a voice asks.

I wish I could say that I handled Orion's sudden appearance beside my treadmill with grace.

Instead, I trip and fall face first, smacking my nose on the treadmill.

The treadmill rolls me off and I thump to the floor with a very unladylike groan.

"Are you alright?" Orion's face hovers above me, his violet eyes sparkling. He's dead serious but based on the way his mouth keeps twitching, he's fighting laughter.

"Fine," I groan. "I'm just going to hide in a hole forever."

Before I can so much as *process* his statement about sparring, I'm being lifted off the ground and pulled into Orion's arms as he sets me on my feet.

Orion's arms linger around me for a few moments longer than necessary, something which I do not miss.

Nor do I mind.

Don't fall for the dragon!

My eye twitches as I fight my own thoughts and I blink it away.

"No, it does not bore me. I enjoy it. The music helps me zone out."

Orion blinks. "Zone out? What does that mean?"

Ah, right. *Ancient dragon.* How *does* one explain ADHD and it's intricacies to a dragon?

I do not know him well enough to warrant a full explanation about the ways in which my brain operates, so I keep it simple.

"I can focus *really* well. It's kind of like…one of my powers. But it's hard to shut that focus off. The music helps. Zoning out is when your mind goes peaceful and quiet."

Orion's face turns thoughtful and he nods, understanding now.

"Would you like to spar?"

His question nearly sends me to the floor again.

"Um, yes, but I don't know how to spar," I admit. I can just imagine Jace punching the air after years of trying to get me to spar with her, and my constant decline.

I love my sister, but she isn't the right person to teach me to fight. I know her too well. I'll hesitate.

"I will teach you, then. We'll start with the basics. First, pick your weapon." He nods at the various weapons decorating the walls.

I walk over to the wall closest to me and pick a long staff with sharp blades at the top. It lifts from the wall mount and slides into my hands. The wood is smooth and comfortable.

I turn and look at Orion, clutching the staff to my chest.

"Good choice." he says.

"And you? Where is your weapon?"

Orion Worldkiller smiles, and it makes me tremble. "I do not need a weapon."

I give him a droll look and he smiles.

"Are you ready?" he asks and I nod. We walk into the middle of the space and face each other.

I assume what I'm fairly sure is a fighting stance—only from seeing it in movies and from Jace.

Orion nods. "Very good. Let us begi—"

A squeaking sound interrupts the dragon and I watch as Boris wheels his traveling aquarium into the room.

"Is that—" I squint, trying to see what he's holding in his tentacles...

Orion snickers and I realize it is indeed what I think it is.

Boris is holding a white flag. Combined with the fabric tied around his head like a sweatband, he's a sight to behold.

"Good, now that we have a referee, we can begin." I say, watching as Orion has to look away and bite his lip, trying not to laugh at my kraken.

Boris squeaks and splashes happily, rolling out of striking range.

I center myself, taking deep breaths and trying to focus on my muscles, but my thoughts run wild.

A predatory light enters Orion's eyes, and I realize he's looking at me like I'm the prey.

Maybe this wasn't such a good idea after all.

CHAPTER 19

SILENCE OF THE KRAKENS

My back hits the soft floormats and I let out a rough *"oof"* as the air is knocked out of my lungs for what feels like the hundredth time today.

"Maybe fighting just isn't for me," I groan, my palms going to the floor to slowly prop my upper body up. Orion crouches above me, a proud smile on his face.

Orion looks away, hiding a smile. "You did very well for your first day. You have the speed; all you need to do is practice."

Boris makes a squeaking sound that sounds suspiciously like laughter. I glare at the red cephalopod but he just blinks at me, pretending to be perfectly innocent.

"How about you use your magic this time?" Orion suggests.

I blink. "Are you sure?"

Orion nods and I force my face to remain unemotional. I show none of the inward excitement I feel.

I roll onto my feet and dust myself off. Picking up the staff from the ground, I assume a defensive position across from him.

Orion's amethyst eyes are sparkling with mirth.

My right eye twitches at the sight of his muscled body. I look away, trying to keep my cool, but based on the smirk on the dragon's face, he fully caught me checking him out.

"Ready when you are," I say with a yawn, as if I'm bored.

"By all means," Orion bows, then gives me a mocking salute.

My eye twitches again and I nearly slap myself in the face.

Neither of us move. Instead, we begin to circle each other. I sweep to the left as he goes right, each of us accessing the other for any moment of weakness.

I don't let my magic out right away. I wait until he goes on the attack.

Just as his fist is about to hit my abdomen, I unleash the magic at my core.

Not my portal magic. Not my spells, but something else.

Something that I probably should not do, but for some god-forsaken reason, I want to.

Pure, nuclear energy bursts from my chest and hits Orion, sending him flying through the air.

The dragon twists in midair to land in a crouch like a cat.

He runs at me and I realize the dragon has been holding back. A *lot*.

But I'm ready.

When he's just about to tackle me, I twirl out of the way and let another wave of nuclear energy burst from me. This time, it sends the dragon flying into the wall. He falls to the ground with a loud thump, various weapons falling on top of him.

Orion stands up and shakes himself off, turning to meet my gaze.

Excitement so raw, so vibrant, it almost *hurts* glimmers in his eyes.

"Nuclear energy? You can control *nuclear* energy?" he asks, awe in his tone.

"Yep." I smirk and pop the 'p' sound with emphasis. "Didn't

read that in my file, did ya?"

There's a beat of silence and then Orion's head falls back at he lets out a loud, boisterous laugh.

His head falls back down and he looks at me, smiling. "Now I see why the UGF keeps you your siblings under watch. Your power...it could—"

"There are many applications for my power, but I have no desire to be *used* as some war tool. All I want is—" I break off.

Orion is next to me a breath later and I gasp at his close proximity.

"Yes? What do you want, Henri?"

He doesn't ask it as a demand, but with insatiable curiosity.

Genuine curiosity, and it throws me off enough that I answer honestly.

"I want to be happy. I want to live in peace, not being hunted down or sold to the highest bidder for my powers. I am a *person,* not a weapon, and I want it to stay that way."

Orion tilts his head and a soft, sweet smile forms on his lips. "I think I finally know why I'm so drawn to you."

I take a step back as my legs turn to jelly. "W-what? You're drawn to me?"

"Not everyone would use a shifted dragon as a wall to lean on, Henri. You are...unlike anyone I've ever met."

DANGER. DANGER. WE ARE IN DANGEROUS TERRITORY! The warning signs flash in my head but I can't look away from Orion's eyes.

"I am drawn to you, Henri, because we are far more alike than you realize."

I am drawn to you. My hands tremble as his words repeat over and over in my head.

I clear my throat, breaking the eye contact. "Tell anyone, any*thing* about what you just learned, and I will portal you into a black hole."

Orion blinks and a delighted smirk appears on his face. "Are you *threatening* me?"

"Why, yes." I smile. "I am."

"How delightful," he responds.

Boris makes a loud squeaking sound as he appears by my side, crawling up my body to glare at the dragon. He waves his tentacles around, smashing two of them together in a way that I'm sure is meant to be *very* intimidating. I cross my arms and nod, as if I'm his back up.

Orion ignores Boris. "If the UGF finds out though? Henri—"

I raise a hand, "I know...I know. They won't. At least, they won't if you don't tell them."

The training room goes silent.

Boris' slimy, red head swivels back and forth, looking at the two of us.

"Are you going to tell them?" I ask, needing a concrete answer.

Orion is silent for a moment. He uncrosses his arms and walks towards me until he's so close, I get a whiff of his tantalizing scent.

"Your secret is safe with me, Henri. I will never tell another soul."

Is it safe with you, though? Or will you use it against me, the way most people would?

"But Henri, I cannot control what happens if others see your power. Use it only as a last resort. Gossip travels fast in space. You're safe to use your portals, but keep the rest locked down."

I grimace and rub my temples. He's right.

"Fine. I will only use it as a last resort." I acquiesce. "You're right. Aliens gossip more than teenage girls."

Orion smiles and goes to say something but gets interrupted by an announcement from the ship.

"Approaching the Hades Outpost," Starfire says.

"Begin docking protocol. Farthest hanger from the center, please."

"Yes, Orion." Starfire responds. The dragon and I look at each other. Time to go meet some space pirates and *hopefully* make it out alive.

We dock without issue. Once Starfire has fully landed, we get changed and make our way down the ramp.

Boris isn't coming with us for obvious reasons.

Nothing says, "Hey! Notice me, evil space pirates!" Like walking around with a red kraken in a rolling aquarium. Instead, Boris will stay back while Orion and I use disguises.

Anonymity is our friend right now. While the Hades Outpost is technically neutral territory, with the UGF officially at war, the rules have changed.

Any sign that we're with the UGF will just result in questions, and that will just cause more problems.

I brought a nondescript gray scarf to wrap around my hair but I look down at what should be my blonde and hot pink hair, I realize a scarf isn't necessary.

"When did you give me a glamour?" I gasp, looking at the

dark plum hue to my hair. It's straight now too, and soft as silk. Then I spy the silver bracelet sitting around my wrist. It's small, so small I didn't even feel it, made of tiny silver links.

"Do you know how illegal this is? And when the hell did you put this on me?" I shake the bracelet at him. My skin glimmers beneath the light of the ship, my arm now a pale, sparkly lavender. Boris watches me with wide eyes.

"This is one of many illegal things we are about to do," Orion mutters casually. "Do not worry about the glamour. It will keep you safe, that's all that matters. And I put it on you in the training room, but I believe I moved too quickly for you to notice. I thought you saw it—I apologize for startling and confusing you."

I blink. "Okay, fine. But if they put us in jail because of this, I'm going to remind you of this moment and say, 'I told you so'." I lift the bracelet again and show him. "I appreciate the help, but next time just ask first. Bodily autonomy, and all."

Orion chuckles. "You are right. I apologize. Next time, I will ask."

I sniff, mollified for the time being. But internally, my mind races. Orion can afford a glamour? Not just one, but two? Holy *shit!*

I look down and inspect my hands fully.

My skin is...*lavender?*

Boris leaves his bowl and wiggles over, looking at me like he can't make sense of this.

"It's still me," I respond and breathe a sigh of relief that the glamour didn't change my voice. "Just...a bit more purple."

I'm wearing cargo pants tucked into leather, steel-toed boots. My jacket is made out of some dark blue neoprene like material, except it's a bit more...leathery. I've never felt anything like it.

"Your brother made it," Orion nods. "The material, that is. It's so new, they haven't even come up with a name for it yet."

The dragon steps in close, dragging his fingers along the edge of the jacket. Despite the fabric separating us, my breath hitches and my heart begins to race.

His glamour turned his black hair silver, and his amethyst eyes now onyx black. His skin was a couple of shades darker and covered in colorful tattoos made up of symbols and languages I don't recognize.

Orion's glamour put him in a black leather vest with a thin cotton tunic beneath. His pants are made of a similar leather material but in a deep navy. Shiny black boots similar to my own finish off his look.

Upon further inspection, I realize the leather is actually the same material as my own jacket. Not quite leather, but it looks so close to it.

"Take your time," Orion smirks, his eyes meeting mine.

Blood rushes to my cheeks, making my face hot and most certainly as red as Boris' kraken skin.

Orion caught me checking him out, and he *knows* it. I know he can hear it thumping away in my chest, racing at his proximity.

"The fabric is made of a new element Shaye created. It's stronger than steel, but as light as air. Light enough it can be turned into thread."

My heart begins to race for an entirely different reason as I try to come up with a logical reason my brother just handed the UGF something that could win them the war...and I'm not so sure I want that outcome, anymore.

Not when they currently have my sister under arrest.

Not when our entire lives have been *monitored*.

On Earth, it was easier to be patient. Out of sight, out of mind, after all. But out here? There was no ignoring it anymore.

Orion steps back and nods at me, his face going cold. "If anyone asks, we're metal traders from the Gallo system. We met at an orphanage on a nearby moon that circled a large, frozen planet."

"And our names?"

Orion smiles, "That's up to you."

I sniff.

"Clara Lecter," I hold my hand out. "At your service."

Orion raises a brow. "Clara Lecter it is, then. Interesting choice."

He doesn't get the joke, or the reference.

"You're supposed to say something about fava beans and a nice Chianti," I tell him.

Orion blinks, completely confused.

"Never mind," I mutter. Jace would have laughed her ass off. Nothing hurts my ego quite like a joke that doesn't land.

I sigh and put my hands on my hips, "What's your name?"

"The Butcher."

I blink, processing.

Clara Lecter and The Butcher? We sound like a bad Broadway show.

"Alrighty, then," I click my tongue. "Let's do this."

Orion hands me two bolters—guns that can shoot both bullets *and* streams of electricity so hot, it burns all the way through muscle and bone; and yet again, HIGHLY ILLEGAL!

"Are you sure you're not a pirate?" I ask him, waving the guns around. His eyes go wide as I point the barrel of the left one at his face. "Cause you've got a lot of illegal shit here, dragon!"

"About that..." he starts.

I instantly am on edge at his words.

"Before the UGF caught me, before I went to Praxis-6...I was rather well-known, particularly in parts like these."

"What do mean by well-known? Well-known for *what?*" I ask, my hands on my hips.

Orion tilts his head and smirks. "I was well-known for being someone you should never fuck with. However, that was many centuries ago. I do not believe anyone will recognize me."

"You were a pirate, then?"

This isn't new information entirely, but hearing it come from Orion himself is different.

"Pirate," Orion shrugs. "Assassin. Thief. Warlord—take your pick."

My jaw drops.

Orion snatches the guns from me and slides them into two pockets built into the jacket. I didn't even realize the pockets were actually gun-holsters, but now that I see it, the design makes sense.

The feeling of Orion standing so close is driving me *insane* though.

With a shaky breath, I step back, and he follows, prowling after me like a hungry lion—or dragon, in this case.

"Something wrong?" Orion smirks, his eyes full of wicked delight. My back hits the wall and he closes in on me, his muscled arms caging me in on either side.

The dragon leans in so close, I can feel his breath against my cheek.

His lips press against mine and I gasp, but he swallows it. Orion doesn't just kiss; he *devours.*

Not quickly, either. Our lips mingle in a slow dance, him leading as I eagerly follow. A low, keening whine escapes my lips and Orion swallows the sound with *greed.*

An asteroid could crash into the ship and I wouldn't stop.

I won't—I *can't.*

I'm not exactly virginal, but it's been a two years since I was with anyone; two years of pent-up need is hitting me all at once.

All I want is *more.*

Boris makes a coughing sound as he wiggles up the wall and stares into my face.

Reality hits me like a bolt of lightning to the brain.

I pull back and unwind myself from the dragon. He sets me gently on my feet and steps back, taking a shaky breath.

I clear my throat and give Boris a quick hug.

My body is trembling. Not with fear though.

My lips *burn* from his touch, and I miss it like a desert snake misses water.

"Right then," I breathe, turning to find him watching me.

It's the *hunger* in his onyx gaze that takes my breath away.

"We better go."

My words are a whisper, but Orion nods as it's back to business.

The heat never leaves his eyes though.

Not once.

Orion Worldkiller, glamour or no, is quickly turning my will to *dust.*

CHAPTER 20

THE BUTCHER SHOP
TANGO

The Hades Outpost is dark and depressing—until you get inside and see the market. Tables lined with aliens of all species selling their wares for a round of cards.

Scantily clad women walk around, dressed in jewels that glow like neon lights.

Drinks are flowing.

Above us, hovercrafts disappear into the fog.

It's huge. So much bigger than I expected.

"Lay low and play it cool," Orion whispers next to me. I take a deep breath and nod. We didn't need re-breathing masks because The Hades Outpost has oxygen generators, but I still feel a bit claustrophobic with the busy crowd.

Nothing to see here. Don't pay attention to us.

One glance around shows me everyone is openly armed.

Orion walks through the crowd and I stay close to his side. We emerge into a wide street lined with storefronts and vendors.

Hagglers shout at us as we pass, but we pay them no mind.

All anyone would think is we've been here before and we know where we're going. We look confident, not out of place.

I *hope.*

Orion slows down and I do the same. We approach a storefront advertising ship parts. As we enter, a bell rings, announcing our presence. The air is stale and musty. Shelves full of unorganized parts line the walls and continue into the room, creating narrow aisles.

Dust covered much of it.

The store seems empty.

Orion approaches the empty cash wrap and rings a bell.

The sound of something hissing comes from the back, making the hair on my arms stand on end.

"What the hell is that?" I ask, but Orion shakes his head, warning me to stay quiet.

A large, scaled body swipes into the room.

I force my jaw to remain closed as it fully emerges, and I get a clear look at the creature.

It has the upper body of a man, although its features are sharper than a humans. Its skin is covered in scales, but instead of legs, muscle merges together, creating a long, snake-like lower body.

"Butcher," the male smiles, flashing huge fangs. I watch as a drop of purple venom falls from one of the fang tips. "Been a long time."

I'll bet my life savings that a bite from him would result in our untimely deaths.

"Yes, it has," Orion says smoothly, a bloodthirsty smile on his face. The two shake hands and I get a closer look at the beautiful green scales on the creature's hand.

"I'm in need of some parts," Orion explains, before producing the list he wrote down.

The male, who I soon find out is named Sven, whistles as he reads through the part list.

"These do not come cheap, Butch. I think I have all of it though."

Orion nods. "Good."

"Except..."

Here we go.

"The nuclear core. For that, you're going to have to ask Aries."

I hide my frustration. Aries has to be one of the Pirate Lords.

"Since when do they control the cores?" Orion scoffs.

Sven shrugs, his long, slit tongue sneaking out from his lips to taste the air.

"Since Aries and his crew took control of the station."

As I suspected.

"How does one go about petitioning this Aries fellow for a core?"

Sven smiles at us, and there's something in it that sets me on edge.

Orion suddenly goes still and grabs my arm. His head cocks, listening to something far away. "This is a trap," he says quietly.

For a moment, nothing happens. Sven's eyes widen, the picture of innocence. Then everything begins to *move*. Orion drags me out of the room, and I sprint after him, but it's too late.

Pirates, armed to the teeth, wait outside of the store.

I grab my bolsters and fire six shots in rapid succession.

Six bodies fall to the floor, and I turn to Orion with a wink. "Did I forget to mention I'm an *expert* marksman?"

Jace and Shaye insisted I get my shooting license the minute I turned 18.

Orion's pupils dilate in surprise.

Blushing, I quickly recharge the bolters as the pirates start to shout, realizing this won't be the easy fight they thought it would be.

Noise comes from behind us as Sven slithers over, two large swords in his hands. More pirates stream in around him, surrounding us.

Orion and I go back-to-back, circling to find any way out.

Shit.

"You're coming with us," Sven hisses, and the sword is suddenly pointed towards my throat. We're handcuffed and dragged along a dark hallway, past the rest of the outpost.

Orion doesn't look concerned, though. Something which I'm beginning to find incredibly annoying.

We're pulled into a small, horribly lit room with a square table. It's like something out of an old gangster movie, complete with the swinging spotlight above us and the metal table.

We're shoved into uncomfortable chairs and then left for a few minutes.

We both stay quiet, understanding that they're watching and monitoring us. After a while, the door finally opens and in walks...*oh wow.*

The pirate is dressed in a billowy white tunic tucked into black leather pants and tall boots. Long dark brown hair billows around him, like something right off of a romance book cover or a fashion magazine.

But his eyes and his skin are *pink.* His skin is a pale bubblegum while his eyes are a deep, pink garnet.

Orion begins to growl, looking back and forth between us as I stare at the pirate, dazzled by his appearance.

"I hear you're trying to buy a nuclear core," he says with a smile, flashing a set of white fangs. "That's a very unusual part to request around these parts, and it will come at a pretty penny.”

“I’ll pay it, Aries,” Orion snarls. “Just let us go.”

“Hmm,” Aries sighs, sitting down across from us. “I don’t think so. You see, I don’t want money. I want something. *Her.*”

Orion’s answering roar shakes the walls.

“Me?” I just sit there, dumbfounded.

Is he serious?

Aries smiles, “Yes. You will be my new bride.”

I choke on my own spit. “As if!”

“Over my dead body.” Orion’s growl makes the pink pirate pale slightly.

The pirate, clearly not understanding the *mortal* danger he’s in, continues, “Eventually you will cave and learn that serving me is in your best interest.”

Oh boy.

The metal table starts to squeak. That’s the only warning we get before Orion flips the table and sends it flying toward my would-be husband, smushing him beneath it and killing him instantly.

“What happened to lying low and playing it cool?” I hiss at him.

“Let’s go,” Orion says, but pirates flood the room, preventing our escape. They step forward to apprehend me when Orion’s head falls back and he lets out a roar. But...a *strange* roar.

Thinking nothing of it, I raise my bolter and take out the pirates nearest to me, when the room begins to shake.

Screams from far away make their way to us, and the pirates freeze, looking at each other in confusion.

The screams get louder, and the shaking gets stronger. I

watch in horror as a giant red tentacle swipes into the window of the room, taking out pirates left and right.

My jaw drops and I whirl to Orion, who smiles at me with glimmering eyes.

"You *colluded* with my kraken behind my back?"

Orion blinks. "It was his idea, but yes."

There are more screams outside and I turn my head to watch as a pirate is thrown past the window.

"You both are in SO MUCH TROUBLE!" I yell as I yank open the door and race outside. Boris is waiting for us, in his gigantic mode, taking up the entire hallway with his large red body.

Boris' large eyes come into view. He squeaks at me and shakes a big tentacle. A pirate sprints at him, daggers and bolters at the ready, but Boris just slaps another tentacle out, sending the pirate flying through the air with a high-pitched squeal.

Boris, acting as our bodyguard, clears the way. Orion dashes into Sven's shop, grabbing some parts that I can't identify, before we all sprint back to the ship. Shouts echo behind us, Aries' followers.

Some pirates clap as we pass. Not everyone is upset about Aries' death, apparently.

"Starfire! Get us into orbit!" Orion shouts as we run up the ramp to the ship. Starfire instantly starts and the ramp raises. The ship quickly gets into orbit, and we race away from the outpost.

"That was close," I pant, sliding down onto a bench seat. Starfire is piloting herself, but we need to get out of sight. "We need to hide though. They'll follow us to Antheri otherwise."

Orion sighs. "We still need a core."

Which is when something occurs to me.

Something that really should have occurred to me sooner.

"I—um. I can try to refill it."

Orion cocks his head, looking at me with realization.

"Your power," he breathes. "You think you can funnel it into a reactor?"

I wince. "I've never tried precision targeting like that but…I'll try. If it gets us home, I'll try anything."

Orion nods. "Right then. Starfire, set course for Phazor-3. We need an off-the-track terrestrial planet to do this on."

"What's on Phazor-3?" I ask. I know many of the moons, planets, and outposts of our universe, but the universe is too vast for any one person to know them *all*.

"It's a neighboring system that orbits around a very old star. So old, in a few thousand years, it will begin to die."

I gasp. "But old stars are volatile."

Orion smiles and grabs my hand, squeezing it lightly. "The most beautiful things always are. But Phazor-3 is safe, you have my promise. Phazor-3 is the third farthest planet. It's small and well-hidden thanks to Phazor-2, a huge gas giant with seven moons."

"Third farthest means it's cold, doesn't it?" I groan as Orion nods. "Fine, but we can't stop there for long."

"We won't. Just long enough to fix the ship, from there it's around a two-day journey to Antheri. We're going to find your cats, Henri. I made you a promise."

Fear is a sudden weight on my heart.

"I'm afraid of what we're going to find. What if they—"

"No," Orion says, pulling back just enough to look me in the eyes. His hand comes beneath my chin. Then he notices the glamour and pulls both of our bracelets off. The smile he gives at the sight of my own, true appearance melts my heart in a way I simply cannot explain. "They're going to be fine, Henri. I know it."

A tear escapes my left eye, trailing down my cheek. Orion lifts a finger and catches it, bringing it to his lips.

I follow the movement, watching him with such intensity it scares me. But he watches me back ever the same.

"Why?" I breathe. "Why are you doing this?"

Orion's smile is sad. "Because a long time ago, I wished for someone to help those I love, and no one came."

I inhale, feeling his pain.

"I'm helping you, Henri Laselle, because I wish someone would have helped me. I wish someone would have cared about me the way *you* care about those creatures. So let me help you. You deserve that."

"Why did you pick this place again?" I shriek against the freezing wind. "Did it have to be snow? Why not a desert planet? This is horrible!"

Despite the gigantic snow suit Orion gave to me, one which I had to get *help* shoving myself into because there were simply too many layers, Phazor-3 was still fucking freezing.

"Would you like to go back inside until the reactor is ready for power?" Orion asks, not raising his voice and yet I can hear him clearly even against the wind.

I scoff and stomp my foot. "I'm not leaving you *alone* out here!"

"I am perfectly capable, Henri."

I narrow my eyes. "The last time I left you to your own devices, *dragon,* you almost fell into a black hole. So, no! I am not going back inside until this is done!"

Orion flashes me a grin full of sharp white teeth. "I'm a dragon, Henri. I'm the most dangerous thing out here. Go *inside!* Get warm!"

Ugh. I hate when males are right. Muttering to myself, I get back inside and quickly close Starfire's hatch. Shivering, I quickly strip out of the snow suit and shrug into a spare set of sweatpants Orion handed me. They smell like him, and I *hate* how much I love it.

I sniff the fabric and nearly moan aloud. *Why does he have to smell so good?*

Boris squeals and splashes me with blissfully warm water as he rolls along the hallway.

"Thanks for making it warm!" I call after him as he disappears. Headed for the sink, surely. There's a squeaking noise as the hatch opens and Orion enters the ship, shaking himself off after. *He* doesn't need a snowsuit—that bastard. He sets the open reactor on the ground, ready to be filled with energy.

Orion nods at me. "Are you ready?"

"Yes. But, uh, here's the thing..." I say, wincing. "I don't...*really* know how to do this. I mean, I know what to do in theory, but I've never tried anything like this."

I can't even think about what happens if it *doesn't* work.

"Okay so there's a very slight chance that if this goes wrong...I blow us and this entire planet up."

Orion closes his eyes and takes a deep breath.

"Right. Snowsuit back on. We're doing this outside."

"Oh, come *ON!*" My pleas fall on unhearing ears, and soon we're back in the freezing wind walking into the middle of the snowstorm. The land here is flat, like an empty tundra. An endless sea of ice and snow, with the occasional snow dune.

We walk for almost an hour, until the ship is barely visible.

"Here should be good," he says, putting the core on the ground. "If you funnel your energy into it, I should be able to lock it into the core."

"Lock it in?" I ask as my nose goes numb.

"While I do not have magic of my own, as you would define it, I have the ability to manipulate magic. In a way. To direct it in, out, or away."

That's cool.

Orion smiles, and I realize I said that aloud. "I think I can lock your energy into the core so that we can close it up. I'm less worried about you filling it and more worried about stopping the flow of power and *keeping* it within the core."

"Alright, let's do it!" I shout against the wind.

Orion nods and I take my gloves off, wincing against the cold. Rubbing my palms together until they're hot, I take a deep breath and call upon my magic. It reacts eagerly, jumping into my palms. I let it flow from my hands down into the core, like a glowing pink stream. The color changes from pink to orange and yellow as the seconds pass.

Within minutes, the core is full.

"Okay, I'm going to lock it in and when I say so, turn your magic off." Orion says, raising his hands. Purple magic appears within them, and I watch in awe as it surrounds mine. The streams of energy mingle, and I gasp.

I can *feel* him. It tickles. Not in a bad way, but it's like his hands are trailing across my skin.

"Now!"

I shut my magic off and there's a loud *clink* as the core shuts.

My jaw drops. "Holy shit. It *worked!*"

"Yes, it did." Orion smiles.

Not even realizing what I'm doing, I'm running and jumping into Orion's arms before I can think of all of the reasons why I shouldn't. He laughs and twirls me in the air.

Which is precisely when we hear it.

A roar. Low and loud. A sound that chills me to the bone.

Orion pulls away from me, both of our bodies frozen. We turn towards the sound, but there's nothing.

Then I see it.

Blending in *perfectly* with the frozen white landscape.

"Is that—" I breathe.

Orion nods. "Yetis."

Dozens of them. Sprinting towards us in a group. They're too far away for me to get much detail but I would know the visage of those fuzzy white bodies anywhere.

"RUN!" I shout. But instead of running, Orion grabs me and jumps into the air. I'm about to scream my head off when wings sprout out of his back, smaller versions of his dragon wings, and we fly back to the ship.

"I KNEW YOU COULD HAVE FLOWN US OUT THERE! YOU'RE A MEAN, MEAN DRAGON!" I scream against the wind.

Orion chuckles in my ear. "You're very cute when you're mad."

"I WILL PORTAL YOU INTO THE SUN!" My shriek meets more laughter as Orion's arms shake around me. I never feel in danger, though.

I only feel safe.

We land softly and I already miss the warmth of his arms. Quickly running into Starfire, Orion shouts a set of commands as he darts into the control room to load the nuclear core. I head to the cockpit in case any manual piloting is needed.

Not that I know how to fly a spaceship, but it's the thought that counts.

The Yetis get closer, their low screams shaking the ship as we take off. I *feel* the moment the core is engaged. The thrusters pulse faster, and we burst into the sky, easily leaving Phazor-3's gravitational field.

Orion runs into the room. "She's never been this fast before. It's like your energy is *more* than nuclear. Better, even. We'll be in Antheri in a little over..." Orion checks something on the monitor before nodding, "30 hours, now."

I breathe a sigh of relief.

I'm coming, Derek. Just hold on.

CHAPTER 22

TRUTH & DRAGONS

"**N**ow approaching Scorpius," Starfire announces.

Scorpius, like Antheri, is a terrestrial planet. But it's so far from the system's sun—large yellow dwarf star similar to the sun near Earth. However, it's only a few hours away from Antheri.

"Puppy for your thoughts?" Orion whispers in my ear, surprising me so badly, I nearly jump out of my seat.

"Sorry," he chuckles. "I didn't mean to scare you."

"What did you say?" I laugh.

"Puppy for your thoughts?" Orion asks, and I snort.

"I think you mean *penny* for your thoughts."

Orion purses his lips, annoyed at getting the Earth idiom wrong.

"Don't worry, I like your version better. And—I'm just watching. I've been in space before, but it's still so new to me. I think it will always be new and terrifying and awesome to me, honestly."

Orion looks at me like he's reading into the very depths of my soul.

"If the universe was filled with more people like you, it would be a better place."

I blink and take a step back, my hand flying up to grasp my

chest.

"I—thank you," I breathe.

One corner of Orion's mouth tilts. "You're welcome, Henri."

I look back at Scorpius, but it's almost out of sight.

"How long?"

Orion answers, "A little over 10 hours. You should get some sleep."

I laugh.

"What's so funny?" Orion's voice is deep and so close to my ear as I gaze out at the stars. I can feel the heat from his body next to mine.

"There's no way I'm sleeping, dragon. Not when we're so close to Antheri."

The anxiety of what's to come has my ADHD in hyperactive mode. I can feel the energy thrumming through my body. Not nervous, just needing to *move*. Even standing here is hard, and I've been absentmindedly tapping my fingers on my leg to an invisible song only I can hear.

If I stop moving...the questions begin to stream through my mind.

What if Derek isn't on Antheri? What if there's nothing to find and it's too late?

No. Lying in bed alone with my thoughts is not an option right now.

"I want to walk on the treadmill," I announce. "And then..."

Orion lifts a brow as I turn to face him.

Crossing my arms, I lift my chin and assess the dragon.

"Then, I want to talk."

Orion blinks. "Talk?"

"Yes. Like we did the day we met, when you were in your

other form."

Orion cocks his head slightly. "I did enjoy that."

"Right. Well, I have questions, you see. I've told you a lot about me, or you've learned it through *nefarious* reasons," I hiss the word, not angry at Orion but my freaking *brother*—I can't believe he has a roommate and didn't tell me! Clearing my throat, I continue, "Anyways, you know about me, and I want to know about you."

"I see. I have told you much, Henri."

I smack my tongue. "No, no. I don't mean...your biography. I mean, I want to know *you.*"

Orion tilts his head the opposite way, clearly confused.

"Okay, how about...what's your favorite color?"

Orion blinks, his purple eyes going wide for a moment before they crinkle and he smiles.

"My favorite color? I've never thought about, to be honest."

This is what I get for trying to play the questions game with a dragon!

"Right, well, maybe think about it? I want to know about your likes and dislikes, and asking questions is a way to do that."

"Then when you are done walking, we shall talk, and you can ask me your questions."

Now it's my turn to blink. A warm blush rises on my cheeks.

"Right, good." I cough and nod at him before heading back to my room—no, *his* room—to change into workout clothes. I washed my other set in the sink with soap and set it out to dry, so thankfully I don't have to wear dirty leggings.

Boris is playing in the sink when I peek into the bathroom, and I press a kiss against his slimy head before heading back out.

When I get to Starfire's gym, Orion is there.

He's shirtless—and his wings are out.

I nearly stumble at the sight.

The dragon turns to face me, his muscles almost *glittering* in the light thanks to the shimmering scale tattoos decorating his body.

He's fucking gorgeous. I can't deny the fact any longer.

"Enjoy your walk," he flashes a wicked smile before launching into a martial arts routine. Orion Worldkiller moves with such grace, it's almost like he's floating through each position.

Like a dance. But there's an aura of such untamed violence it steals my breath. Orion remains calm, never losing his cool, never losing that peaceful reserve, but still manages to be the most dangerous creature in *every* room he's in.

He doesn't even have to try.

With a shaky breath, I walk past him and inhale his scent in the air. I step onto the treadmill with shaky hands and hit the start button.

"Starfire? Play electropop."

A fast beat filters through the speakers, and I let myself get lost in the music as I increase the treadmill speed, walking to the tempo.

Before long, an hour passes, and I'm covered in sweat. I added an incline this time and my calves and thighs are on *fire*.

Panting lightly, I get off and realize my legs are jelly as I face plant towards the floor.

Just before my nose hits the ground, hands catch me and I'm pulled up to stand.

I turn and look up at Orion. The position puts me more or less in his arms. His chest brushes against mine.

Oh God.

Orion takes a deep breath and steps backwards, motioning for me to sit.

I fold into a crisscross position, sighing at the comfortable, cushy flooring.

Orion mirrors me, his eyes never once leaving mine. "Let's talk." He smiles.

We talk for hours.

About our likes, our dislikes, our families.

Everything.

To my eternal shock, Orion Worldkiller answered every one of my questions.

Eventually, I left to go shower off the sweat while Orion made a quick dinner.

I let out another moan at the delicious veggie stir fry.

Orion sits beside me, gripping the counter so hard I'm surprised he hasn't ripped it right off bolts. He lets the counter go and flexes his hands, taking a shaky breath before turning to me, all business.

"How much do you know about the PSDS?"

My brow furrows and I sit back, having finished my bowl.

"Do you mean PTSD?"

Orion takes a deep breath. "No, I don't mean PTSD. I mean the PSDS. It stands for Planetary Shield Defense System."

Oh. "Never heard of it."

Orion sighs. "Right. The PSDS is made up of twelve docking stations that orbit around the planet. Between the 12, they cover every possible angle of entrance into the atmosphere."

"And these docking stations hold big ass guns, I'm assuming?"

Orion grumbles and nods. "The problem isn't what we're going to do when we land...it's making sure we don't get blown up before we ever get the chance."

Shit. Just when I think it can't get any worse, Orion continues, "The other problem with this is nothing can tie us back to the UGF. If they see us, they need to think we are an individual enterprise."

Of course. "More pirates, then?"

Orion nods. "We don't need glamours for this, but yes."

"How do we get past the docking stations?"

There's a wet slapping sound as Boris hauls himself onto my lap. His big brown eyes narrow and he lifts two tentacles mimicking punching something.

"Yes, I agree," Orion is thoughtful as he looks at Boris.

They turn and look at me in unison. "Care to fill in the peanut gallery?"

"We have to split up."

"Excuse me?" My voice raises a few octaves. "What do you mean, we need to split up?"

"The second we take out one of the docking stations, it will alert the others. The best chance we have to get past the stations is to take out all 12 of them."

I sniff and cross my arms, side eyeing my kraken companion.

"I think that's a bad idea."

Now it's Orion's turn to look surprised.

"Yes, it would give us the best chance at taking out each docking station. But then we would be leaving an entire planet without defense. There is no way to do that without it looking like a big ass red arrow pointing right at the UGF. Look at how much they stand to gain if Antheri had no defense."

Orion processes my words. "What do you suggest, then?"

My jaw desperately wants to detach off my face and fall to the floor with the amount of shock coursing through me. Orion is neither upset nor offended that I'm challenging his idea. He seems genuine in his desire to know my plan.

Which means...I need to come up with a plan.

Shit. I didn't think this far ahead!

Wait, hold on...

"A spell. Not to destroy the docking station, but to disguise the ship."

Orion's eyebrows raise. "A spell?"

I pull Boris into my arms and glance at the shell-shocked dragon. "Do you know what a spell is, dragon?"

His cheeks turn red and his dark brows furrow. "Of course I do. But spells are...small magic. What you want to do with it seems out of the realm of what a spell is capable of."

"And are you, Orion Worldkiller, a spell expert?"

Orion's eyes go wide.

"No, I am not. I also have the sinking feeling that I'm digging myself some sort of hole here."

I snort, "I'm just messing with you. Let's just say, there's a *lot* missing in my file. The UGF only knows a *tiny* part of what my siblings and I are capable of."

"Tell me about these spells, Henri." Orion leans forward and places his hand on my leg.

I nearly jump out of my skin at the feel of his warm palm through my pants. I'm shocked my pants aren't catching on fire.

"You tell me first. Give me the rundown on what you know about it."

Two can play this game, dragon.

Orion smirks. He likes these little word games we play.

"As you wish," Orion says in a sultry voice that makes my nerve endings tingle. "Spells are sayings and poems that rhyme. The Witch species, which makes its home on Earth, uses spells to control and funnel their magic."

"Not bad. *Most* witches need to use spells to channel their magic." I let my words fade as Orion catches on.

"So, what, you just...*will* your magic into a new form?"

I can't help but laugh. "Not quite. My mother was one of Earth's most powerful witches. She and my dad used to joke that Mom was a cougar because she was 700 years older than my dad."

"Witches live that long?"

I smile. "Some do. Mom came from a long line of powerful witches. Many Earth stories were written about her; all false, of course. Mom was the first witch to spell cast without speaking aloud."

"Did she *think* the spell?"

"No, but that's a fair guess. It's more like..." I falter, trying to find the right words. "A spell has a certain goal. For example, you could cast a spell to keep a fire burning all night. The goal is to keep the *space* warm all night, the fire is just the method of which this happens."

Orion leans forward, his eyes on mine. Boris gets comfortable in my lap. He reaches out one tentacle, wrapping it around my finger like a little kraken hug. Absentmindedly, I caress his slimy head.

"I just focus on the goal and will my magic to make it happen."

"And does it work?"

I cringe. "Well, sort of."

Orion blinks. "Sort of?"

I clear my throat and squeeze Boris' little tentacle, needing his comfort.

"Yes. I have ADHD, it's a human thing that a good amount of us are born with."

"ADHD?" Orion asks, not in judgement, but in clarification.

I snort. Now it's *my* turn to teach him an acronym.

"Yeah, it stands for Attention-deficit/hyperactivity disorder. It affects focus and impulses. I'm always thinking about a dozen things at the same time, which can make it hard to focus on just *one* thing. It's not my *magic* that is the problem, it's more the focusing part. Sometimes it's easy, but if I'm stressed or busy, or just having an *off* day, it can be hard to shut everything else off. Right now, I'm thinking about Derek and the kittens, how we're going to Antheri, what we're going to do there, what happens if we're captured, if my animals are safe at home, if my siblings are okay," I pause and take a deep breath. "It's like there's so much in my head, when I try to focus on just *one* thing I just...*can't.*"

Orion smiles.

"What? Is this funny to you?" Indignation rises within me, burning hot through my veins.

"Not at all," he tilts his head. "I am smiling because I am very honored to have your trust in telling me this, Henri. Thank you for explaining."

I nearly fall out of the fucking *chair.*

"Um—I, uh, yes. Of course." I squeak.

Orion smiles wider. "And I think I can help you, in this."

"You can?"

The dragon before me nods.

Then he stares at me for an obscenely long time.

"You're an anomaly, Henri Laselle." Orion leans forward, lifting his hand and gently tucking s a stray blonde curl behind my ear. His fingers brush against the skin of my cheek, leaving goosebumps in their wake.

Slowly, so slowly, Orion leans in and places a kiss on my cheek. I can't help but gasp as his face brushes against mine.

"An anomaly," he whispers. "And a *wonder.*"

I've always felt like a bit of an outsider. A freak, even. It's why I feel so at home with my creatures; I *am* a wayward creature. But Orion Worldkiller makes me feel like my differences are my strengths. He makes me feel *special.* Not wayward; *belonging.*

"Yes well, you are a *dragon.* If I'm an anomaly, so are you."

Boris makes a series of squeaking sounds and the corner of Orion's mouth twitches.

"Quite right, my tentacled friend," he says with a polite nod to Boris. The way he indulges the kraken makes my heart *melt.* Orion clears his throat. "Boris would like it known that *he* is the special one."

"Oh, of *course* you are," I coo to the kraken, petting one of his eight legs. "You're the *most* special, buddy. Anyone who says otherwise is a liar!"

"Yeah, a kraken in space? It doesn't get more special than that."

Oh no. Nothing will make me cave to this male faster than him babying my creatures.

Sure, power is hot. But what is *truly* sexy is *kindness.*

I lower my voice in a conspiratorial whisper. "And, you totally beat Orion in that wrestling match."

This time, it's Orion's jaw that drops. "That is—" he pauses, looking down at Boris, who is hitting him with the puppy-kraken eyes. Orion sighs, "That is *true*. You did beat me."

Orion lowers a hand and gently sets a single finger on the tip of one of Boris' legs.

Boris flinches, slightly. He's cuddly with *me,* but my little friend has had a hard life—and most people who meet him, not that many people *do* meet him, they're *afraid* of him.

Hesitantly, Boris winds a tentacle around Orion's finger, squeezing it lightly.

"Just don't tell anyone, okay? My reputation would never recover!" Orion teases, winking at Boris.

The kraken lets out a series of squeaks that I know to be a laugh.

"30 MINUTES TO THE ANTHERI ATMOSPHERE," Starfire announces, scaring Boris, who makes a loud squeak and inks all over my pants before wiggling down my legs and hiding in his bowl of water.

I take a deep breath, trying to calm my thoughts and clear my head. When I close my eyes, all I see are flashes of Derek in various, torturous situations. Then it switches to Orion staring at me. Another image; my house on fire as I'm far away, unable to save my friends, my *family.*

"Hey," Orion whispers. I open my eyes as he grabs my hand. "You can do this."

"Yeah..." The doubt in my own voice is clear.

Orion shakes his head, "No. No doubt. *I* do not doubt you, so do not doubt yourself, not even for a moment. You deserve more than that. I know you can do this, Henri. I trust you."

Oh wow.

Hearing a millennia old dragon from the outer reaches of space say that he, of all beings, *trusts* me might just make me melt into a puddle on the ship floor.

Get a fucking, grip, Henri! Ew, why does my inner voice sound like my older sister? *Focus, get your cats, and **then** moon over the sexy space dragon!*

Annoyed that Jace is somehow right even when she's not even HERE, I stand and crack my neck. Orion winces a little at the loud pops.

Orion stands and I have to crane my neck back to meet his eyes.

He nods at me, not an ounce of doubt in his starry gaze.

I take a deep breath and lift my chin, "Alright. Let's do this."

"5 MINUTES TO ANTHERI ORBIT," Starfire announces, startling me so badly I nearly jump.

"Where would you like to do the spell?" Orion asks, facing me.

"Here. Let's do it here, where we can see out."

Orion nods and we take a seat; him in the pilot's chair and me in the copilot spot.

"As soon as we reach orbit, the PSDS will lock in."

"Great, no pressure," I mutter.

Orion smiles. "You can do this, Henri."

God, I hope so.

"I would like to help you focus, if that's alright with you."

I nod, although a part of me is scared as to what he has in mind.

Orion surprises me by leaning forward and pressing his forehead against mine. His hands come up to cup my face. His thumbs absentmindedly brush through my hair.

"Relax." His voice is lower and infused with pure magic. My body complies, unable to do anything *but* listen when he speaks.

"I'm going to calm your thoughts and mind. It might feel a bit strange, but trust me. Please."

I give him a subtle nod.

"Begin the spell," he orders in a normal voice.

I shut everything out and try to focus.

Derek, please don't let it be too late. Other thoughts fight for dominance as I picture the goal of my spell.

I imagine Starfire, her outer hull completely invisible. No heat sensors will pick it up. Nothing will be able to tell we are here.

The pop song I listened to on my run a few days ago pops into my head and the chorus repeats. I hum to the tune without a second thought.

Orion nods. "Good. Keep doing that."

The humming helps.

A tingling, ticklish feeling washes over me, like a slow wave of water all the way from my head to my toes.

The outside thoughts drift away. Even the music in my head quiets.

Wow.

This is *amazing.*

"15 SECONDS UNTIL ORBIT."

I focus on the spell and with a deep breath, punch my magic into it. My eyes burst open and I watch as a wave of purple magic drifts over the window. It settles into the hull without ever making a sound.

"Did it work?" I ask.

The ship suddenly groans and jerks as we're pulled into Antheri's orbit.

"I think we're about to find out."

"NOW IN ANTHERI ORBIT." Starfire's voice fills the cockpit.

"Strap in." Orion nods at the complex seat belt hanging at the sides of my chair. I quickly buckle in, tightening it so I'm secure. Orion does the same.

"Starfire, tell Boris to prepare for turbulence!" I say to the ship.

"Certainly."

An alarm sounds on the dashboard as an orange light flashes.

"They're scanning us," Orion mutters.

I hold my breath. The alarm continues for 30 more seconds before finally falling silent.

Orion glances at me with a mischievous smirk and a twinkle in his eyes. "It worked."

I laugh and a feeling of warm pride fills me. I did it.

"Very nice job." Orion's compliment makes me want to *burst* with pride. "Starfire, I'm switching to manual for re-entry," Orion flips a switch on the dash and the ship shakes as he takes the wheel. The dragon increases the engine as we begin to circle the planet, using the orbit to power our re-entry.

Orion dips down as the ship goes faster, tucking us gently out of orbit and down into the planet's exosphere.

Antheri is a pretty planet. Pale blue water covers 30% of it.

The rest is made up of rocky mountains covered in thick green and blue trees next to sprawling tundras covered in purple flowers.

This is not what Antheri is supposed to look like. Not that I expected the UGF to be the pinnacle of honesty and morality...but for centuries they've maintained that Antheri is a lawless hellscape full of bloodthirsty aliens.

The colors were so vibrant from up here. The colors quickly disappear, though, as we enter the atmosphere. Starfire begins to shake as Orion fights the wheel. Turbulence hits and we plummet to the ground. An orange glow encompasses the window as Starfire heats.

"Hold on!" Orion shouts, yanking the wheel. We go sideways as Orion tries to control our fall. After 15 minutes of miserable turbulence, we finally slow. Orion uses the cloud cover to hide the ship. If it weren't for my seatbelt, I would be plastered to the ceiling, covered in blood and bruises.

"Starfire! Is Boris okay?" I ask with concern for my tentacled friend!

"The kraken is safe in his bathtub."

I let out a breath. Thank god.

The mountains and valleys of Antheri shimmer beneath us.

I wish I could say that getting into Antheri was the hard part. Now we have to figure out where the hell to *go*.

Where are you, Derek?

CHAPTER 23

TO THRAXIA

"Starfire, initiate camouflage mode."

As we descend from the clouds, the ship becomes invisible to the naked eye. We fly over a vibrant city made up of short cement houses all encircling a colorful market. The city is surrounded by a large wall and outside of it, the land is lush and filled with thick forests.

"We'll start in Thraxia," Orion nods to the city. "It's the equivalent to their capital city and the hub of trade for all planets outside the UGF. If someone stole your creatures, Thraxia is where they'd go. There's a forest to the north of the city that we can use for cover. We'll land there."

I have to trust that he knows what he's talking about.

"I've been here before, but a very long time ago. Before the UGF was created. The planet was still young."

I shake my head in amazement. "You're so *old.*"

Orion laughs. "Yes, I am. We'll land in the forest near the city. The tree cover will hide the ship. I don't want to take any risks, even with the spell."

"What's the plan if we need to make a quick escape?" I don't want to jinx us, but I can't help but ask.

Orion lifts his left hand, and I notice a thin, silver band around his wrist. "Starfire can self-pilot. At my call, it will come get us."

"Fancy."

Our descent quickens as we lower out of the clouds. Orion pilots us down to the forest. Several trees are broken as we land, but he's right; this is a good hiding place.

Starfire shakes lightly as we land. The ship quickly quiets down as Orion hits several buttons.

A tentative squeak behind me, followed by the creak of wheels and the splash of water alerts me to Boris' presence.

I unbuckle and turn, leaning down to pet Boris.

He makes a very poignant squeak followed by a slap of his tentacle against the floor.

"Boris says he's coming with us," Orion translates.

"Buddy, it's not safe—"

Boris slaps his tentacle down on the floor again and glares at me, his big brown eyes menacing—and adorable.

I hear Orion sigh and take a deep breath, as if grasping for strands of patience.

"Boris would like me to share that he is not asking—" Orion pauses as Boris makes another series of squeaks, followed by some bubbles. "And he would like me to remind you that he has saved both of us, on many occasions, over the past few days. He is just a much a part of this as we are."

My heart sinks. I know that he's right.

I want to say no. I hate this, but Boris deserves to make his own choices.

I nod reluctantly, and Boris crawls into my arms, hugging my neck with two tentacles. "It's not at *all* that I don't value your help, buddy. I ask you to stay back because I'm *terrified* something will happen to you and I can't—" emotion makes my voice wobble "—I can't lose you, too."

Boris lifts one of his tentacles and brushes it against my cheek. His eyes are such a dark brown, they're almost black. While a few seconds ago he was glaring at me, now Boris gazes at me with understanding and love. How can anyone think that creatures like him aren't sentient and *worthy* of love?

It baffles and *infuriates* me.

"Alright," I sigh and press a kiss to his tentacle. Slime coats my lips, but I don't care. "You can come with us."

Boris makes a high-pitched, happy shriek and hugs my neck tighter.

"But, BUT, if I tell you to run, you run. Okay?"

Boris deflates slightly and makes a low, quiet groan.

"He is annoyed, but agrees to your request."

"Thank you," I whisper and press another kiss against his tentacle. Boris pulls away slightly and looks at me.

"How exactly are we going to hide him?" Orion cocks a dark brow.

An idea pops into my head and I sigh.

"I might have a solution..."

Orion stares at my belly with wide eyes, weaving slightly as if his legs might give out. Beads of sweat form at his hairline. Come to think of it, this is the first time I've even seen the Dragon truly sweat. And look...well, rather woozy.

"Uh, that's...certainly an idea."

"What?" I protest, looking down. I tucked Boris into my shirt and instructed him to maintain his *blob* form. Sometimes when we snuggle, Boris will tuck his legs around me and it will look like he's just a small round blob on my belly.

Which means it looks very much like I'm pregnant.

"You know what people will think," Orion says, his voice cracking slightly.

I stare at him, "Of course I know what people will think. They'll think you're my baby daddy and I'm knocked up with a little dragonette."

Orion chokes so hard he coughs up a smoke cloud. "Drag-on*ette?*"

"Yep," I remind him, waving a hand through the air to clear the smoke. "Or maybe I have a hot side piece that knocked me up and you're just here to keep me safe."

Orion stands straighter at that, and the air turns hot. Now *I'm* the one overheated.

"A side piece?" He snarls, flashing a sharp set of pearly white fangs. His eyes glow as silver stars burst in his irises. "Are you telling me that you have a...*lover?*"

Oh my god. Is Orion jealous?

I shrug, egging him on, and his eyes start to glow as the air around Orion shimmers with heat and energy.

Angry dragon alert.

"No, I do not have a *lover.*"

Orion's anger disappears and a pleased, possessive smirk takes over his gorgeous face. "That's very good to know, Henri."

Shit. Why does hearing him say my name make my legs almost give out?

Clearing my throat, I try to get my thoughts away from the way a certain dragon is making me feel.

"However, my love life doesn't actually matter. What *does* matter is whether or not anyone can tell that the bump is actually a pygmy kraken." I lift the neckline of my shirt and look past my bra-bound breasts.

"Hi," I whisper. "Is this comfortable for you? Will you be okay out of the water for this long?"

Boris waves a tentacle, slapping it lightly against my skin.

"He says it's fine but maybe get a drink of water somewhere and 'casually' pour some down your shirt."

I stare at Orion who smirks.

"That last part was my idea."

I blow Boris a kiss and let the neck of my shirt fall back into place, tucking my coat around me. "Can you see him at all?"

Orion cocks his head and walks around me, inspecting my belly further. I changed into black leggings that Jace bought me for my Birthday a few years back. They're made out of a material that automatically adjusts to keep your body the perfect temperature, regardless of the temperature outside. A long sleeve shirt that matches now covers my top half. Boris is tightly wound around my abdomen beneath it.

Calf-height black combat boots and a long navy coat that looks something like a mix between a trench coat and a cape, completes the look.

"I can't tell at all. It really does look like you're pregnant."

Boris makes a pleased squeak.

"You'll have to stay quiet, mister," I warn him and he blows a bubble at me.

Orion wears something similar to me, but his pants are tapered and gray, while his jacket is in a style more akin to a blazer.

"What's our cover?" I ask as we walk to the ramp. The weapons are stored in metal trunks near the door. Orion unlocks them and I whistle at the absolute armada he brought.

"The best cover is one that is both a truth, and a lie," Orion says, handing me a bolter and a silencer.

"I'm a merc and you've hired me to help you find your son. He was kidnapped a week ago."

I nod. That was easy enough to remember.

"Where are we from? Clearly, I'm human."

Orion shrugs. "I'm not worried about that. Many alien species can appear to be human. For all they know, *this* is your glamour."

Orion grabs his own weapons, strapping them onto his thighs. He shrugs off his jacket and holsters two short swords to his back, a bolter attached near his right shoulder, and a gun near his left shoulder.

My eyes focus in on how his muscles are straining beneath the fabric of his shirt. I force myself to look away.

"You are a lady from the Lower Houses of Diomedes. If anyone asks, you're from Era. One of the main species that inhabits Era looks remarkably human."

"Got it. And you? How did we meet? Where did I hire you? What form of payment did I use?"

Orion shrugs his jacket on with a smile. "Jacinda taught you well."

"This is what happens when your sister does...whatever it is she does. It's her fault that I'm a *menace* with contracts."

"I'm sure," Orion murmurs. "To answer your questions, we met on Era. I was finishing a job and returning an heirloom to a client when we met by chance. You're friends with the woman

I returned the heirloom to. She recommended me, and we've been tracking your son ever since. You paid me in credits."

Ah. I'm glad I asked.

The one detail I often forget about space is that most planets— outside of Earth—use credits as currency. Tangible money is worthless out here.

"Half up front, half upon delivery. Your son has a tracker, something very common on many of the affluent planets. We've been trailing a pirate ship that landed here and traced it to Thraxia."

"You're good at this," I note, one hand cradling my belly—erm, my kraken.

"It's not my first rescue mission."

His words make me pause. There's a sadness in them.

"Thank you," I say quietly. "Truly. The closer we get to Derek...the more I realize I'm not sure I would have survived if I was doing this alone. You did not have to help me, yet you chose to. So, if I haven't said it already...thank you, Orion."

Orion meets my eyes and smiles. "You're very welcome, Henri."

How could this...kind, caring creature destroy a world? It doesn't make sense. The more that I learn about Orion, the more I question.

Orion hits a button on the wall and the ramp lowers with a low buzzing, jerking me out of my thoughts. The lush forest of Antheri beckons.

Here goes nothing.

CHAPTER 24

CUTE BUT DEADLY

We walk through the forest outside of Thraxia for a good half hour. The terrain is steep at certain moments, but the closer we get to the city, the more it levels out and rocks turn to soft dirt and moss.

The trees remind me of the Pacific Northwest. Like some distant relative of a Sitka Spruce, but taller and narrower, with fluffier leaves and needles in a vibrant emerald. The bark of the trees glows in shades of pink and purple where the sap flows down to the forest floor, looking like something out of a fairytale. The trees are tightly packed together, making it difficult to navigate through them. I follow behind Orion, who confidently weaves through the branches and tree trunks with a knowledge that speaks to his previous times here.

Boris is quiet, but the suckers on his tentacles pulse and move under my shirt.

"Here," Orion stops and hands me something out of his pocket. "We'll be out of the forest soon, and you'll need this."

It resembles a black flat stone, but it's curved slightly and only the size of the tip of my pinky.

"It's the latest in comm tech. It will translate any language you hear and allow you to speak any language in return. And if for any reason we get separated, it will allow us to communicate."

I grab the small stone and inspect it. Something brushes against my magic and the taste of bubblegum coats the tip of my tongue.

"These are Novan," I glance up at him. "Where the hell did you find these? There's no *way* they would ever let tech like this go off planet, let alone into the hands of the UGF.

Novans are notoriously tight lipped. Proxima Nova is the most powerful neutral planet. The UGF tried to get them to join for centuries, but Novans keep to themselves. *Including* all of their advanced tech.

"I have my ways." Orion winks at me.

I place the bead behind my ear. There's a slight pinching feeling and I feel the magic enter my system. The feeling soon goes away, and it's as if the communicator bead isn't even there.

Soon we reach the edge of the forest and make it to a dirt road.

A village, or what used to be one, greets us. A dirt path making its way to the city bisects it.

The village is empty.

"Was this abandoned last time you were here?" I ask. A sour feeling rises in my stomach as I glance over to see Orion's furrowed brow.

"No, it wasn't. There was a big field here, to the east side of the village, but it looks dried up."

We take a minute to weave through the abandoned cottages, built with stone and straw. A large empty field sits to the east, like Orion said.

But it's wilted and rotten.

"A plague?"

Orion clicks his tongue. "Or drought."

We fall silent for a moment until Orion takes a deep breath. "Our mission is still the same. Let's keep walking. We're close to Thraxia."

Thraxia is in one of the many valleys of Antheri. A tall stone wall lines the outside of the city. I could see it from the abandoned village, but it looked small. Now as we approach it, I realize I was wrong. The wall is huge, maybe as tall as the Statue of Liberty.

Noise, even from this distance, travels from beyond the city walls, illustrating how populated it is. As we walk closer, the noise gets louder, as does the smells of food. Spices waft through the air, making my mouth water.

As we approach the wall from the road, we're met with a line of armed Antherien guards and Oh. My. God.

"You didn't tell me they were so cute!" I hiss beneath my breath at Orion, who snorts as if to say, "does it matter?"

The guards in front of us resemble something between a large moth and a caterpillar. Their bodies are mostly mothlike, with large, multi-colored wings protruding from their backs and two big antennae sit in between their fuzzy, pointed ears. Their bodies are also fuzzy, but with dozens of caterpillar-like arms on either side. The arms go all the way down their thoraxes, acting as legs, should they not want to fly. Their eyes are giant and pitch black.

"Halt!" a high-pitched voice squeaks. "State your business and present your papers."

My first instinct is to hug these adorable moth-like creatures. *No! No hugging! Bad brain! We do not hug beings we do not know like a total WEIRDO! DO NOT BE A CREEP. BAD HENRI!*

Even adorable strangers are still strangers. They do not know me, and I do not know them—or their culture.

When it comes to aliens, just because something looks like a creature, doesn't mean they are not intelligent, consenting beings. So, I wrestle my cute aggression into submission.

I'm also thoroughly impressed with the comms bead. The translation is seamless; there isn't even a millisecond of lag as it translates the Antheri's words into English.

Antheriens are supposed to be dangerous. This whole *planet* is supposed to be dangerous. Surely there must be more to them than meets the eye. It takes every ounce of my willpower not to stare at them.

Orion hands over two pieces of paper I haven't seen before.

"I am on a job for..." Orion pauses. *Shit, we didn't decide on our cover names! I knew I forgot to ask something.*

"—Lady Cygnus." I blurt. "I'm looking for my son. We tracked him here. All I want is to get him and return home. We mean no harm and will make not a single fuss."

I sniffle a little bit, amping up the heartbroken mother façade. Orion glances at me in surprise. *Yes, I know about Era too, dragon.* Cygnus is the real name of one of the Lower Houses. Granted it's because I watched a few too many seasons of the Real Housewives of the Galaxy, but he doesn't need to know that.

"Mr. Lecter is escorting me," I add and Orion snorts, but it's so subtle, the Antheriens wouldn't notice unless they were paying attention. They're too busy reading his papers.

One of the moth-like creatures prances over to us, surprisingly nimble for such small legs, before handing us back our papers.

"Cleared! You may enter."

That was...surprisingly easy. Suspiciously so.

The city wall creaks as the large stone door is pushed open, revealing several Antheriens hovering in the air with ropes, pulling the doors.

The wall is thick and the stone, heavy. Heavy enough I would expect it to take far more of them to operate, which means the Antheriens are stronger than they appear.

Orion offers his arm and I gladly take it as we make our way in. The city is a bustle of activity. Alien species of all kinds meander through the streets. Even a few humans, which makes me almost stumble in shock.

Vendors with carts offer food for sale. Fruits of various kinds are handed off. My stomach chooses this moment to rumble.

Orion glances at me with a soft smile and stops at one of the carts selling something that resembles a fruit skewer. He grabs me two, one with a pink fruit and one with an orange fruit. He pays but something about it bothers him. I can tell by the way his eyes narrow for the briefest second.

"Thank you!" I say and dig in. The pink fruit tastes like if a watermelon and apple had a baby. It's delicious and tart. The orange fruit tastes surprisingly floral, like jasmine and pistachio. It's like nothing I've ever had before.

"Oh wow, these are amazing."

"I am glad." Orion says as we walk through the streets. Nobody pays us a second glance.

"What upset you back there?"

Orion pauses, looking at me with confusion.

"The payment. Something about it bothered you."

"Ah, I wasn't bothered, but very surprised. It was significantly more expensive than it was the last time I was here. Whatever affected that field we saw must be affecting food production."

"Hmm. Interesting."

Nobody notices as I casually drop some of the fruit down my shirt where a tentacle happily awaits. Boris makes quiet, happy squeaks as he munches on the sweet fruit.

Orion grabs some fruit juice from another nearby stand, as well as some water in a wooden cup. I drink both gratefully, spilling some down for Boris to keep his delicate skin wet.

We meander through the streets, but Orion clearly has an idea of where he's going. Eventually we lose the crowd and make our way to the center of town.

"This part will be difficult," the dragon whispers.

I nudge him, wanting more information and Orion frowns.

"We need to visit the Market."

My heart clenches to the point of pain. I've heard plenty of the Market—a place to trade all sorts of rare treasures...and rare *creatures*.

If a rare creature is being sold, the transaction will happen at the Market.

Which means we're going to see lots of creatures in various conditions.

My instinct has always been to save every animal I come across, alien or otherwise. Having to turn away from animals in need...it kills me.

Boris squeezes me tighter and lets out a soft, comforting bubbling sound. Orion looks thoughtful as he translates.

"Someday, we will save all the creatures but today is not that day. Today we just have to save four creatures."

I sigh. I know he's right, but it doesn't mean I have to like it.

I caress my kraken belly.

"I know we will, buddy."

With a deep breath, I look up at Orion who gazes at me with knowing eyes.

"Let's get this over with."

Orion nods. "We're going to find the Market Master. He goes by the Ringleader, but his real name is Jala Zigu."

Right then.

Orion grabs my hand and I nearly yank it back, shocked by his touch. I've spent so many years on my own, I've become used to only knowing the touch of tentacles, fur, and claws.

His hand is huge, but he cups mine so gently, a small part of me wants to weep.

The dragon's touch grounds me. It reminds me that I am not alone.

I can do this.

Orion pulls me along and we come to a set of two grand red doors that open in the middle. The doors are closed and guarded by two guards that resemble some sort of werewolf/human crossbreed. Werewolves are a common sort of alien, so I'm not surprised by their presence, but I *am* surprised that they're on Antheri. The Were planets are part of the UGF.

What are UGF loyalists doing on Antheri?

Are they deserters?

"What business do you have in the Market?" the wolf-man on the left asks.

His head is that of a Wolf, but his mouth moves like a person. It has furry hands with claws, but the rest of its body appears human. I can't help but stare.

"We're looking for a feline creature and heard there are a few that would be here. We're interested in putting in an offer."

In sync, both wolf-men turn to look at me. "You don't look like the type that frequents the Market. You're a buyer, are ya? You sure you can handle this?"

Oh, they did *not* just say that.

I lift my chin and glare. "I can assure you, I am well prepared. I have been to many auctions and trades. I am here looking for a feline creature to be my companion, and I happen to know the Market is the best place to look for pristine specimens."

Calling animals "specimens" makes me want to throw up, but I keep the confident smile on my face. I refuse to show them even an *ounce* of fear or doubt.

"As you wish." The wolf-men turn in unison and open the two red doors.

The smell hits me first. Feces, urine, and sweaty bodies.

Then the sound. High-pitched shrieks of pain and cries of sorrow. Howls of sadness and shouts of anger.

This is going to kill me.

Traders walk around with creatures in collars and chains. Some of the enslaved beings are humanoid, some look like normal, Earthling pets.

Most of the animals are in terrible condition. I watch as multiple are jostled around and slapped.

I hate this.

Boris trembles slightly beneath my shirt and I keep one hand on my belly for both of our sakes.

With my other hand, I squeeze Orion's palm and picture punching every single one of these animal abusers in the face.

I know, logically, it's more complicated than that. Many of the traders here rely on this business to feed their families. It doesn't excuse or justify any behavior, but the creature trade won't be dismantled overnight, even if I start throwing punches.

This system has been ingrained in their societies for decades, if not centuries. It will take time to dismantle it without starting another war.

So, for now, I will keep my violent fantasies to my imagination. For *now*.

I zone out, overwhelmed by the sadness in the animals' eyes. Orion leads the way, pulling me through the Market until finally we get to a small, stone building. It looks almost like a small house, and I would wonder if it *was* a house, if it weren't for the large gold sign on the wooden door that says, "RINGMASTER."

As Orion knocks on the door, the reality of what we're doing fully hits me.

This Ringleader is in charge of everything that comes in and out. They know about every single creature. The abuse here happens under *their* watch.

Anger is hot in my belly as we wait for Jala Zigu. The air feels tense, as if we're standing on the edge of a cliff.

If Derek and the kittens are here, Jala Zigu will know. Which means I can't nuke it out of existence.

I picture Derek in my mind.

I will do this for him. I promised him I would always keep him safe, and by all that is fucking right and holy, I will keep that promise. Even if it kills me.

The door opens with a low creak, and out from the shadows steps Jala Zigu and—

Oh my *God.*

Jala Zigu is a giant spider.

CHAPTER 25

IT'S ALWAYS GIANT SPIDERS

My heart stops in my chest and all of the air rushes out of my lungs with a slight wheezing sound as I take in the sight in front of me.

The sight of Jala Zigu.

Jala Zigu, who is a giant spider.

The giant spider who is Jala Zigu.

I wish I was joking, but as I look into their eight beady eyes, my life briefly flashes before my eyes.

I can do a lot of animals. Even the scariest, creepiest creatures and critters. But I draw the *line* at giant spiders.

I don't know precisely what happens, but I have the sudden, overwhelming feeling that something is wrong. It's a yawning pit that opens in my stomach and the hair on my body stands on end. Goosebumps rise on my arms.

Boris instinctively hugs me tighter, sensing my anxiety.

I can't react.

Not with Jala Zigu's eight eyes staring at me, missing noth-ing.

Their body is thick and covered in wiry brown fur.

"What do you want?" The voice is horrific, equal parts hiss and shout. Fear makes my hands tremble.

Jala Zigu stares at me, but the question is clearly directed at

Orion.

"My client is looking for a rare item, and we were hoping you could help us find it. My client is happy to pay."

"What is it you ssseek?"

Orion shouldn't tell him. I don't have a good reason for feeling this way but something tells me we shouldn't trust the spider.

I want to scream at Orion but if I react, all it will do is endanger us all.

I refuse to risk Boris. I can't lose him too.

It's like watching a terrible car crash as Orion leans in and whispers, "We're looking for a hellcat. A young one—unspoiled. Or a breeding pair."

I want to throw up.

"I have what you ssseek." They nod, clacking their fangs. The sound makes my blood pressure spike. *"But it will cosssst you."*

"There is no price too high for my client," Orion says smoothly.

"Very well. Follow me."

With a nod, Jala lifts one of their eight legs, beckoning us to follow as they leave the stone house and head into the market.

Everyone clears the way for Jala Zigu, bowing in submission as they avert their eyes. I keep thinking we're going to see Derek and the kittens, but Jala Zigu keeps walking. We pass creature after creature until it feels like every step tears a hole in the very fabric of my soul.

The rows of creatures eventually thin out and we go into a quieter, more high-end area of the market.

This has to be where they keep the biggest sellers. The treasures.

"You will ssstay here for the nighttttt." Jala Zigu says suddenly

and we come to a halt. *"Tomorrow, I will get you the hell beastsssssss you sssseek."*

Uh, tomorrow? That won't work.

"That is very kind, but we unfortunately have lodgings already set up. We can come back in the morning if it is a time sensitive matter," Orion says in a tight-lipped, polite voice.

Jala Zigu smiles and it's a thing of horror. *"It was not a quesssstion."*

I glance to the side at Orion, trying to signal to him that we need to get the fuck out of here.

Rule #1 in any world: *Never trust the giant spider!*

Noises come from all around and I gulp, not even wanting to look.

Please, not more spiders.

Something touches my foot, and I look down to see a cabbage-sized spider with spikey red fur and onyx black eyes sitting on my foot.

With a pained sigh, I gently nudge it away.

Nice spider. Please don't bite me, spider.

I pretend it's something less scary. It's still an animal. A misguided one, possibly, but—

"Kill them, my children." Jala Zigu suddenly announces, and the formerly-docile-cabbage-shaped spider suddenly *leaps* at my face. *"Feast!"*

The scream that explodes from me could wake the dead. Instinct kicks in and I punch it so hard, the spider is shot put into a wall.

But there are more.

So many *more.*

"Try a spell," Orion grunts he pulls a dagger out of his boot and waves it at the spiders but they keep coming.

Dozens upon dozens until the ground is just a sea of spiders.

I adjust my stance until we're back-to-back. I try to shut the fear out and concentrate. It's difficult because everywhere I look, there's another *spider!*

Ignore it, I tell myself.

SPIDER! My thoughts respond.

Shut the fuck up!

For a moment, my thoughts quiet and I jump on the opportunity and focus on my intention, but...

I can't kill them. They're just doing what they're told.

Then a solution hits me. I shove magic into the solution, imagining it being real.

My magic bursts from me, invisible to the eye but each spider it touches falls over.

Not dead.

"They're asleep," Orion chuckles beneath his breath. "Brilliant woman. That was well done."

I know that I could have killed them. A part of me wanted to. But it's not right. Who am I to decide if a species lives or dies?

I am one speck of dust in this wide, wayfaring universe. I am no one. I might have the power to kill...but I do not like using it in that manner. Only as a last resort.

"What have you done to my children? Murderer!"

Orion flashes his fangs and stalks up to Jala Zigu who is cowering slightly just ahead of us.

"Where are the hellkittens, Zigu?" A bolter is suddenly in Orion's hands. With one hand, Orion holds a dagger to their neck. With the other, he points the bolter into the center of their beady eyes.

"I'll kill youuu for thisss—"

Orion sighs and shoots the bolter at one of Jala Zigu's legs. The skin burns as a giant hole appears. The spider writhes in agony, crying out.

"The moths! The moths haveeee themmm."

The moths?

Oh.

"You mean the Antheriens?" Orion clearly came to the same conclusion I did.

"Yessssss. They have what you seeeeeek." Jala Zigu chitters, trembling slightly.

"How do we get to them? Where are they being held?"

"Belowwww the keep. Beyond that, I do nottt knowww."

Orion sniffs. "That's not good enough."

The bolter goes off again, hitting another leg, and I wince. I don't enjoy killing people, and I don't enjoy violence, but I *do* understand that sometimes a little...non-life-threatening incentive is required.

Besides, all bets are off when it comes to my creatures.

"Stoppp! Stoppp! No moreeee." Jala Zigu pants. *"I know only one more thing. The catsssss will be used as bait in the gamesss tomorrow."*

My legs nearly give out. Orion asks Jala Zigu to explain but all sound fades.

They would be used as *bait?* Over my dead body.

"How do we get into the games?" I ask, not giving a shit about any cover.

The spider glares at me.

"Ssssilence—"

I backhand the spider, letting my *true* strength flow through my muscles and bones. The giant spider is flung into a wall with a hard *crack*. I allow myself a short moment to feel bad about it and then I let the feeling pass.

"I will repeat myself. How do we get into the games?"

"Onlyyyy mothsss and competitorssss."

"How do you become a competitor?" I ask.

"Prisonersss are forced to compete. You cannott enter."

I approach the spider, the anger making me confident. "Where are the games happening?

"Southhh part of city." Jala Zigu says, their voice weary. *"Go! Leave me be."*

"Fine, that's all we needed anyways," Orion says, dropping the bolter. His sword disappears again and he gently grabs my arm, leading me away.

Jala Zigu scuttles away, holding their injured legs tightly to their chest.

The spiders on the ground slowly wake up and follow them, and I see Jala Zigu let out a sigh of relief at the sight of their children in one piece.

Just as we're about to leave, a something darts in the corner of my vision.

I walk closer, trying to see what it is. By the far wall, crouched in a corner, is a spider.

Much smaller than the ones that attacked us, it must be the size of my palm.

Where the other spiders were all shades of red, this one looks different. This one is purple, with pink stripes along its body and blue eyes.

It's...well it's actually kind of cute!

And it looks so scared.

I bend down and it shrinks away from me.

"Don't be afraid, we won't hurt you. You didn't attack us like the others…did you?"

The little creature shakes its head.

So, it can understand me.

"Why didn't you follow your maker?"

The word "father" is very human. Creator or maker will be more universally understandable.

The spider looks at me, blinking. Jala Zigu had eight eyes but this spider only has four, two on either side.

It crawls out of the shadows, approaching my outstretched hand slowly.

Its body is covered in soft fur.

"She says her maker was very cruel to her for being so small."

My heart breaks.

Then I hear a squeak and Boris pokes his head out of the collar of my shirt, looking down at the spider. At the sight of her, he wiggles out quickly. She spider freezes at the sight of him.

Boris coos and bats his eyes at her and—

Oh my god, is he flirting?

"Boris, this is not the time to flirt!"

Orion chuckles. "He's reassuring her that there's nothing wrong with being small. And he's telling her that she can trust you."

I smile at that. Looking around, I try and find a solution but find none.

I bite my lip and look at Orion before facing the spider again. I crouch down further, getting to her height and I reach out my hand oh so slowly. She freezes, clearly still scared, but the spider lets me gently pet her soft fur.

"I know that you're scared, but we won't harm you. If you want, you can come with us when we leave here. I have a home on a planet far away, where no one would ever harm you. You will always have a full belly, there are plenty of nice animal friends, and you can lay in the sun as much as you want. No more hiding in the shadows."

The spider blinks, looking at me with wide eyes and then slowly leans into my finger still brushing along her back.

"She says that she would like that," Orion says softly.

Boris squeaks and coos.

Clearly he likes the idea too.

"Her name is Dora."

I smile at that. "Hello, Dora. My name is Henri. Let's get you out of here, okay?"

Dora nods happily.

Then I look at my kraken, who gazes at the small spider with such care and love it brings tears to my eyes.

"Buddy, it's time."

Boris' eyes whip to mine and he glares.

"Nope, I mean it. We have to separate. I need you to get back to Starfire and take Dora with you, okay? Keep her and the ship safe. We have to figure out how to get into a competition full of alien prisoners. Knowing you're safe will get me through this. I need you to be safe, okay?"

Boris deflates a little and I know he understands, even if he doesn't like it.

Dora slowly walks over to him and leans slightly against the kraken.

Boris inflates and looks down at the spider before lifting his chin and giving me his "brave" look.

"That's my guy. I wouldn't trust this job to anyone else but you."

Boris nods.

"Crawl back into my shirt and when we get outside, I'll give you the signal to leave. You stick to the shadows and get out of the city. Can you make it from there to the forest?"

"He can follow the trail by smell," Orion adds.

It didn't occur to me that a kraken could track by smell, but that makes sense.

"Okay, Dora? Until we get outside, can you hide in my hair?"

I take my hair out of the ponytail so that it drapes down my back and Dora crawls up my body to nest at the back of my neck. She's quick and I barely feel her.

Boris returns to his spot beneath my shirt. As we emerge from the Market back into the city streets, I realize Boris was looking a bit clammy when he emerged.

"We need more water," I tell Orion. "Boris won't make the return journey without it."

Orion nods and finds a vendor, grabbing two large wooden cups of water and handing one to me. I drink half and pour the other half down my shirt subtly. Boris lets the first few drops wet his skin. His kraken eyes close in bliss. Then his mouth opens, and the red creature gulps the water down gratefully.

His tentacles loosen a bit as his body relaxes.

"He says thank you." Orion nods at the lump.

We start walking as Orion and I split the remaining cup of water, although we both instinctively refuse to take the final sip, choosing to let it drop down to Boris instead.

I *pretend* my heart doesn't melt into a damn puddle at the smile Orion flashes me.

"So, what's the plan?" Orion asks. I blink.

"You would follow *my* plan?"

He smirks. "Maybe. It depends on said plan."

I take a deep breath.

"The plan is...we get into the games."

Orion cocks his head. "Jala Zigu said only prisoners get entered."

I wince. "Yeah, I know. Which is why we need to become prisoners."

CHAPTER 26
WILLING SUBJECTS

Two things happen simultaneously after that. As if they heard my idea and came running, Jala Zigu appears in the corner of my eye, barreling down the street as they drag their injured legs. Guards are with them. More of the were-soldiers.

The second thing that happens is my realization that *this* is when Boris has to leave.

"Boris, Dora, go! Quick!"

The kraken obeys and slithers down my leg, Dora next to him, and they disappear into the shadows of the crowd. The distraction of the soldiers and Jala Zigu is, in some way, a blessing.

Then we're surrounded. Eyes of all kinds watch as the guards surround us.

There's no way to get out of this unscathed.

"Let them capture us," I say beneath my breath as I turn and face the guards.

Orion glances at me and nods. I can't believe he's going along with this.

"Weren't youuuu with childddd?" Jala hisses.

Shit.

I scramble for an excuse and find one. "For your information, I was bloated!"

"You attacked my children! Arresssst them. Murdererssss!"

Orion bares his teeth before throwing his bolter and dagger to the ground. I follow suit, dropping my own bolter.

Soldiers rush us and we're forced to our knees as they slap tight metal cuffs around our wrists. No chain connects them, but no chain is needed. The moment the cuffs *lock* around my wrist, pain explodes through my body. My magic is suffocated until all that's left is a looming void within me and it *hurts*. The lack of magic *hurts*.

Orion grunts, clearly feeling the suppression tech too.

Hands pull us to our feet and Orion headbutts the nearest guard, a tall blue humanoid creature with white hair, whiskers, onyx eyes and sharp black claws. The guard whimpers in pain as his face shatters. Orion just snarls, struggling against the cuffs.

He's swarmed and we're walked into a dank, dark, empty building just off the streets. The air is acrid and smells of sweaty bodies.

Cages lines the edges of the room.

Cages full of *beings*. Some are humanoid, some are not.

These are the contestants.

The two of us are separated and shoved into two large cages in the far corner. Only inches separate the two of us.

The cages close and the guards lock each of the doors with a loud *click*.

Jala Zigu scuttles forward to stand in front of us and I struggle not to tremble in fear. The fur along their body is spikey and dense. But those eight eyes watching me are *terrible*.

"*Tomorrow, you dieeee.*"

I sigh. "Your pep talks need a lot of work."

The spider hisses at me and opens their mouth, showing two

sharp fangs surrounded by hundreds of tiny ones.

One of the guards throws something into each of our cages that resembles bread. It's hard and looks extremely dry.

Dinner. How lovely.

Then we're left alone. The guards and Jala Zigu leave the building and it's just the contestants, each of us locked in our own cage.

Some of the contestants begin talking. Others start shouting threats to each other.

Then, the threats start being shouted at *us*.

"You're gonna die tomorrow, new girl!" something calls.

Orion's head whips around and he glares at whoever said that. His amethyst eyes glow in the dark of the room and it's not just me who shudders at power within them. "Touch her, target her, look at her for more than a second, and I will end you. The girl is *mine*."

The contestant laughs, not believing the threat, but a glance around the room tells me the other contestants *do* believe the threat.

Eventually the conversation dies down. Some go quiet as they eat their own loaves of dry, old bread.

"Hey," a voice whispers. I look over to see Orion leaning on the bars of his cage, staring at me, nothing fear worthy in his eyes anymore, only warmth.

"So, what's a girl like you doing in a place like this?" His voice is low enough that no one else will hear. Despite our circumstances, I can't help but smile at his words.

"I never knew dragons were so *bad* at pickup lines." I whisper back, making sure no one would hear tell of his true identity.

Orion's eyes wrinkle as he huffs out a silent laugh. Then we both fall quiet.

"I won't let anything happen to you," he says quietly, reaching through the bars to grab my hand. He interlaces our fingers until we're connected, as one.

"I know. But I'm not helpless, you know. I'm...more afraid of hurting people than I am of getting hurt."

It's something I have always felt but never said aloud.

Orion nods. "I will do everything in my power to get us out of here without having to cause any pain, but...it might not be possible, Henri."

I flash him a sad smile and squeeze his hand. "I know. Tomorrow, whatever happens...we save Derek and the hellkittens, and we get out of here. Alive."

Orion squeezes my hand back. "I'm going to get you out of here, Henri. You and your creatures."

It's the way he says it. So sure, like he would do *anything* to ensure his words become truth.

Which is why I finally ask the question that's been eating away at me this entire, wild journey.

"Why? You could get out of here safely, without bothering with all of this. Why are you willing to risk so much just to help me?"

The dragon cocks his head and reaches an arm through the cages, placing his hand on mine.

"Do you really not know?" he whispers.

Words fail me at the sheer emotion in his voice and face.

"I—no. I don't," I admit. "I don't understand any of this."

Orion leans his forehead against the bars, and I do the same, needing to be closer to him for a reason I can't explain.

"All I've ever wanted was to be ordinary and invisible," I

breathe, tears suddenly beading at the corner of my eyes.

Orion exhales as if punched. "Henrietta Laselle, you are *anything* but invisible and ordinary. You shine brighter than a thousand burning stars. You and I are not meant to *hide*. We are meant to *burn*."

Orion's thumb caresses my hand. The movement is so minute, so small, but just like his words, the touch lights a fire in my belly.

"As for the rest," Orion continues. "I do not know why they picked your creatures. The entire situation is suspicious, and I do not like it. I haven't liked it from the beginning. Antheriens don't leave their planet often, let alone to go all the way to Earth."

"Lots of alien creatures have been appearing on Earth lately, and there's no explanation."

Orion cocks his head.

"I found an Armasidian Pony in my local romance bookstore."

"An Armasidian Pony? That doesn't make any sense."

I nod. "It's been more and more frequent. Like someone is ditching them on Earth."

"Earth is a protected planet, why is the UGF letting this happen?"

I shrug and Orion purses his lips, considering the situation.

It *is* weird.

And how did the kidnappers know to target *my* house for the hellkittens?

"Something about it doesn't feel right," I admit. I've felt it the entire trip but now, I can't deny it. "Once we get out of here, we can figure out how the hell this all happened."

Orion's gaze snaps back to me and I shiver under the weight of his attention. His eyebrow lifts. "We?"

I blush so hard it feels like the air around us raises 20 degrees.

"Don't worry about anything besides winning the games, Henri." Orion interlaces our fingers. It grounds me, providing a lifeline to reality that I so desperately need right now.

"Right. Tomorrow."

"Try to get some sleep," he suggests.

I wince and let out a deep sigh.

He's right, although I doubt I'll find much rest in this place.

We could escape. I don't feel stuck, exactly. Just scared. But the consequence of unleashing our combined magics would be devastating.

I'm not sure I can focus my power enough to keep the innocent citizens of this world safe.

"Calm your thoughts," Orion whispers, lifting his other arm and pushing it through the bars of his cage to brush my hair with his fingers, tucking it behind my ear.

After seeing his full form, nothing is more shocking than the fact that this giant, ancient dragon is so unbelievably *gentle*.

Then Orion's hands lower to my waist and he *pulls*. I'm dragged closer to the bars until I'm lying on my side, mirroring Orion. He maneuvers so his arms are pushing through the bars of the cage. They strain around his biceps, but Orion merely grunts and the metal *bends* to allow him through, and he clasps my hands, drawing me closer until his thumb brushes against my cheek.

Words form on my tongue as I look at him but the fear swirling within me keeps me silent.

We lay there, side-by-side, separated by a metal cage, staring into each other's eyes.

"Sleep, Henri. I will watch over you," he whispers, lifting our clasped hands to press a warm kiss against my fingers.

Despite it all, despite the fear and danger, I find my thoughts calming and my mind goes quiet as I drift to sleep, thinking of amethyst eyes that sparkle like the infinite cosmos.

Sounds in the distance wakes me. Confused, I blink away the blurriness of sleep.

A warm hand holds mine.

Turning my head slowly to the side, I sleepily take in Orion's tired figure watching me.

Orion never let me go. Never stopped watching over me.

My heart *thuds* at the realization.

"Up and at em'!" someone calls. "The Games are starting soon!"

There's a harsh blast of light against my eyes as a guard opens the front door, letting the light in.

Has it really been an entire day that we've been in here?

"How long was I asleep?" I ask in horror.

"About 6 hours."

I sit up so fast that I hit my head on one of the bars of the cage. Wincing in pain, I glare at the offending inanimate object.

"You let me sleep for 6 hours? Orion!"

He laughs. "You needed the sleep, so I let you sleep. Besides, it's not like we can do much else here."

Okay. That last part is true at least.

"You should have woken me so we could switch. You need sleep too, you know."

Orion shrugs. "I'm fine."

Dragons. I sigh.

Soon a Guard comes over to unlock our cages. The same guard from yesterday with the white hair and blue skin. The guard moves to grab my arm but stops at Orion's enraged growl.

They don't know he's a dragon, but they know he's something not to be fucked with.

"Follow me," the guard hisses, while other guards surround us, pointing their various weapons in our direction.

"Fine," I mutter. Orion steps forward and walks next to me, refusing to obey the single line they're trying to make. He relaces our hands and my heart skips a beat.

Dozens of additional guards do the same with the remaining contestants. Surprisingly, no one causes a fuss, but then again, there are deadly weapons pointed at us.

We're marched outside and I wince at the bright light. The weather is overcast and I'm thankful; if it was any brighter, it would burn my retinas.

The guards bring us to another building, this one smaller and even brighter. Inside are walls lined with weapons.

"Pick your weapons. You have five minutes," the blue-skinned guard calls. "Try to kill each other—or one of us—and it'll be your head."

A question pops into my head, and I can't help but ask.

"Will we get our cuffs off for the games?"

The guard smirks. "Nope. No unfair advantages."

Of course not. They couldn't make this easy, could they?

I look at the weapons on the walls more closely now that I know exactly just how badly I need them.

"Grab what you can carry but make sure you can still move with it," Orion says quietly, and I nod.

The guards signal that we can pick our weapons and for a moment, nobody moves. Someone twitches and, like the start of a race, we all sprint towards the walls of weapons, grabbing them like moms at a grocery rush hour.

I manage to snag two bolters and a dagger the size of my face with cruel serrated edges. The blades and bolters go first. Then it's the more unique weapons.

Orion grabs a staff with four sharp blades at one end, as well as a curved sword. He somehow managed to grab three bolters and two smaller daggers on top of that.

"How the hell did you grab all of that?" I mutter.

Orion just flashes me a smile that nearly lights my pants on fire.

"Dragon."

Right. I fall silent as I look up into Orion's eyes and that's when I realize—I stopped seeing the glamour.

"I can see you," I breathe. "Orion I—I can *see* you."

Orion pockets his weapons and lifts his now empty hand, cupping my cheek. "I can see you too, Stardust."

My jaw drops and my cheeks flush at the nickname.

"Why?" I ask. "How? I don't understan—"

Orion quiets me with his lips. His hands sink into my tangled hair and he pulls me close.

While people stream around us, Orion Worldkiller devours me whole, leaving nothing behind but an empty husk as I lose myself to his kiss.

Our lips move in sync, perfectly reacting to every action, every movement matched and mimicked. I can't help but lean into him, pressing my body against his. I need to be closer.

Quiet, so quiet no one else would be able to hear, I let out a mournful whine as Orion pulls back, panting lightly.

His amethyst eyes are brighter than ever before. He presses his lips against my forehead, wrapping his arms around me.

"You have my heart, Stardust. That is why you can see through the glamour. Everyone else still sees it, but not you. You see the truth, and the truth is you are *mine*—and I am yours."

My own heart stops beating at his words.

"Orion, I—"

My response is interrupted as the guards arrive.

"Time's up! Let's go."

The guards move into the room and open up a door that was previously locked. The guards shoulder past the contestants, ignoring their newly acquired weapons.

The door swings open and the guards shove us forward, forcing us into the awaiting, empty space.

This one has a sliding door that opens into a large, open roof stadium. It rather resembles a football field, but it's made of stone. The stands are full of Antheriens and other alien races that scream and chant in anticipation.

But I don't see Derek.

Where are you?

"Patience," Orion whispers.

I stick my tongue out at him. "Patience sucks."

He snickers. Names start being announced through some sort of speaker system as contestants are shoved into the light of the stadium.

This is the last moment we have before...before I don't know what.

I'm not sure what's about to happen.

So, without thinking and without preamble, I turn to Orion and reach up to fist his shirt, pulling him down towards me. My lips land on his. I break away before he can react.

"I'm yours...and you are mine. When we get out of this, we'll figure out what that means, okay?" I press one more kiss against his lips before the guards pull me away. I slap at their hands, but they just shove me out onto the sand. I trip and almost fall to my knees, but Orion is already there, catching me before I meet the sand.

Large columns are bolted into the sand just a few feet away from us. The guards surround us and one of them pulls out what looks to be a fancy tv remote. The guard hits a button and the columns light up. I'm suddenly dragged towards it. I squeak, startled at the fact that I can't stop moving. But the *pull*. The columns are giant magnets and the cuffs around our wrists ensure we can't go far.

The pressure eases as I get to the column, panting and sweating.

Orion is at the column to my right, with the other contestants on my left.

We're not chained to the columns, but it will be extremely difficult to walk away from them. I don't think I like these Antheriens after all.

A voice calls over the loudspeaker, rambling on about the games. I'm not paying any attention. Instead, I'm frantically surveying my surroundings.

The air is chilly, and I wince against the glare from the clouds overhead.

I have weapons, but no magic.

I'm not chained down, but it's not exactly easy to run away.

My thoughts falter as a cage is brought out by the guards. It's only then that I start paying attention to the announcer.

"—and here we have THE BAIT!"

That's all I catch.

But it's enough.

I already know what's in the cage before the creatures are shaken out onto the sand. They fall, thumping to the ground.

"Derek," I gasp.

CHAPTER 27

NOW OR NEVER

D erek.

Oh my God, it's Derek! Three flaming kittens surround him. They've grown, but they're still smaller than my longtime feline friend.

They're alive. They're all *alive.*

The crowd begins to scream and shout as large cages are rolled out on the other side of the stadium. The cages are full of giant, dangerous monsters; a minotaur, a giant spider that looks like a zombie version of Jala Zigu, and something that looks like a worm the size of a draft horse but with teeth. *Lots* of teeth.

"Orion!" I hiss, but he's already watching.

"I see them."

A plan forms in my head. A desperate, fool-hardy plan.

"Derek!" I yell. My cat hears me and his head swivels, looking around. The moment he sets eyes on me, he lets out a happy, *"Meow!"*

"Derek, help me! Use your claws!"

Derek blinks.

Out of all of my animals, he is the one who seems the most normal.

The thing about aliens is nothing is ever what it seems.

Derek's eyes narrow and he meows at the kittens, sitting down so that he can raise a paw. He gets to work chewing off the pink claw caps I force him to wear—something I know he finds terribly annoying. But if I didn't, my furniture would be in shreds!

Derek is what's known as a Pantera. A critically endangered species of cat that looks like the domestic felines that inhabit Earth, but is ten times more deadly. With claws made of a metal so sharp and so strong, they can cut through any substance.

The hellkittens chew off Derek's remaining claw caps and then run across the sand to me.

I'm yanked out of my thoughts as a large bell sound rings throughout the stadium. It's so loud, I'm wincing against the sound.

Orion snarls and steps forward as cages open.

"Can you distract them?" I shout at him.

"Already on it."

The minotaur charges Orion. Even with the cuffs, the dragon is so strong, he's able to move *almost* normally. Whereas I can barely move.

The giant spider follows the minotaur, but it gets distracted with the other candidates. Their screams sound as it closes in and bites their heads off in a show of blood and gore.

I have to look away.

"Derek!" I motion to the Pantera. "Derek, come here baby!

He meows and runs over to me, the kittens following just behind. They seem ambivalent about the giant, cat-eating monsters just a few feet away.

"Can you cut these?" I show Derek the cuffs. He leans up, his paws on my legs, and sniffs the metal. Sitting back down, Derek nods and raises a paw, letting his nails brush against the metal.

The cuffs drop to the ground. I didn't even feel it. Derek's claws cut through the suppression tech like *butter*.

A large shadow suddenly blocks the glare from the sun.

Oh no. I FORGOT ABOUT THE WORM!

"DEREK, RUN!" I scream, glancing behind me just in time to see the worm opening its mouth full of dozens of tiny sharp teeth.

I bend down and scoop up two of the kittens as Derek grabs the smallest by its scruff and prances away. I follow, clutching the fluffy kittens to my chest. They burrow closer, scared and finally realizing something is wrong.

Or maybe they noticed the giant worm roaring behind me.

Spit hits my hair, and I nearly gag, but force myself to focus on not falling as I sprint across the sand.

"GIANT WORM!" I screech as I pass Orion as he chops off one of the spider's legs.

"Fuck," Orion sighs loudly as he abandons the spider and runs behind me. I'm annoyed with how quickly he's able to arrive at my side, not even panting—while I'm flat out sprinting.

Derek gallops along at our feet.

I wonder if the spider is related to Jala Zigu—NOT NOW, BRAIN! WE'RE TRYING NOT TO DIE!

At this point, the crowd can clearly tell something is wrong.

Boos and other jeers are hurtled at us.

"Can you shift and kill the worm?" I ask Orion, breathing hard from the fast pace.

"Yes, but then our cover will be blown."

"Do you have any better ideas?!" My voice turned into a high-pitched shriek without even trying.

"Cast a spell that weakens it and makes it tired!"

I nearly trip.

"What?!"

"We need a distraction. Making them fall asleep will allow me to kill the worm without causing suspicion."

Oh. Okay yeah, that's a good idea. Unfortunately for us, my mind is *racing*. The fear is making my heart pound. I know we can make it out of this but Orion is right; we cannot break our cover. Between my galloping heart and the overstimulation from the fact that thousands of cute but terrifying aliens are *screaming* at us which is like nails on a chalkboard inside of my own HEAD, spells aren't looking like a good option right about now!

Because if I get it wrong...my heart leaps into my throat at the thought of just how badly things could go if I got the spell wrong.

I try to focus, but the giant spider suddenly leaps at us from the left. I scream, jumping out of the way, but it knocks me to the sand. I clutch the kittens tightly to my chest, using my body as protection.

They will not get hurt. I refuse to let them get hurt. Shut up, THOUGHTS, and let me save my creatures!

The thought *changes* something in my head. Where there was chaos there is now calm. I turn, refusing to run anymore, and face the monsters.

Sometimes when my adrenaline is really high, I can force my brain to hyperfixate on just *one* thing. It doesn't always work but it's working now and I will take it!

"HENRI! WHAT ARE YOU DOING?" Orion shouts as he takes on the Minotaur, who has appeared at our right, covered in blood.

A quick glance behind us tells me that we're all that's left.

The other contestants are dead—and we're next.

Fear turns to determination. I force my mind to go quiet and focus on the monsters heading towards me.

YOU ARE GROWING WEAK! I think. I repeat the words over and over again, using every ounce of willpower in me to force the words into reality.

The worm pauses and the spider suddenly cries out in pain. The minotaur slows, panting and stumbling.

Orion flashes me a wicked grin. "Good girl."

I blink as my body floods with heat at his praise.

UH NOT RIGHT NOW, PLEASE! I shout at my traitorous body.

Orion quickly gets to work killing the monsters. While I dislike death, it was us or them. And I will not let *any* harm come to my cats. Soon, it's just me and the dragon, standing amongst piles of gore and dead bodies.

The air reeks of blood and sweat.

Orion still doesn't look the least bit winded, which is both intensely attractive and a bit annoying. I'm covered in sweat and blood—not mine, I think—and if I smelled my armpits, it would probably make me pass out.

But the dragon isn't fazed. Orion jogs over to me and wraps me and the kittens in his arms.

"Are you alright?" he whispers in my ear, cradling my face.

"Yeah, just winded and in shock."

"It'll be okay."

I take a deep breath, inhaling his scent. He doesn't smell sweaty or gross. He smells like the stars. Dark and musky, slightly fruity.

I force myself to step away, which is when the crowd begins shouting.

I look around, suddenly hyper-aware that we're not safe yet. The crowd is *angry*. The bloodbath left two alive.

That, apparently, was not the goal.

Words in various language are screamed at us, and the translator only tells me some of them.

"KILL THEM! KILL THE TRAITORS!" is the most common sentiment.

The entire stadium rages until a voice comes on from the loudspeaker. A door opens in the wall across from us, and Antheriens fly out, followed by guards.

I spot the blue-skinned one again. They surround us, weapons aimed.

"You were not meant to survive," an Antherien says.

"Okay." I blink at its honesty. "Well, we did. You need to let us go now."

"You stole our cats!"

My vision turns read.

Theirs?

Perhaps playing it nice isn't the answer here.

Because suddenly I'm feeling very, *very* mean.

CHAPTER 28

THE RED HERRING

"**T**hief!"

"**Liar!**"

"**Kill them!**"

The shouts from the crowd filter quickly through my translator, stoking my anger until it's a blazing inferno, burning its way through my skin, desperate to surface.

"Thieves?" I ask, my voice trembling. "These creatures belong to no one. They belong to themselves. But they happen to live with *me*. No. We are not thieves," I pause. "*You* are."

The Antheriens laugh. It's a high-pitched buzzing sound.

Then they strike. Running at us from all sides and I—I panic. Derek and the kittens still clutched to my chest, I let my magic rise to the surface.

My body begins to glow as nuclear energy swirls around me, lifting my hair into the air as if it's riding a phantom breeze. The cats are unharmed. I don't know how I knew they would be, but something in the back of my mind knew my magic won't hurt my creatures.

I won't let it. Not now, not tomorrow, not ever.

Orion fights off the Antheriens while I power up. With a roar he leaps back and shifts into his true form. There's a flash of light and then his mortal skin becomes scales as his body grows infinitely.

The dragon that is Orion roars at the Antheriens, but it only seems to make them angrier.

"STOP!"

The voice is so loud, we all go still.

It's the most bizarre moment of my life. One moment we're on the brink of war, and the next, the stadium is silent.

The crowd of soldiers parts like the sea as something small moves through them.

An Antherien emerges. A very old Antherien. The moth uses a specialized cane that helps it stay up. Its wings are almost dried up and transparent. Its fur is white and gray.

"Stop. No more fighting!" The Antherien pants lightly. Even with the translator, I can hear how old he is.

To my shock, the soldiers stand down.

A scaled snout noses my back and I turn to see Orion. There's a flash and then he's back to mortal form. He quickly steps in front of me and strikes a protective stance.

"Step aside." The Elder Antherien motions at Orion with his cane. "Please, son."

I don't drop my magic, however...

"Do as he says," I say quietly, never letting go of Derek and the kittens. I want to see what this alien has to say.

Orion growls and steps to the side, but I can tell he's not happy about it.

The elderly Antherien steps closer, taking a closer look at me.

"They are your family, are they not?" He uses his cane to point at the cats in my arms.

Nervous and unsure, I nod. "They are."

The Elder motions to the crowd watching us, and to the

guards that surround him. "These are all my family, and I would like it if you did not kill them."

I stumble back. "I—I don't want to. But, I also want to go home safely."

"You may leave without anyone bothering you."

I take a step forward and crouch slightly, getting eye level to the elder.

"Why are you doing this?"

"Because I am tired and my people are suffering. There has been enough death. We have lost so many, I cannot lose any-more."

"Then why do you host this awful game? Why do you have the cruelest market in the galaxy where you treat creatures *terribly?*"

The Elder tilts his head and I get the feeling that he…pities me? But that doesn't make any sense.

"Dear girl. You think we chose this?" The Elder takes a deep, rattling breath. "We do this because we have no other choice. The UGF kills our crops and raises our taxes, torturing us until we give them whatever they want. These games are the only way we can make enough money to keep everyone in the city safe. The market is the only way we have money to buy food. Otherwise, we would starve, and no one would spare us a sec-ond glance."

I fall fully to my knees in front of the moth-like creature as his words sink in.

A shadow falls over me as Orion approaches. "You said they're killing your crops? How?"

The Antherien sighs. "Biological weapons. We suspect next they will begin poisoning our water. They use long range drones to enter the atmosphere and bypass our defense system. There is nothing we can do but watch as they rain death upon us."

The village outside of the city.

The UGF did that.

"How—how are you getting the creatures for the Market? Can't you leave the planet?"

The elderly Antherien takes another rattling breath. A younger Antherien flies up and tucks itself under the Elder one, helping to prop him up.

"Thank you." The Elder says to the youth, before he sighs and looks back at me. "The UGF destroyed all of our ships. We couldn't leave even if we wanted to. But this is our home. We have no desire to leave."

I wait, knowing what comes next.

The Elder Antherien continues, "As for the creatures? The UGF delivers them on a weekly basis. Anyone who asked questions was killed on sight, so we stopped asking questions. When a creature doesn't sell, the UGF takes them and drops them off somewhere. I've heard they're using Earth as a dumping station, is that true?"

My hands begin to tremble, and Derek lets out a nervous meow.

"It's true," I say, my voice despondent.

We all go quiet for a moment before the elderly moth shuffles over, the younger one still at its side.

"Please forgive us for being a part of your family separation. Know that you can leave safely, and we will not follow."

At his words, the sky goes dark. I stand and look up, expecting to see clouds, but nearly choke on my own spit as I see Starfire hovering above the open-air stadium, blocking out the sun.

It's the terrified screams of the crowd that knocks me out of my stupor.

"Did you call the ship?" I ask Orion.

"No," he grits out. "I did not."

We both stare at Starfire hovering above the arena. There's a noise as one of Starfire's escape hatches opens.

No. Oh, he wouldn't.

He's not really going to—

I nearly suffer a heart attack as Boris slithers down the walkway and leaps into the air with glee on his face. He waves his tentacles at me and lets out a high-pitched *SQUEAK!*

There's a flash of light and he goes from small to as big as the spaceship.

A giant, roaring kraken lands on the stadium sand before us.

The sand shakes under the weight of his massive form.

Boris glances back at us, his brown eyes alight with happiness. He winks at me before turning back to the Antheriens and letting out a roar so loud, it nearly bursts my eardrums.

"Uh, actually, Boris...I think we're all good here."

The roar cuts off and the kraken turns to look at me, confusion in his eyes.

I motion to the elderly Antherien who looks at Boris in absolute terror.

"Yeah so, this is all...well, a big misunderstanding. No need to terrorize them. Not anymore, at least."

Boris deflates and makes a petulant sound, flashing back into his regular small form. He slithers over to me and leaps onto my shoulders, letting out happy squeaks at being reunited with Derek.

Surprisingly, Derek lets out an equally happy meow and head butts the pygmy kraken.

Something about that moment breaks me.

It also makes me furious. Furious at the UGF.

I turn to the elderly Antherien, and in that moment, I make a decision. A decision that might change the course of our universe. A *stupid* decision...but the right one.

"I would like to see your crops. The first that fell, ideally."

CHAPTER 29

NOVUM

We fly Starfire to the first of the dead crops. Only an hour outside of the city, dried up ground greets us.

The Antheriens flew, but I invited the elder to join us on Starfire. He accepted gratefully and now, hobbles down the walkway as we emerge into the dry dirt.

He lets out a shaky breath and motions to the field. "This...this used to be grain. For a thousand years, this field provided enough grain for our cities. Then the UGF dropped their weapons and in days, every crop was dead."

Hundreds of Antheriens fly in the sky above us with light buzzing noises.

The Elder looks at empty field before us. "We've tried to fertilize the ground using the ways of our ancestors, but nothing has worked."

It's like visiting a cemetery. I can feel the way they mourn as they gaze down at the dead, withered ground.

With a deep breath, I walk down and join them. Orion follows, but the creatures stay on the ship like I asked.

Orion didn't ask any questions. He hasn't said anything since the arena.

I turn to him and let the fear bubbling within me grow. Fear and regret. Because this is one secret I never planned on sharing with him. Or anyone. Not ever. But I have to do this.

Before I can see his reaction, I turn and crouch, sinking my hands into the dirt.

20 years ago

"Mom! Come quick!"

Jace's shout echoes through the garden and my parents come running, Shaye at their side.

My older brother sprints over to me, kneeling in the dirt.

"Look!" I give them my brightest smile and show them the flowers in my hands.

My father's eyes go wide and he drops to his knees.

"Can I see it?" he asks gently. I nod and stand, still small enough that even though he's kneeling, the top of my head barely comes to his shoulder.

As I stand, more flowers appear from behind me, as well as the fruit tree now full of bright, shiny red apples...in the middle of the Arizona Desert.

My dad takes the daisies from my hand and shows them to my mom, who trembles lightly as she touches the petals.

"I didn't use a spell or anything!" I beam, but the happiness dwindles.

No one else is smiling.

"What's wrong?" I ask, suddenly nervous. "Did I do something wrong, Daddy?"

My dad lets out a shaky breath. "You didn't do anything wrong. But, sweetheart, you need to promise me you won't do this again."

I don't know why, but tears instantly fill my eyes. It felt so *good* to bring these plants to life. I look back at the tree full of fruit and frown.

"But why, Daddy?"

My mom's arms envelop me, and I breathe in her jasmine scent.

Then Jace joins us as she hugs my back, tucking herself against me. I can feel the way her body trembles.

"Why is this so wrong?" I ask, the tears falling in earnest. "Am I...bad?"

"No! No. You are not bad," my father says, joining us in the hug. Their arms fall away, and I lean back into Jace, who still holds me tightly as I look up at my parents. A hand slides into mine and I glance to the side to see Shaye, worry in his bright blue eyes.

"You are wonderful and kind and so, so special, my darling." Mom cups my cheek. "You didn't do anything wrong. But you know how you and your siblings have...special powers?"

I nod, sniffling.

"This power that you just used, it's *extra* special. If anyone found out, you could do this...they would want to use you. They would take you away from us."

My heart skips a beat.

"They would...take me away?"

My dad lets out a sharp breath. "They would try. But we will never let that happen, okay? You just need to promise not to show *anyone* this power. No one outside of the family can know. And you two—" Dad looks at my siblings and nods. "I don't care what happens. You never say a word of this to anyone. Ever."

They both nod.

"But...what is it?" I ask quietly. "This power? Isn't it like my other powers?"

My dad lets out a laugh but there's no humor in it. "This isn't like anything else, sweetheart. This is a power that comes from my side of the family. Every thousand years, someone in my family is born with something very special. The ability to create life."

I look down at the flowers surrounding us.

Life.

Is that...what this is?

"I created life? I thought it was just...growing some plants."

My mom points to the desert around us. We went on a road trip to the Grand Canyon this fall and stopped to walk around a bit after being in the car for hours.

That's how we got here. In the middle of nowhere, surrounded by cacti and dried shrubs.

"You grew things that do not grow here. The seeds your power locked on to must be...maybe thousands of years old. You grew something from a different age. You created *life*, my darling girl."

They sound terrified.

"I'm sorry," I sniff, feeling emotional again. "I promise I won't do it again."

Mom wraps her arms around me and Jace. A yank and Shaye is pulled into her side. He pretends to not like my parents' snuggles, but I know he secretly loves it.

"Never apologize for being yourself," she whispers. "Never, ever."

"Okay..." I breathe, inhaling her scent.

"What's it called? This power?"

The question isn't mine, it's Jace's. I'm only 10, so I don't know much about our history. I'm still learning. But Jace is grown and understands what I don't.

My mom pulls back and straightens, glancing at my dad. He's the one who eventually answers.

"The power does not have a name, but the person who wields it does."

I hold my breath, terrified for some unknown reason at what he's about to say.

"It's called the Novum. You are the Novum."

13 years ago

"Just tell me!" I stomp my foot and Jace lets out an angry sigh.

"I don't see the point, Hen. You can't use the powers anyways. Besides, Mom and Dad explained—"

I interrupt her. "No. No, Jace. They provided a very *vague* explanation. All I know is that if I use this power, someone is going to come find me. I want to know how. I want to know *why*. Can't you at least tell me that?"

"Shaye should be the one doing this." Jace rubs her temples.

I was going to say something else, going to press her for more but...I know she didn't ask for this.

To become my *parent*.

Mom and Dad have been gone for 2 years, and in their absence, my older siblings have stepped into the role of "parent" for me.

"If I'm the Novum, whatever the hell that means, then I have a right to know. Who would take me away, Jace? Walk me through it. If I use my creation powers, what happens next?"

Jace plops down on the couch next to me, deflating slightly. I slide my hand into hers, squeezing.

"Please," I breathe. "It will make it easier to keep it a secret if I at least know *why*."

Jace turns to me, her blue eyes full of sadness—and fear.

"Okay. I will tell you. I don't know *how* you became so wise, but...you're right. You deserve to know the full truth."

I inhale sharply.

She's going to tell me!

I hug my Pantera cat, Derek, close to my chest. He lets out a soothing purr and tucks his head beneath my chin, his paws on my shoulders.

Jace smiles sadly at the sight of us.

"If you use your powers, one of two things might happen. The first option is that the UGF finds out. If they do, they will take you into custody by declaring you a threat to Earth's sanctuary and the galaxy all together. They will test you and then use you as a weapon."

I—what?

I go to ask a question but Jace holds up her hand. "Let me finish."

I nod and save the question for later.

"The second option is that Proxima Nova finds out first. If that happens, *they* will be who comes for you, and you will be taken back to Father's home planet. You will be tested and then installed as the King's second."

I stop breathing.

"Actually, I lied. There's a third option, although it's less of an option and more of an inevitable." Jace pauses, chewing her lip. "If the UGF finds you, they will use you in their war. But if Proxima Nova finds out they're using you, they will go to war too. Not for the UGF, but against it."

My mouth opens as shock courses through me.

"If Proxima Nova thinks that the UGF has been hiding the Novum, willingly withholding information related to the planet's royal line, Proxima Nova will destroy the UGF."

"But they don't get involved," I note.

"For you? They wouldn't hesitate."

"So, if I use my powers, I will become a pawn for the UGF or Proxima Nova, and I might start an intergalactic war...ending in thousands upon thousands of deaths?"

My sister's head falls back onto the couch cushion as she looks up at the ceiling.

"Yes. And you will be forced into service for Proxima Nova for the rest of your life. You will not be able to say no."

"Is this why Dad went no contact with his family?" I ask.

Jace laughs and looks back at me. "Proxima Nova is talked about like it's this...magical Elysium. But the reality is, they're a brutal, cut-throat, prejudiced species. Dad left because he had no other choice, but it was long before you were born, Hen."

We fall silent, our hands intertwined.

"I will keep my promise. I won't use the power. Ever. I won't be a pawn. Not for anyone or anything."

Jace squeezes my hand and leans over, pressing a kiss against my temple. "I know you won't. But if something happens, because accidents do happen, know that Shaye and I will do *anything* to protect you, okay? We will not abandon you to some cruel fate. We Laselles stick together. That's *my* promise."

I ignore the way deep within the far reaches of my mind, I can feel my magic sleeping. Waiting to be used.

Now

A little under two decades of keeping my true power a secret is erased in an instant as I *reach* with my magic into the dead Earth beneath my fingers.

I barely have to try.

It's like it was waiting for me to use it. My magic dives deep into the ground, invisible to the naked eye. Then I feel them.

Seeds. Thousands of seeds. I expected they would be dead, but *no*. They're *alive*. Weak and small, but they are alive. The Antheriens attempts worked.

With an exhale, I breathe magic into a single seed.

I don't know how else to describe it. But this magic—it feels like breathing. My magic joins with the seed, supercharging its growth. Gasps sound in the distance.

I open my eyes to see a single stalk sprouting from the ground.

I turn to the shocked Elder Antherien. "I can bring your crops back to life, if you would like me to. What you tried, it worked. The seeds are alive again thanks to you; I just sped up the growth. Would you like me to speed up the rest?"

The Elder gasps. "Oh, please! We would be forever grateful."

I nod and move my focus back to the dirt beneath my fingers. I fall back into the depths of my mind, where my power resides. My connection spreads, touching every single seed. I breathe more life into each and every one of them. Then I use root paths to find the other crops, until they are all brought back to life.

Then I use the seeds like networks, forcing my magic to spread even farther until I can feel *every* field and all of the seeds planted on Antheri. The weight of it makes sweat start to drip down the center of my back.

But I never stop breathing.

I push and I push until my magic begins to tremble under the strain. It's the noise that pulls me out of it—and a hand on my shoulder.

"You're using too much. Pull back," a voice whispers. "Come

back to me, Stardust."

I gasp, breathing oxygen instead of magic and my eyes burst open as I let my magic disconnect. It hums, happy and tired within me as it goes back to sleep.

Then I realize what's in front of me.

I kneel in a field of wheat stalks. As far as the eye can see, plants sway in the wind.

There's a choked sound nearby. I move my body but it's stiff as I turn and see the Elder Antherien falling to the ground. His small arms touch the stalks, and then he bursts into tears.

The Antheriens in the air all land, some of them crying out with joy at the sight.

"How?" the Elder gasps, turning to me. "How did you do this?"

"I cannot tell you," I breathe. My voice is a bit scratchy, like I went into some sort of stasis for days instead of minutes.

Pearlescent tears fall from the Elder's eyes. "You *saved* us."

I stand on shaky legs and Orion's steadying hand helps me. Walking over to the Elder, I crouch and hold my arm out to him.

He leans into it. "Who are you? How can you do this?"

I shake my head, unable to answer.

"Never mind that. Whoever you are, you have saved my people. I don't—" the Antheri's voice cuts off in a sob. "I don't know how we can ever repay you."

I smile and reach out my hand to gently grasp one of his. I make sure to move slowly and to be extra gentle, not wanting to offend or crush him—while also giving him time to decline the gesture. To my surprise, he clasps my hand back, pulling me closer.

"Saving you *is* the payment," I tell him. "These crops should never have been attacked in the first place. What I've done should make them resistant to the UGF's weapons. They will not starve you again. I promise."

I close my eyes for a moment and wake my magic. Not the life force at my core, but my witch magic.

"Resist." The spell is simple. But I feel it take hold as each plant is instantly safeguarded against future biological attacks.

Exhaustion comes quickly. I've never used this much magic at once.

"It's time for us to go," I tell the Antheri, and he nods.

"Please know, you are welcome on our planet any time. Let all who will listen hear this: the Life-Giver and the dragon are friends of Antheri."

The Life-Giver.

With exhaustion, comes reality. *Fuck.*

"Please…don't tell anyone I did this. Or what happened here. If anyone asks, this happened naturally." My voice trembles under the weight of realization. If anyone finds out…

"They will never believe us," the Antherien Elder protests, but I pull my hand back and he sighs. "But we will not say anything. I promise."

"Thank you." I smile and turn to Orion who gazes at me with an awestruck look. But that awe turns fierce.

He understands, then. My smile drops and I nod to him, touching his shoulder as I walk back to the ship. I hear him fall in line behind me and soon, we're walking up the ramp to Starfire.

"Starfire, take us into orbit," I order the ship.

"Certainly," she replies. The hatch begins to raise when I feel something touch my hand.

I look down, expecting to see Boris, but am surprised to see the Antherien spider, Dora.

"Hello."

She tugs on my finger, having crawled up my leg without me even noticing.

"She says she can help."

I turn and look at Orion.

"She says that she can make them forget."

CHAPTER 30

FAMILY

Through Orion, Dora the spider explains exactly what she means.

"She wasn't just outcast from her nest because of her size. Her web is different."

I bring my hand up so that I can look into her eyes.

"Starfire, hold ascent," Orion orders, before turning to me. He continues translating. "Dora says her web *should* be like other Antherien spiders. Physical and strong. But her web it..." Orion trails off and his cocks his head. "Hmm. She says it's...shiny."

"Shiny?" I ask her, and the spider nods.

"I don't have the words for it in English but...I believe she means that her web is metaphysical. She says she can hypnotize people with it."

My eyes widen. "Really? How?"

"She says, if you will allow her, that she will show us."

I nod and the spider makes a happy squeaking sound.

"She asks you to bring her down the walkway and hold out your hands so she's facing the Antheriens."

I follow her orders and do just that, Orion following close behind. Dora takes a deep breath as she looks out at the Antheriens. They wave at us, thinking we're saying goodbye.

She lifts her two front legs and a web shoots out.

Not a physical web at all. But one made of *energy*.

"Shiny," I laugh.

"Wait! Don't!"

I pause, and Dora's web does the same.

The Elder Antherien looks up at the web, understanding it's significance.

"We made you a promise, and we intend to keep it. You can choose to do this, but you have saved our lives. For generations to come, we will think of you. But we will not speak of you. I promise that every generation that comes will know to *never* tell anyone about what happened here today."

I let out a shaky breath.

"You said it yourself; our methods worked. No one need know why the crops grew quicker other than that we brought the seeds back to life. That is the only story that will ever be told. But we will know," The Elder flutters his wings and the others follow suit. A low buzzing sound becomes louder and louder, like a *hum* from all Antheri. I feel it in my chest. "We will know about the woman who came from the stars, who helped our crops grow. We will know. But we will not speak of you; not once. This, I swear."

I want to be afraid.

But I have been afraid for so long.

Orion is right.

Maybe I am not meant to be invisible.

Maybe I'm meant to *burn.*

"Okay," I nod, before I can talk myself out of it. "Okay. I trust you. Drop the web, Dora."

The little spider nods and her web disappears.

Today, I choose hope.

"Thank you. No one outside of my family knows this. But your kindness, your love for your people, it makes me want to be better. So I will trust you in this, and I thank you for your confidence."

The Elder nods and smiles at me, his antennae fluttering.

"Thank *you* for trusting us." Then he calls me a name that my translator doesn't pick up. I turn to Orion for help.

He tsks his tongue. "There is no word for it in your English. But it roughly means...girl-from-the-stars. Or star girl. I'm not sure."

Star girl. I crinkle my nose, fighting a smile.

I like it.

Hope will always prevail over hate and evil. It has to. So, I will be brave. For them, for my family, for my *creatures,* I will be brave.

Even though my siblings might just kill me if they ever find out about this.

I clear my throat and mutter. "Don't tell my siblings about this."

I glance at Orion, who nods.

"I will tell them...*eventually.* But not yet."

Orion flashes me a small smile. "As you wish, Stardust. Or should I call you Stargirl now?"

I elbow him. "I like Stardust too."

He chuckles and looks back at the ship. "Now, might we head home please?"

I return his smile and nod. We wave goodbye to the Antheriens.

"Starfire? Continue ascent. Take us into orbit!" Orion shouts. We quickly walk back up the ramp and it raises, shutting with a loud click.

In silence, we make our way to the cockpit. Dora in my hands, and Boris slithering at my feet. Derek and the kittens are already there, waiting in my chair of all places.

"Keeping it warm for me?" I ask as we approach them, but every step feels heavier and heavier. Derek meows, the kittens letting out their own tiny mews in response. I nudge them off so I can sit in my chair and buckle up, and they crawl back into my lap. It feels so good to hold them again.

Antherien disappears as Starfire ascends into the clouds.

Soon, stars greet us, and the planet disappears.

It's only then that I breathe a sigh of relief.

Seeing Antheri disappear means we did it.

We did it.

It hits me all at once and I start sobbing.

The sound of something unclicking is the only warning I get before I'm swept into Orion's arms, Dora included. The cats jump to the floor, but Dora moves so that she's perched on my shoulder.

"Come on," Orion whispers. "You need to sleep. I can feel how tired you are." He presses a kiss against my temple and that only makes me cry harder. Meows and squeaks follow as the creatures trail after us.

I barely remember the rest of the journey to the bedroom. All I know is I can't stop crying. Relief, fear, confusion, frustration, and pure happiness run through me. It's too much.

Orion sets me down and I wobble over to the bed as he rifles through my bags.

Making a noise of frustration, he abandons my bags and instead grabs clothes from his own drawers. He hands me a white t-shirt, and a pair of boxers covered in tiny dragons. For some reason, the fact that the dragon has boxers covered in a print of tiny dragons only makes me cry *harder.*

But I grab the clothes and walk into the bathroom, changing quickly before I lose all energy. In seconds, I'm naked and sliding into the t-shirt. It comes almost to my knees, and I have to double roll the waistband of the boxers, but besides that, it's shockingly comfortable.

Depositing my dirty clothes by my bag on the floor, I collapse on the bed, gathering all of my creatures close. We sink into sheets covered in Orion's scent.

Derek and the hellkittens tuck themselves against my chest. My beloved Pantera, my longtime companion, purrs and makes biscuits against my cheek as he headbutts me before curling himself around the kittens.

"You're safe," I whisper to him, petting his soft fur. "You're safe, and we're going home. I'm never letting anything happen to you ever again."

Derek *mmrp's* and licks my hand. I don't know when I fall asleep, but sometime later I wake to Orion climbing into bed behind me. He carefully joins the cuddle pile, wrapping his arms around my waist and pulling me until my back is pressed against his chest. A tension I didn't even realize I was holding relaxes at his touch.

We fit together perfectly.

My eyes feel swollen from crying and sleep still tugs at my mind.

"Get some sleep, Stardust," Orion whispers, placing a kiss against my head. "I'll be here when you wake up. You're safe now. You're all safe."

To my surprise, I can feel the way the creatures all adjust and cuddle around our bodies.

They've accepted Orion.

My mind and body relaxes at that thought and I'm quickly pulled back into a calm slumber.

When I wake up a second time, I'm alone.

The creatures are gone—as is Orion.

Panic is a knife to my heart as I frantically look around, startled by my sudden aloneness.

Then the door to the bathroom opens and a shirtless Orion strides out.

The relief I feel at his presence is tangible.

"Feeling better?" he asks with a soft smile. His black hair is mussed from sleep. Amethyst eyes watch me, sparkling with mirth and happiness.

"Yes, still tired though."

"You've been through a lot." He nods.

"How long until we reach Andromeda?"

My stomach sours at the thought.

Orion sees the way my face must fall because his own smile disappears, and he lets out a long sigh.

"Three days."

Quietly, he pads over to the other side of the bed, sliding beneath the covers.

"How long was I asleep?" I ask, trying to think of anything but the UGF.

"About 12 hours."

Not too bad.

My stomach suddenly lets out a noise reminiscent of a semi-truck.

"Hungry?" he asks.

I nod.

"How about breakfast for dinner?"

CHAPTER 31

THE DRAGON & THE WITCH

What happened on Antheri—no, not just on Antheri but on this entire journey—it's changed things. It's changed *me*.

All my life, I have tried to be human. I have tried to be invisible—*normal*.

Then I met a dragon and all of the sudden...I don't want to be invisible any longer.

Orion sets a plate down in front of me, full of steaming pancakes in front of me and I nearly orgasm on the spot. Then he's next to me, his arms wrapping around my waist as his lips meet mine.

"Do you want syrup?"

I gasp and he swallows it.

Then he's gone and I'm left gaping like a wounded fish!

"You're so *fast.*" I say with a shaky voice. Syrup is deposited in front of me along with a cup of water, and then Orion slides into the chair next to me, focusing on his own plate of pancakes.

He smirks, his amethyst eyes twinkling. "I didn't want to scare you, so I do what I normally do around humans; tamper my speed. It took many years of practice, but I've gotten quite good at it."

I pause with a piece of syruped pancake poised just before my mouth. I set it back on the plate, my fork clattering.

"You keep telling me to not hide who I am. Well, the same goes for you. Don't minimize yourself or your true powers around me."

Orion laughs. "Yes, I suppose I should take my own advice, shouldn't I?"

We fall into a comfortable silence as I finish eating. A few minutes later I groan and lean back in the chair, full and content.

Then two hot hands are on my bare thighs as Orion turns the chair so that we face each other. His leg brushes against mine.

"Hi." The dragon smiles, and my heart nearly flutters away at the sight of it.

"Hi," I laugh.

Something blinks to life in the corner of my mind. Something I've wanted to ask.

"Can you tell me about it?" My voice is gentle. "Can you tell me about the planet you destroyed?"

Orion shocks me when he nods.

"What would you like to know?"

Blinking rapidly, I blurt out my questions. "Did you really destroy a whole planet?"

Orion dips his chin. "I did."

Shock courses through me. "How—no, why? Why would you do that?"

Orion exhales. "It's a long story, and a complicated one. So I will answer it in a different way, because I can *feel* what you're getting at."

I bite my lip, worrying at it.

Orion leans forward and cups one hand beneath my chin,

forcing me to look into his amethyst eyes.

"I did destroy a planet. That much is true. But what the UGF has never figured out is that planet was empty when I destroyed it. No lives were lost, Henri. Not one."

I jerk back in surprise, almost losing my balance and falling off the chair, but Orion's hands steady me.

"It was empty?" I gasp. "You—how?"

Orion smiles. "That's the long and complicated part, but the UGF is not nearly as smart as they think they are and never verified that the planet was occupied when they came to investigate. When they found craters and debris, they didn't question it."

Something clicks into place and I realize distantly that it feels a bit like trust.

I trusted Orion before, but there was still a seed of doubt. Of wondering if maybe he really *was* a criminal mastermind, someone who deserved to be in prison. Except from the moment I met him, he's defied every one of my expectations.

Having food in my belly clears the exhaustion as I begin to pepper Orion with more questions, which is when I smell something...unsavory. I look around before glancing down.

"Oh my God, I need a shower!" I realize, seeing the dirt and blood covering my arms. "Orion how could you let me into bed like this? I bet your sheets are disgusting now! Gah!"

I jump off the chair as Orion laughs. "Fuck my sheets. You needed sleep."

"Okay well now I've slept, and I need a damn shower. I feel so gross! Thank you so much for the food, but I need to go shower. Right now. Immediately. *Yesterday.*"

I fast walk out of the room, my bare feet sticking lightly to the cold metal floor. Even my *toes* feel dirty. I make it to elevator and smash the button, cheeks flaming with embarrassment.

The elevator doors open a few seconds later with a soft *beep*. I walk in and turn.

Orion stares at me, watching with amusement. I almost scream at the sight of him. He's so quiet!

But I did tell him to be himself, so I guess that includes almost scaring the shit out of me.

"Would you like some help?"

I inhale so sharply, I nearly choke on my own pit.

He doesn't mean...

"What do you mean?" I ask, my voice visibly wobbly.

The corner of Orion's mouth twitches. "I think you know exactly what I mean."

It's like being zapped by electricity. Knowing Orion wants me.

"Let me take care of you," Orion murmurs, stepping closer. He reaches for me, his hands landing on my waist. "Don't make me beg, Stardust. Because I will."

Ohmygod—

"Yes." The word leaves my mouth before I can think better of it.

Orion backs me against the elevator wall. I distantly hear the doors close as the floor below us *lifts*. He leans down presses a hot kiss just below my jawline.

Before I can take my next breath, Orion's hands are around my waist and he's lifting me, my legs wrapping around his waist in a single movement placing his hardness right against the apex of my legs. It's like being struck by lightning. Every nerve ending in my body comes to life.

Then his lips are on mine and the dragon *consumes* me. There is no gentleness in this kiss. A keening whine escapes my lips and Orion swallows every second of it.

Then he pulls away, panting hard. The elevator is beeping at us. I didn't hear it behind the cloudy haze of need, but now I do.

He carries me to the bathroom, kissing my jawline and neck.

Boris, the cats, and Dora are all still asleep, cuddled together on the bed, and Orion walks us straight into the bathroom as the bedroom door closes behind us.

Then he's setting me on my feet. Orion steps around me and presses a combination of buttons on the wall.

Shower heads descend and turn on, creating a smooth rainfall from the ceiling. Then the far wall turns cloudy, before becoming clear.

"Oh!" I gasp. It's like showering among the stars. Distant planets and swirling galaxies glitter in the distance.

It's beautiful.

Without thinking. I shed my clothes and step into the water, sighing at the feeling of the warm water covering my skin.

I turn and immediately blush at the heated look in Orion's eyes. He looks me over from head to toe, missing nothing. It's so vulnerable—and terrifying. A second later, his own clothes hit the floor right alongside my jaw.

"You're beautiful," I breathe, taking in his bare form.

He reminds me of a Greek God. Like a statue in a museum, only better.

As he steps forward, every muscle in his body *flexes* and his tattoos shimmer like something out of my naughtiest daydream.

I force myself to look at *all* of him and holy shit, he's big *everywhere.*

To be honest, I don't usually see the naked male body and think, "sexy". But Orion Worldkiller oozes sex appeal. I could look at him all day. Suddenly, I can't look away, like I've been hypnotized by Dora's web.

Orion grabs a bottle from a small shelf and the smell of citrus and lavender fills the space as the air turns steamy. Still, the glass to the outside never fogs up.

"Turn around," he orders softly. I obey.

Hands run through my hair as he massages my scalp. I moan and lean back against him, unable to hold myself up at the delicious sensation.

"Relax," Orion whispers. "I've got you, Stardust."

"I think I like that nickname." I let out a contented sigh as he begins rinsing the suds away. "What made you think of it?"

Orion finishes rinsing my hair and then adds some conditioner before resuming his massage. I lean even more against him, unable to ignore the way his hard length presses against me.

He's enjoying this just as much as I am.

"Dragons are known for hoarding treasure. It's one of the few legends about us that is true." Orion falls quiet for a moment, and I let my eyes close, drifting into a half-sleep until his low voice brings me back to reality. "I was thinking of a treasure. Something rare and utterly irreplaceable."

He rinses the conditioner out of my hair before squirting a different smelling soap, this one a rosemary and tangerine, onto his hands. Then he starts massaging my shoulders, soaping up my bare skin.

I let out another moan as he works my sore muscles.

"I treasure you, Henri. My dragon wants to hoard you like the finest treasure and hide you away, keeping you all to myself."

My body flushes at his words.

He...thinks I'm treasure.

His treasure.

"Somehow, in all of that, I just came up with Stardust. Precious, treasured, perfect—just like you."

I turn and face him, gazing up at his face as the shower head rains water over us.

"I'm not perfect," I laugh. "Not even close."

Orion gives me a soft smile. "You are to me."

I fall silent in shock as he soaps up the rest of my body. When his hands brush against my chest, I stop breathing. Every nerve-ending on my body is alight with his touch, but the dragon is polite. He doesn't linger. He cleans with precision and care.

Like I really am his treasure.

When he kneels, I almost melt on the spot. He cleans each leg slowly, going higher and higher with every pass. I feel like I might spontaneously combust. I'm panting and trembling when finally, his fingers brush against the outer edge of my core. I let out a strangled sound at his touch and immediately flush with embarrassment.

Maybe it was an accident.

He uses water—no soap, the smart dragon—and carefully cleans between my legs.

One finger dips inside of me and my knees give out. I place my hands on his shoulders to keep myself from faceplanting.

Definitely not an accident.

My thoughts go blessedly silent as he cleans me—inside and

out.

"There." His finger pumps slowly. "Now you're all clean. I wouldn't want to miss any dirt, Henri." His finger thrusts in time with his words, and I'm hypnotized. "I'm a dragon that keeps his promises, you see. I promised I would get you clean."

I moan his name as Orion inserts another finger. He increases his speed, looking up at me with such emotion that it—*God*. It *melts* me.

"Orion—" I gasp.

"There it is," he murmurs. "Let it come, Stardust. Let me see you *shine*."

At his words, I'm coming apart in his hands as stars burst behind my eyes. I moan his name, writhing against him. I'm too turned on to be embarrassed. Then he's gently drawing his fingers out. Orion finishes cleaning me, straightening up, and I sigh happily as I lean my cheek against his chest.

"What about you?" I ask, reaching my hand down. But he stops me, grasping my wrist.

Orion chuckles. "This is about you. We have plenty of time for that later. Besides, you're about to fall asleep."

I go to protest—and yawn instead.

"Oops," I giggle, and in my stupor, I press a kiss against his chest. He's so warm.

"Let's get you dry before you fall asleep standing up." He kiss- es my forehead, and I sigh happily as he turns off the water and ushers me out. A thick blue towel is wrapped around my body a few seconds later, and Orion uses a thinner, microfiber towel to gently scrunch my hair. Then he surprises me by pulling out a wide-toothed comb. One suitable for maintaining my curls. The dragon gently combs through my damp hair before twisting each individual strand one by one.

I blame my wide eyes and complete and utter silence combination of exhaustion and the fact that I'm in fucking shock because *hello a hot space dragon is doing my curl routine? Am I HALLUCINATING? AM I DEAD?*

I just stand there, watching him, unable to look away as Orion Worldkiller *pampers* me. When he's done, he dries himself off before wrapping a towel around his waist.

When we exit the bathroom, we're greeted to a scandalized Boris who stares at me with wide eyes. Dora hides behind him and—is she cuddling his tentacle?

I raise a brow at him, and Boris looks away, embarrassed.

With a laugh, I pad over to bed and crawl under the covers. Too tired to care, I ditch the towel and sigh as the cool sheets brush against my bare, clean skin.

A movement at the other side of the bed signals Orion joining me.

He pulls me close, and the creatures arrange themselves around us once again. Boris, on my nightstand, in a bowl filled with water. Dora is perched on the edge of his bowl, watching him with her four eyes.

Derek and the kittens are at the foot of the bed, cuddled all together and snoring lightly.

Orion wraps his arms around me, and I sigh, using his warm body as a pillow. Our legs tangle until we're pressed against each other.

I fall asleep in the arms of a dragon, happy and treasured.

CHAPTER 32

BURN DOWN THE HOUSE

"We land on Andromeda in 30 minutes." Starfire's announcement wakes us up.

Orion makes a frustrated sound, and I pry myself out of his arms.

"I don't think I've ever slept that hard," I croak. My voice scratchy from sleep.

Orion nods. "Me neither. We're already there? Shit."

Then there's a flurry of movement. In seconds, Orion is dressed. My jaw drops as I take him in.

He winks at me. "Get dressed and meet me in the cockpit."

"Don't you tell me what to do!" I protest, but he simply laughs and walks over, leaning over me before pressing his lips against mine. I sigh into him as his tongue gently pries my lips open. He tastes delicious. Like plums and vanilla. I already miss his kiss when he starts to pull away.

"Fine," I sigh. Orion winks at me and leaves me alone to dress.

I look to the side at Boris, who watches me carefully. "Well buddy. I think it's time we go home."

Which means...it's time to say goodbye.

When I get to the cockpit, something's changed. Orion acts the same, but the moment he looks into my eyes, I watch as he comes to the same realization that I did.

We don't talk about it. I don't even know what to say.

Come back to Earth with me, I don't want to end whatever this is? Be my space dragon boyfriend? No. I can't say that. Because what if—what if he says no?

Even after all of this. The worry is present. Starfire begins to slowly descend, and I take my seat in the chair beside him, buckling myself in. Entry is smooth—but the quiet is awful.

As we make it through the atmosphere, Starfire self-pilots to the Arc. The sight of it appears in the distance, getting closer and closer every second.

Starfire descends further, and I hear the whirring of her landing gears releasing. Something about the noise—it sets me off. I turn to Orion, suddenly *bursting* at the seams. Just as I open my mouth, he beats me to it.

"Do you want this to end, Henri? Or do you like what's happening?"

The words freeze on the tip of my tongue, and I swallow.

"I don't want this to end. But..."

At my hesitation, he stiffens.

"What about the elephant in the room?" I ask quietly.

Orion's brow furrows.

Oh. Right.

"I mean, the big secret we haven't talked about but that you *definitely* know about."

Orion relaxes at my words.

"Henri, you don't need to tell me if you're not ready. Yes, I know what you are. I am old enough to know what your magic is and what it means. But I can feel that you are not yet ready to talk about it fully."

I lean back, startled at just how well he can read me.

"I need you to promise you won't tell anyone. I know that you won't. But I want to hear it, Orion. I think I need to hear it to believe it."

Orion smiles and leans forward, grabbing my other hand so that both of mine are clasped between his.

"Henrietta Jane Laselle—"

"How do you know my middle name?"

He rolls his eyes. "I read your file. Now hush, I am making a grand declaration."

That shuts me up quickly.

"Henrietta Jane Laselle—" Orion repeats, "—I will never tell another soul about what you are. Hurting you is the last thing I ever want to do. I will keep your secret for as long as I live and beyond then. I give you my word, on my honor as King of the Dragons."

The worry in my soul and heart withers away at Orion's promise

"Thank you." I whisper, squeezing his hands.

The words settle into the space between us as we turn to look at each other.

This time, when Orion speaks. It's not the man, but the dragon. "I won't let you go, Henri. Not when I just found you."

I nod. That's exactly how I feel too, but...

"Do you trust me?" he asks, glancing back at the Arc. "Promises aside, when we land, do you trust me enough to follow my lead?"

We're almost on the ground and soldiers stream out of headquarters. I have to take a second glance when I see a bear.

Harold and Jace! And there's Shaye!

My family. They're here and—they're being held at gun-point?

"Oh shit," I groan. "I don't think Jace's stay went well."

Orion chuckles. "Yes, I had a feeling that might happen. But I have a plan."

I turn to look at him, exhaling slowly.

"I trust you, Orion. Perhaps I shouldn't, but I do."

Orion smiles and the pure joy on his face makes me smile right back.

Falling silent, I take a deep breath as Starfire finally lands and begins to power down.

I turn to Orion and nod. "Alright. I'll follow your lead."

We walk down the ramp, Boris in tow.

He insisted on joining us, but Derek, the kittens, and Dora stayed behind. I don't know what we're walking into, and I don't want to risk them getting hurt. Boris is on my shoulders, hovering like a tentacled guardian.

Jace smiles when she sees us. Harold makes a happy chuffing sound and in seconds, the bear is barreling towards me. Instead of running into me, he stops and gets up on his hind legs. He yanks me off my feet and I get a face full of Harold fur.

"Harold miss Henri. Harold glad Henri safe." His voice is low as he hugs me tightly. I caress his back, careful to avoid his spinal spikes.

"I missed you too. So much."

Boris makes a squeaking sound of agreement.

Then Jace is butting in. "Let me see my sister!"

Harold sighs and lets me go, setting me on my feet and going back on all fours. Jace replaces him as she nearly tackles me with a hug.

"I'm so glad you made it back safely. I was so worried." Her voice trembles and it's then that I realize just how scared she was for me. "Did you find Derek?" She pulls back and I smile.

"I did. And the kittens—they're all safe."

Jace lets out a sigh of relief. "Oh, thank God. I'm so glad. How did you—no, never mind. Now is not the time. Let's get the fuck out of here. I never want to see another UGF soldier in my entire life! I am *sick* of this place!"

My brother approaches and I'm wrapped in another tight hug.

"I'm glad you're safe," he whispers before pressing a kiss to my hair. Which is when I remember I've been betrayed. I shove my brother away and poke him in the chest.

"You didn't tell me Orion was your roommate! What the hell?"

Jace's head nearly falls off she whips it to the side so hard as she looks at Shaye with wide eyes. "You have a hot dragon as a roommate?"

My brother pushes his glasses up and pinches the bridge of his nose in exasperation. "Not the time, ladies."

"Why didn't you tell me!" I demand, not caring about the damn timing.

"Because I knew you'd go and fall in love with him, that's why," my brother snaps, and my jaw drops. Jace giggles. "I mean look at him! He's charming and rich and all polite and shit—it's my worst nightmare." Then Shaye leans in. "You know he's like 10,000 years old, right? I mean, he's kind of a cradle robber!"

I roll my eyes. "Seamus Laselle, I am 30 years old. I am not an *infant,* I am an adult."

Jace nods. "Yeah and age gaps are hot. I love books with that shit."

Shaye exhales and his eyes nearly roll into the back of his head. "I swear to fuck, you're both going to give me high blood pressure one of these days."

We snicker at him and someone clears their throat, interrupting us. We turn and face General Sirius, who watches our reunion with twitching eyes. But it's the man standing at his side that is the final needle on the haystack of my dwindling patience.

William Fairfax stands next to the General, looking smug and decidedly upset about how closely I'm standing to Orion.

"What?" I ask, and all of the anger, the frustration about this entire situation rises to the surface. "What's the problem now?"

Shaye coughs into his hand to cover his laugh.

"Provide a report of your little trip, Ms. Laselle. And I'm not asking," the General orders.

I think of the UGF. I think of everything the Antheriens told me. I think about the dumped creatures on Earth—and as I do, I get mad. I get really. Fucking. Mad.

Before I can open my mouth to say anything, the General continues. "You and your goddamn creature terrorized the Hades Outpost, that's what. Do you know how that makes us look? I'm arresting you—and your sister. You're both too dangerous to be left to your own devices."

My jaw drops and my sister instantly has her guns trained on the General. Red dots cover her chest in return, but she doesn't lower her weapons.

Damn. Jace is *pissed* if she's ignoring their threats. Even Shaye looks ticked off.

What happened here when I was gone?

"Don't do anything you'll regret, Henri. Why don't you come over here and we can talk about your trip?" Will smiles and it makes my stomach turn.

"She's not getting anywhere near you, you fucking creep," my sister snarls.

"Agreed." Shaye adds.

Boris squeaks indignantly, adding his agreement.

"Don't be like that, Henri. You know we're good together!"

I make a gagging sound. "Don't ever say that again. We're never getting back together, William. I would rather sit naked on a cactus for a year straight than be with you."

William's face turns red and his eyes narrow in anger.

"Enough of this," the General sneers and he make a motion with his left hand. Soldiers step towards us, their guns at the ready.

Until Orion opens his mouth. "No, I don't think so. No one is getting arrested today, Leonard. Your little power trip over the Laselles is done."

Follow my lead. I didn't realize that meant challenging the UGF but you know what? As I watch the General's face turns a very satisfying shade of red at Orion's words, I realize that I'm done living under their microscope.

Orion glances to the side at me and winks before returning his focus to General Sirius. "Also, Henri quits."

Wait—what?

I briefly give Orion a panicked glance but then I remember his words.

This is what he wanted me to trust him on, and I said I would.

With a deep breath, and a few concerns that I'm making a terrible mistake, I say *fuck it* and nod.

"He's right. I quit."

The General sputters.

Jace's jaw is almost on the ground. She shakes herself out of it and then gives me a wide smile. Shaye just raises a brow at me, and I shrug.

"You can't quit," the General grits out.

"I can and I did," I smile. "I quit. I fucking quit."

Then I flip him the bird.

Jace lets out a loud laugh. "That's my little sister!"

"Everyone knows that," Shaye hisses, but Jace just elbows him in the gut. Shaye lets out a low groan and Jace snickers.

"Arrest them!" the General orders. Soldiers take another step closer which is when my patience runs out.

With a growl worthy of a dragon, I unleash my nuclear powers. The air begins to glow as I let it build. Jace cracks her neck and whispers a spell that causes a strong wind to bear down on them. Harold roars and it's terrifying. Shaye raises his fist to the sky and the air suddenly becomes electric as a metallic taste coats the tip of my tongue. Lightning gathers in his fist as he slams his hand down. Bolts of lightning encircle the soldiers, protecting us.

When the lightning clears and the wind slows, the General is left sputtering in front of us.

"The days of you controlling and monitoring us are over, General." I step forward and point at the General, "And if you come for me, if you try to hurt my siblings? My *creatures?* I will tell *everyone* what's going on in Antheri. I'll tell everyone the *truth* about your so-called war."

"STAND DOWN."

The soldiers put their guns down as they click on their safeties.

General Sirius is breathing heavily as he approaches.

I wave my finger and let a wave of my power hit him. The General is pushed back 10 feet. "Nuh-uh. No closer. This isn't a discussion. I am telling you that I quit, and there is nothing you can do about it."

"Your business will fail without our funding and support," he hisses.

"No, it won't," Orion's voice is smug. "I'm going to fund it."

Will decides this is the perfect moment to insert himself back into the situation. He stalks up to Orion and pokes him in the chest. "You're not going anywhere, you fucking crimi—"

SLAP.

A giant tentacle swipes William's feet out from under him. He hits the ground hard, like a sack of potatoes.

I didn't even feel Boris leave my shoulders. I was so distracted I missed him super-sizing! But a giant kraken now glares down at my ex-boyfriend.

Then another of Boris' tentacles bumps into Orion.

Did they just...fist bump?

Orion returns his focus back to the General, who is shaking so hard I almost suggest he sits down. "Here's the thing, *Leonard.* I could have left supermax anytime I wanted. I stayed there because I wanted to learn. I let you think you were in control of me, but that ends today. I am leaving with Henri, and I am backing her business. If you or the UGF try to come after us, I will kill you."

Then Orion steps forward until he's standing over a groaning

William Fairfax. He crouches down and smiles at him.

I don't hear what's said, but the way William's eyes go wide, his pupils dilated as the blood rushes from his face tells me that Orion is unleashing a verbal threat worthy of his immortal lifetime.

As Orion pulls back, Boris replaces him, still in his supersized state. A vicious series of squeaks leaves the kraken. Then Boris narrows his gaze and—

We all cringe as Will gets inked. Black liquid shoots into his face and Will chokes on it.

Boris snickers as he returns to his normal size. He slithers over to me and crawls up my leg.

Then I'm being nudged aside. Harold ambles over, slow and steady, and sniffs Will, who is trying to get up but can't.

Harold sits back on his hind legs and reaches around for his sword. Unsheathing it, he moves faster than a Bear should be able to do and—

We all cringe again as Harold *bonks* Will on the forehead with the flat side of his blade. Will flops down to the ground, moaning.

Harold sheaths his sword and turns to face us, pausing for a moment. He makes a strange face, like he's concentrating really hard—

We all let out various sounds of shock and hysterical laughter as Harold drops a big pile of steaming poo right on William Fairfax's prone body.

Jace is laughing so hard I'm actually worried she might collapse. Orion makes a snorting sound and my brother just shakes his head but can't hide his smile.

I watch Harold, trying to hold back my laughter as the bear

faces me.

"Harold defend Henri's honor."

"Yes you did, buddy. Thank you."

"Nice job," Orion murmurs to my Ursine friend.

Harold looks mighty pleased as he ambles back into line behind us.

"I quit too."

We turn in unison and look at my brother. But Shaye just stares at me, something indescribable in his gaze. Regret, maybe.

"I've been away from home for too long," he says quietly. "If you would have me...I would like to remedy that."

My cheeks flush with surprise.

"Shaye, I've always said it's your home too. You're welcome there as long as you want to stay."

Shaye smiles.

"You can't—You're our chief science officer!" the General squawks. Orion abandons him and walks over to me, grabbing my hand and interlacing our fingers.

Shaye doesn't spare the General a second glance as he respond, "Oh and I'm taking my work with me. All of it."

I think the General might be having a heart attack.

"You—you—"

Orion's hand squeezes mine.

"Come on," I say. "Let's go home."

We walk over to Starfire and Orion nods. "I'll fly you over to The Menace, then I will follow you to Earth."

It hits me then, and I feel stupid for not realizing earlier.

I turn to Orion with wide eyes, and he smiles at me.

"Are you sure?" I whisper, but he lifts my hand and presses a soft kiss against my knuckles.

"I've never been more sure of anything in my life."

Oh wow.

A neon, fizzy type of joy bursts through me. I feel like I could jump a thousand feet into the air and fly into the clouds.

Orion wants to come with me. He wants my home to be his home. We don't have to say goodbye.

As my siblings walk into Starfire, we follow. It's a quiet journey over to The Menace, and when it comes time to separate, they don't question when I stay with Orion.

"There will be plenty of time to catch up later," Jace winks at me before bodily shoving my brother out of the hatch. He protests, muttering something about not trusting a dragon around his sister, but Jace just shoves him again until he shuts up. Harold follows them and in minutes, The Menace is lifting into the sky and we follow, leaving the Arc and Andromeda behind.

CHAPTER 33

WELCOME HOME, HENRI

Come and Get Your Love by Redbone

I would say I didn't spend the entire flight home making out with a millennia old space dragon...but then I'd be a liar.

Soon, far too soon, Earth appears before us. It's beautiful from up here. The swirling clouds atop deep blue oceans and lands of green.

In minutes, we're landing, and I instruct Starfire to set down in the forest behind my house. My cloaking spells will hide the ship. The Menace sets down next to us and my siblings unload, Harold right behind them.

We all disembark, Orion carrying our bags. I told him I could help but he ignored my protests.

I'm giddy with excitement, almost jumping out of my own skin as we approach the house.

A horsey head pokes out of the barn and Mable lets out a loud *neigh!* Soon, lots of animal calls follow and we're surrounded. All of the creatures crowd me. The Kluckies brush against my legs and the horses run their velvet lips along my head, messing up my hair.

I giggle, hugging each and every one of them.

"I missed you so much!" I press a kiss against Bob's cheek and ruffle Petunia's mane.

Once everyone outside has been properly greeted—and they inspect my siblings and my guest, we head inside and—

I nearly fall on my face at the sight that greets me.

"What—" I choke on my words as I take in the conga line.

The weenies—who, admittedly do look like Earth Dachshunds but are actually a nearly identical species from Proxima Nova, known as the dog of the royal houses called Weinérs—fly through the air, using their *very not supposed to being used* powers of levitation.

My siblings come up behind me to see what's got me in a tizzy. Jace lets out a strangled laugh at the sight of Betty and Carolyn sing the Conga song as the Weinérs fly behind them, each of them in colorful doggy sweaters. Frankie wears goggles and a party hat. Barbara has on fairy wings and a tutu, and Jinx is sporting a bowtie and a...

"Is that a pink wig?" I mutter.

"Somebody pinch me!" Jace hisses.

It's the sight of Kevin and the other Kriblets swinging around on Mardi Gras beads in their aquarium that knocks me out of my stupor.

"Henri! You're back!" Betty spots me and runs over, a wide smile on her face.

"I'm guessing everything went well?" I ask tentatively.

Carolyn flashes me a thumbs up as she swings Frankie into a ballroom dip, breaking the conga line. I point at the weens as they spot me and fly over, landing at my feet.

"Looks like we all broke some rules, huh?" I laugh as they lick my face. Jinx tries to shove his tongue up my nose, and I squeal, falling on my ass as I'm covered in a pile of happy creatures.

"We'll head home later, but anytime you need babysitters, let us know. This is the most fun I've had in years!" Carolyn shouts happily. "Oh, and the pony you got? Yeah, it poops glitter."

Jace makes a strangled sound. But to my surprise, it's Shaye who lets out a loud laugh.

"Yeah! Thought you'd wanna know!" Betty agrees.

Carolyn nods, still dancing to the music. "Agreed! You should have told us you were a magic-alien thing sooner. This has been the best time ever!"

Shaye's eyes nearly bug out of his head at my being called a 'magic-alien' thing.

Jace shrugs and joins in on the dancing, pulling Harold with her. Watching the bear shake his butt to the music is a sight I'll never forget. Even Shaye cracks up before Derek meows at him, demanding cuddles. My brother relents and picks up the cat, hellkittens and all. He taps his foot to the beat, swinging them gently like a rocking baby.

When the weens finish their love attack, I get to my feet and face Orion.

To my surprise, he bows, holding out his hand. "May I have this dance?"

Oh wow. Is this what it feels like to swoon? Cause I'm swooning. I swear to God I'm swooning.

My blood turns into bubbling champagne as I place my hand in his and the dragon sweeps me into a twirling dance.

"Woo! Get it, Henri!" Betty whoops, picking up Jinx and dancing with him. Barbara flies around them, refusing to be held.

Something pink flashes in the corner of my eye and I turn to see Boris driving around on his mobile aquarium, Dora on his head. His tentacles wiggle in the air in a kraken-y dance as he bobs his red head. Dora taps her legs on him to the beat.

"He's cute!" Carolyn adds and I have to hide my face in Orion's chest as I turn redder than tomato. "Does he have a brother? Two brothers? Three?! Or maybe a twin?"

I make a shrieking sort of giggle. "He doesn't—and he's mine."

Orion chuckles and whispers in my ear, "Yes I am. And you're mine, Stardust."

I look up at him and in an act of pure bravery, I lean up and press my lips against his, ignoring the cheers in the background—and the grumbling from my brother.

We're interrupted as Harold gets up on his back legs and begins attempting to dance for real.

"Go Harold!" Jace claps.

I turn and face the creatures, completely and perfectly happy with my family and loved ones around me. Orion wraps his arms around me as we swing to the beat.

"I already love it here," he whispers in my ear, pressing a kiss against my neck.

"Good," I smile and motion to the scene in front of us. **"Welcome to the Home for Wayward Creatures."**

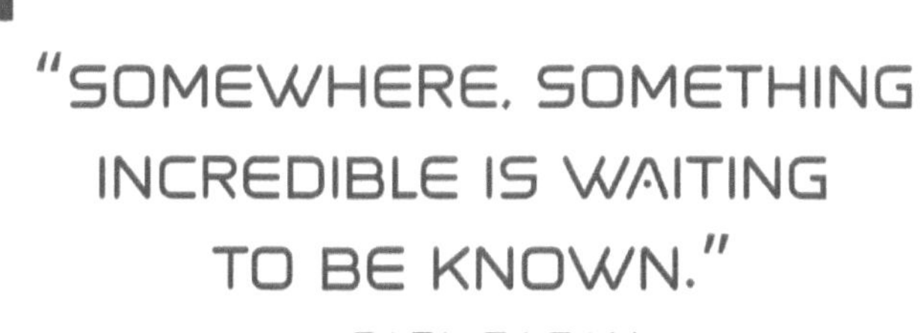

THE END

...FOR NOW

HENRI, ORION, JACE, SHAYE, AND ALL OF THE
CREATURES WILL RETURN IN VOLUME 2, COMING SOON

SOME THANKS

This story came about after I finished my debut novel, The Forgotten and The Feared. TF&TF is extremely dark, as is the majority of my work, and while I love writing dark stories, particularly in first person, it also means I go through the traumatic moments with my characters. That can be hard on a writer mentally, and thus, The Home for Wayward Creatures was born. It's a warm hug to my readers and to myself, in those moments when we need happiness. It's my coping mechanism and the story I work on in between all the dark stuff. It helps me stay centered and not sucked into a depression. I put all of the things that make me happy into one story, and this is what I ended up with.

For all of the darkness, there must also be light.

The Home for Wayward Creatures is also my love letter to the animals who have changed my life. **Boomer, Luca, Flynn, Beau, Blue, Xena, Stanley, Tosh, Artemis, Sophie, Kid, Evie, Carmen, Jinx, Lady**...your kind hearts inspire me. **Frankie;** thank you for being my best friend and my muse.

Mom and Dad; thank you for the endless support. I am so lucky that you are my parents; truly.

The entire **Schaeffel, Wolski, and Garrett Clans;** thank you for making me feel like I'm not alone in this world.

To the friends who have become family; **Tiffany, Corrine, Becky & DJ, Marilu, Molly, Lindsay, Betty, and Carolyn**. It is your friendship and love that inspires me the most.

My writing group, **The Trash Bandits;** you keep me going when I feel like throwing in the towel.

To my amazing editor **YarnWyvern**; infinite thanks and gratitude for your friendship, mentorship, and your keen eye. You improved this story so much, and I am so thankful. To my proofreaders, **YarnWyvern & Molly**; thank you for the enthusiasm, the notes about when a sentence didn't make any sense, and for your friendship. You both are a gift I am so grateful for. And again—to **Molly.** Not just my proofreader but my PA, friend, confident, and emotional support person who talks me down when I get spirally. Team Aries ftw.

To my **Alpha and Beta readers; t**hank you for the honesty and thoughtfulness behind every opinion and answer. I am beyond grateful for all of you. To my **Inner Circle Community;** Thank you for going on this journey with me! Your feedback was essential and made this so fun. I can't wait for Volume 2.

To my **Kickstarter backers**; Thank you for taking a chance on me and showing me that my ideas are worthy. I'm still in shock at your generosity and am endlessly grateful.

To the team at **Under the Cover;** thank you for being my muses and for what you've done for the Kansas City community. It's an honor to be on your shelves. Thank you for how you champion indie authors. I can't wait to make more aliens eat your books (sorry not sorry).

And **you,** dear reader. To you for reading this, and making my dreams come true.

ALSO BY ECG

<u>REPUBLICA HELVETORUM</u>
gothic monster romance
Here There Be Monsters
Here There Be Witches – *coming 2026*
There Are Monsters Beneath – *coming 2026/2027*

<u>THE DRAGON QUEEN</u>
dark epic fantasy
The Forgotten and The Feared
The Broken and The Brave
The Defiant and The Damned
TDQ3 – *coming 2026*

<u>THE HOME FOR WAYWARD CREATURES</u>
paranormal romantic sci-fi
Vol. 1
Vol. 2 – coming 2027

<u>SHORT STORIES & SERIALS</u>
Rescue Me – *contemporary fiction*
FERN – *sci-fi horrormance*
DARKMOOR – *gothic why-choose romance*

EC Garrett is an Alaskan transplant now living in Kansas City, MO who writes fantasy/sci-fi speculative fiction. She has her bachelor's degree in English literature with a focus in Early Modern and Medieval Literature from the University of Nevada, Reno. EC is currently getting her master's degree in English: Print, Manuscript Culture, and Editing at the University of Missouri-Kansas City.

In her spare time, she's either reading or watching the latest fantasy releases, riding horses at the barn, spending time with her family, or playing with her very cute but extremely ornery senior dachshund mix, Frankie.

She dreams of becoming a dragon Rider.

Midnight Pages

indie publishing house + bookish candles
handmade in kansas city, mo